PSYCHIC CITY

Page Turner

Andrea,

Psychic City

May you have
the best of
a̲l̲l̲ possible
futures.

Page 💙

Published By: Braided Studios, LLC

https://braided.studio

ISBN: 978-1-947296-06-0

A special thanks to my Patreons

Elan

Andrea

Alex

Heidi

Jason

Jennifer

Kit

Nada

Reino

William

Allyson	Jenny
Andrew	Kaizen
Anna	Larissa
Beverly	Marion
Brendan	Maureen
Endre	Milagros
Gregg	Pour
Jason	Tom

For my father, who knew more about tomorrow than most people know about yesterday

Projective Tests

"Pull over," Viv said.

"...and so I said to him," Penny continued, not even taking a breath, "don't you know that color does nothing for your complexion? You look like an untoasted bagel, you really do."

"Penny," Viv said again.

"An untoasted bagel? That's great," Karen mused. "I wonder what flavor he'd be. Martin *thinks* he's an everything bagel, that's for damn sure."

They both laughed.

As Penny launched into a story about the first time she ever ate bagels, Viv gritted her teeth together. When the two of them really got to talking, you couldn't count on conversational lulls. Instead Karen and Penny had a way of stretching a thick fence of words between them. A wall of energy. Forget about getting a word in edgewise. If you were lucky, you could peer between the slats. And you weren't always lucky.

Normally Viv just let them talk, especially on long car rides. Eventually, they'd tire, and the fence would fall naturally. But there was no time for that now. Viv knew she'd have to be more insistent to pierce the barrier.

"Penny!" Viv snapped.

"Yes, darling?" Penny replied.

"Pull. The. Car. Over."

"Is it your stomach again?" Karen asked from the backseat.

"It's always your stomach," Penny said. "I told you that you shouldn't have such a big breakfast. Not with your new medicine anyway."

"It's not my stomach," Viv said. "Something *happened* here."

Penny pulled the car to the shoulder.

Viv didn't wait for her two companions. As soon as the car stopped, she opened her door and started walking off into the knee-high grass.

"What do you think?" Karen asked Penny.

"I think she's going to get Lyme disease that way," Penny replied.

"Well, when she does, you get to be the one who says, 'I told you so,'" Karen said.

Penny laughed.

"Don't you think we should go after her?" Karen asked. "There's no telling what's out there."

Penny shrugged.

Viv was walking at a such a brisk pace that she had already become a small dot in the distance. At any moment, she would vanish into the tree line.

Karen suddenly felt a huge wave of anxiety. The hairs on her arm stood on end. Karen looked at Penny and raised an eyebrow. "So you're worried. You can't hide it from me, you know."

"I hate that empathic power of yours." Penny replied. "Absolutely no privacy."

"Not when Viv leaves, no."

Karen could feel Penny's annoyance swell up in response to what she had just said. They stood next to the car staring at each other for a few moments. Finally, Penny sighed. "If I get ticks, I'm blaming you."

"That's fair," Karen said.

Together, they set off to follow Viv.

"Oh Great and Powerful Empath," Penny teased, "Time to make an official report. How are the ticks feeling today?"

"I dunno," Karen joked back. "I'm having trouble sensing *anything* over the extreme levels of sassiness that are emanating off you."

"Sass, class, whatever," Penny said, flippantly tossing her long blond hair.

Her dramatic hair flip was a gesture that Penny often affected in order to look unfazed by whatever was going on. Most people bought it. But Karen knew the truth. When Penny was frazzled, she usually looked very composed. It was a secret Karen could have shared with everyone, but as with most of her insights she kept it to herself, rarely even telling Penny that she knew, let alone anyone else.

Karen had learned that lesson when she was young. People weren't always aware of their own feelings. Even when they were, they didn't want others to know. And they certainly didn't want to talk about it. It was usually better to keep her empathic revelations to herself.

Suddenly, the wall of Penny's feelings fell away. Karen couldn't feel them anymore. *We must be catching up to Viv*, Karen realized.

For some reason, and Karen had never figured out why, if Penny and Viv were both within 100 yards of her (give or take a few), her powers went away completely. No constant intrusions from other people's emotions. But only if they were *both* there, Penny *and* Viv. One or the other wouldn't work.

It was what had first drawn Karen to them in the first place, the fact that she felt like a normal person when they were both around. It was the first time in her life she could remember it ever being that way. And that sense of calm was worth putting up with a lot for. It was the most precious thing she'd ever found.

That sense of calm stayed as she and Penny reached the tree line and started to work their way slowly through the thinner spots in the forest. A mix of white birches, pines, and – what the Hell kind of tree was that? Karen remembered seeing it when she grew up in the Maine woods, but she could never remember the name of it.

"Penny," Karen said.

"What, sweetie?" Penny asked.

"What kind of trees are those?"

Penny laughed. "Seriously, Maine girl, we have to get you into a course or something. Botany for Fourth Graders. Hooked on Tree Phonics."

"I know, I know, I'm hopeless."

"The worst, really," Penny joked. Before adding, "But you're the *best* kind of worst. Those are *cedars*."

It was hard for Karen to explain to Penny, how easy it was to take the woods for granted having grown up right next to them. To know the feel and shapes of trees and leaves. To recognize them like you'd recognize your own feet in the shower. But not have the right words to name them.

Emotions were the same way. Her entire life, Karen had been drowning in other people's emotions but couldn't begin to explain what *that* felt like. You would think being so close to something would make it easier to describe it. But being familiar with something and describing it were entirely different things. Sure, Inuit tribes had 50-some-odd words for snow. But fish weren't exactly guest lecturers on water, despite being surrounded by it.

Most days Karen felt like she had more in common with the fish than the Inuits.

But Karen knew all too well the particular thwack of cedar leaves as they hit against her skin.

"Cedar leaves are funny," she said to Penny. "Rough, yet plasticized."

"Hey, I resemble that remark," Penny joked back. And she had a point. Her curls were still in place, even though both of them had been smacked in the head by several tree branches already.

"If the leaf fits – " Karen began, before stopping dead in her tracks.

In the clearing was a horrific scene. Penny, Karen, and Viv had been working together as a team for PsyOps for three years now. And if pressed, none of them would have been able to give you an accurate count offhand of exactly how many crime scenes they'd dealt with. Although Viv would likely have been the closest, on account of her photographic memory – which posed an unfair advantage in most guessing games and in Trivial Pursuit, the cause of much consternation.

But all three of them knew one thing for sure: The crime scene they were standing in was one of the worst they'd ever seen.

As usual, Karen didn't want to look at the scene directly. She stood at the edge of the clearing sneaking peeks in her peripheral vision, challenging the nausea rising in her chest bit by bit, slowly taking the whole scene in, one piece at a time.

Viv was focused on performing her usual duty, surveying the scene from a variety of different angles. Memorizing the positions of anything that seemed even remotely relevant. While trying not to touch anything, on the off chance a fingerprinting crew would come in later and start dusting things.

Viv had made enough mistakes in the past to know the headache that would result if her prints were found on anything important. And of course, because the three of them made the foolish decision to take the day off for a change to visit Viv's mother in the countryside (instead of yet another insidious seven-day work week), none of them had packed gloves in the car before setting out.

"Well, you have to be careful with that sort of thing," Penny had joked when Viv had suggested maybe keeping a box of gloves in the car would be a good idea. "Wouldn't want to give people the idea that we're kinky lesbians or anything."

That had gotten a rare laugh out of Viv. "Oh, let 'em talk," Viv had said, cracking a smile.

But then Karen had said something else even more funny and distracting, upping Penny's ante and changing the subject, and no one had packed the gloves.

To the casual observer, Viv would look a bit like she was vogueing at crime scenes. Striking odd poses and freezing. At least on the first pass when she memorized a scene with her mind. Her movements always looked a little more natural on the second or third sweep, when she'd capture the images with the camera that hung around her neck, a way of documenting things for non-psychics, or "normals" as they called themselves, the back-formation emphasizing that psychics were viewed as abnormal by society.

Penny had pointed out Viv's vogueing thing the first time they'd worked a case together but had quickly learned her lesson. Viv might have a freakish memory, but she was often lacking in the patience department. And like most people, Viv could dish out criticism to others, but rarely ever enjoyed jokes at *her* expense.

No matter. Penny knew how to work around it. Usually humor was a helpful exploratory tool. A safe way of testing to see where Viv was at any given time without sincerely committing to a position.

There were two corpses in the clearing. The closest one had so much damage to its face that what was left over was barely recognizable as human. As Karen stole progressively longer glances at the remains, she thought that the blood on the victim's chest reminded her of a Rorschach ink blot she'd seen when she was inpatient on a locked ward some years ago.

It looked like a demon with its wings outstretched. Or perhaps two women sitting back to back.

If Karen were asked by a psychological examiner about what she saw in the pattern, she'd know to tell them it was two women and not the demon. In general, seeing living things in ink blots is considered the "correct" result. Animals are good. But people are even better. Especially if you can come up with a story where there's some kind of relationship between them. Ideally, a positive one.

Projective tests are all about getting an honest glimpse into a subject's psyche, and a healthy person, theoretically speaking, is a social animal and will see people when presented with ambiguity.

In any event, the women in the bloody splotch on the victim's chest seemed much more alive than the person sporting it. And Karen found her eyes oddly transfixed on the pattern.

A handbag lay a few feet from the corpse. It looked as though it had been overturned, rummaged through. Could this have been a robbery?

Penny's walked over to the handbag and crouched down on the ground next to it.

"Is that right?" Penny said.

For a second, Karen thought Penny was talking to her, like she always did when Penny saw one of her "friends." But Penny was using that tone. *The* tone. The one that Penny used whenever she talked to those who she had known the longest: The dead.

To Karen and anyone else who would have been watching (including Viv, if she weren't busy documenting the scene), it would have looked like Penny were talking to a purse. To the living, mediums looked like they were talking to themselves or inanimate objects.

But Penny saw something else altogether. She saw a woman standing next to the purse with her hand on her hip, shaking her head in disgust as she watched Viv taking photos. Penny thought the woman was probably a spirit – although she never really knew for sure. The living and the dead looked quite similar to Penny. The only difference was that other living people couldn't see the dead.

"You won't find what you're looking for," the spirit said.

"Is that right?" Penny said.

"I don't know. Is it?" the spirit said mockingly.

Penny sighed. Definitely a spirit. She was used to them playing games. The dead were rarely cooperative. Evasive at best, they frequently lied. If she were lucky, they'd speak in riddles.

"I know you are, but what am I?" Penny said.

"What?" the spirit said.

Penny stared and blinked, trying not to laugh.

"Don't you want to know my secrets?" the spirit teased.

"How do you know I don't already?" Penny replied.

The spirit frowned.

Penny had found this to be the best tactic over her decades of dealing with the dead. The usual motivations that work on the living rarely made a dent. Flattery was often useless. You couldn't exactly trade favors, that didn't work. Neither did bribery. What do you buy the ghost who has everything?

That left confusion. Or at least a powerful cognitive interrupt. Baffle the riddler. Flip the script.

"You're an odd one," the spirit said at last.

"I'll take that as a compliment," Penny said.

"It wasn't meant that way."

Penny ignored that. "So, hot stuff," she said.

"Hot stuff, I'm d—"

"Right. Dead. Whatever. You might be dead, but I'm not. I'm a woman. A woman with needs."

The spirit blushed. "Um, thanks, but you're not my typ—"

"Honey, I'm everyone's type," Penny continued.

The spirit looked even more confused. This conversation wasn't going to plan.

"So hot stuff, seen anything interesting lately?"

The spirit sighed. "Alright, you win. I'll spill it."

"Penny," Viv said suddenly.

"Not now, Viv," Penny said. "I'm channeling."

"Channeling which one?" Viv said.

"What do you mean which one?" Penny said.

"Which *spirit*, Penny? Which spirit?" Viv said impatiently.

"Viv, what is wrong with you? There's only one spirit here," Penny replied.

The spirit glared at her, clearly irritated that their conversation had been interrupted by a third party.

"Really?" Viv said to Penny. "One spirit? That's odd. Because there are *two bodies*."

"Your friend is dumb," the spirit told Penny. "That other person isn't dead."

"What?!" Penny said.

"What is it?" Viv said.

"Are you deaf or something?" the spirit said to Penny. "There's only one corpse here. Mine. And I was thinking… could you do me a favor? I'm thinking I'd like to be cremated. Have my ashes spread somewhere real nice. As you can see, an open casket is out of the question."

"Well, that really depends on what the police want to do. They might need to hold your remains for a while until the investigation is over," Penny replied.

"Penny," Viv said sternly, laying a hand on her shoulders.

Penny stood up. "Sorry," she said to Viv. "The spirit says that you're dumb."

"Penny!" Viv said, clearly getting irritated.

"Well, that you're dumb, and that they want to be cremated. Oh, and that the other victim is alive," Penny said.

"Alive?" Viv said. "But that's not what I saw in the car. Are you sure that spirit isn't lying to you?"

"I'm not lying to you," the spirit said to Penny.

"Well, she says she's not lying to me," Penny said to Viv.

"She could be lying about lying," Viv said.

"Oh my God, why would I lie about lying? What would be the point of that?" the spirit said.

"Well, to be fair, other spirits have lied to me about lying. It's not unheard of," Penny said to the spirit.

The spirit rolled her spectral eyes.

"I don't think she's lying, Viv," Penny said.

"But the woman I saw in the car in my vision… she was so still. She looked like Snow White did in the old cartoon. When she ate the poison apple."

"I know what you mean," Penny said, laying a hand on Viv's arm. "She looks pretty dead from over here. Well, dead or sleeping."

"Sleeping with her eyes wide open?" Viv said.

"You'd have some weird dreams, wouldn't you?" Penny said.

"You know, I never dreamed when I was alive," the spirit piped in.

"No one asked you, hot stuff," Penny replied.

Viv and Penny slowly walked together over to where the second body lay on the ground. Seriously, Viv wasn't kidding. She looked like Snow White did in the old cartoon. Lying on her back with her arms folded on her stomach. The only different was that *this* Snow White wasn't in a fancy glass case. And Viv was right, her eyes were wide open.

"Karen, get over here," Viv said.

Karen was still staring into the bloody blotch on the first victim's chest.

"Seriously, Karen, stop ogling that corpse and get over here," Viv said.

She did.

Penny nodded knowingly at Karen. Giving her a look Karen had come to recognize. "You want me to *feel*, don't you?" Karen said.

"Good girl," Viv said.

Karen sighed. "It's been a long day. I don't know if I can..."

"You can," Viv said. She took Karen's chin in her hand and stared directly into her eyes. "You're stronger than you think."

Viv had some pretty sharp edges in general, but when she softened, there was nothing sweeter. At least not to Karen.

"Okay, Viv," Karen said. "I'll feel."

"Karen, meet Snow White, Snow White, Karen," Viv said, gesturing to the woman lying on the ground.

"Who's leaving?" Karen said.

"I'll go," Penny volunteered. "The other victim is annoying me."

"You're no picnic yourself," the spirit said to her.

"You're not even the *ants* at a picnic," Penny snapped back at the spirit, as she headed away from the scene.

"If you need me after, I'll be here. And Penny will be back in just a few minutes. You know we'll be here," Viv said.

"You've always been good at aftercare," Karen replied.

"Shhh, don't tell anyone," Viv said.

"Who would I tell? No one would believe me anyway," Karen said.

Viv smiled. They held one another's hands and looked into each other's eyes, waiting, while Penny walked away.

But the moment Penny was out of range, Karen felt the wind get knocked out of her. She hunched over sharply, like anything that folds for storage when you kick in its joints. "Oh God," she said. She felt like she was going to throw up. Everything started to spin.

Viv waited. Watched.

Karen crumpled into a ball on the ground. She suddenly couldn't remember who she was. What she was doing here.

Karen looked up at the stranger standing over her. A woman with a camera hanging around her neck. A tall thin redhead wearing a pair of paint-splashed overalls with striking eyes, eyes which seemed to change color every time she looked at them. Who was this Amazonian woman looming over her? Where were they? And who was that person lying on the ground next to her? Why was she sleeping with her eyes open?

None of it made any sense.

"Karen, are you okay?" Viv said, crouching down. When she did, the camera around her neck swung close enough to Karen for her to bat feebly at it like a baby swats at a hanging mobile. Viv stood back up to protect the camera.

"Who's Karen?" Karen replied. "Is that Karen?" she said, gesturing towards Snow White. "Are you Karen?"

"Karen, cut it out," Viv said.

"Do you have a knife?" Karen said.

"This isn't funny. I'm not Penny," Viv said. "Stop the lame jokes. I don't like them."

"But you said to cut it out. How am I supposed to cut it out if I don't have anything to cut it with?" Karen said. Karen started to cry.

This wasn't normal. Karen typically maintained her composure when channeling someone else's feelings via empathy. She could detect what the other person was experiencing but never lost herself in those emotions the way she seemed to be doing now. And she never forgot her own identity or who she was.

Viv stared impatiently at the edge of the clearing. C'mon Penny. How long could it take to walk a spirit around the block?

"Cut me," Karen said to Viv. "If you want it cut, you'll need to cut me yourself."

Viv picked Karen up off the ground. "Alright, knife player, we're gonna go on a little trip," Viv said.

"Where are we going?" Karen said.

"You'll see," Viv said, moving Karen back into the woods.

"Ahh," Karen said. "I see. You're gonna cut me with the tree branches. How romantic. Maybe a lash with ash?"

"This has to be the weirdest feel you've ever done, Karen, honestly," Viv grumbled.

"Who's Karen?" Karen said again.

"It's what I call the trees," Viv said, shaking her head.

Karen started to mumble incoherently. It didn't sound like any language that Viv had ever heard.

When they emerged from the woods, Viv could see Penny again, off in the distance. Karen collapsed on the ground as they got closer to her.

Penny jogged up through the grass to meet them.

"Geez, Viv, what the hell did you do to her?" Penny said.

Viv shrugged. "I don't know what happened. Those were some weird feels, whatever they were."

"Did you get enough pictures?" Penny said.

"I think so," Viv said. She pulled out her cell phone. Called in the scene to emergency services. Read off her agent number. Let them know that there was one person dead but that the second one was still alive but unresponsive. A quick call, one she'd made hundreds of times at different scenes. Something she could do in her sleep by this point.

Viv put her phone away. "We should probably go see Martin at headquarters, let him know what we found," she said.

"Guess we'll have to visit your mom another time, Viv," Penny said.

"Guess so."

PsyOps

The Department of Psychic Operations, or PsyOps for short, was located underground in a building whose ground level storefront housed a variety of failing businesses. Around Halloween it became a costume shop that sold cheap trinkets that probably wouldn't give you cancer and could make you look like a passable witch. Or a sexy nurse. Or a sexy nurse witch.

Another time it had been a bakery that made low-fat donuts that tasted terrible. They did cause you to lose weight though since most people didn't want to eat for the rest of the day after choking one down. So that was a plus.

Initially PsyOps had posted a guard on the premises. An invalidator, the kind of tuey that implanted thoughts into people's heads that made them dismiss their beliefs. The idea behind this was that the guard on duty would sit in the shop, and if anyone wondered why random customers were going out back, ones who didn't work behind the counter, then the invalidator would cancel that out with doubt. Within a minute or two, the customer would dismiss their suspicions as silly. Why would they ever think that? There were plenty of crummy shops, just like this one. Nothing to see here, folks.

But after a while, the department realized it could cut costs by not posting a guard at all. The businesses themselves were sufficiently terrible to keep people away. A few folks inexplicably bought things, but most people found the stores depressing and left.

As a result, the original invalidator guards were laid off. This was a big problem at first. Formerly confident residents were plagued by nagging doubts. Others reported issues with the neighborhood street lamps. They seemed to be dimming at random. But when PsyOps went to check, other witnesses swore that the lighting had been just fine. Nothing had ever happened.

The matter was never resolved and was moved indefinitely to the gaslighting division.

Several hundred psychic intuitives worked in this one branch of PsyOps, in the heart of Skinner, the Psychic City. The agents passed through the tacky shop. Pretended to the use the bathroom. Sneaked into the service elevator.

And down they went.

It wasn't glamorous. But in a weird way, it was home.

"Well, if it isn't the Three Bears," Martin said as Viv, Penny, and Karen stepped off the service elevator.

"I keep telling you," Viv said. "We're not bears. Bears are something else entirely."

"Viv, you act like I haven't traveled," Martin said.

"Only because *you* act like you haven't traveled. Haven't you ever been to San Francisco?" Viv said.

"It's an analogy," Martin said. "Do you have to take everything so literally?"

 Martin Meek had been their boss at PsyOps for four years, which was an awfully long time for anyone to have the same supervisor there. Especially since all the supervisors were normals, and most normals couldn't stand tueys. But not Martin. He'd been managing them back when the team was just a duo, when it had been just Penny and Viv, before Karen joined the investigative team.

"And besides, when would I have time to travel? Have you seen our current case load? Poor Amarynth's buried up in Connections."

"Bad news for you then, Martin," Penny said.

"Oh for fuck's sake," Martin said. "You didn't find another one, did you?"

"Yeah. One. Well one and a half. Called it in. The normal police will be there soon. And the paramedics," Viv said.

"Still ours though," Penny said. "Definitely not something the normals will crack."

"Damn," Martin said. He looked at Karen. "What's wrong with her?"

Karen pulled the hoodie she was wearing further over her head so that it completely obscured her face, slouching. A makeshift cloak of invisibility.

"She's had a rough day," Viv explained. "Feels."

"Right. Feels," Martin said. "Okay. Fine. Whatever. Don't tell me."

"*Martin*," Penny said. "Don't be difficult. It's literally feels. She read the second victim's emotions, and it fucked her up. Be nice, okay?"

Martin wasn't kidding when he said that Amarynth was buried up in Connections. He'd accused Viv of being too literal, but he was just as bad sometimes.

They couldn't even see Amarynth at first due to the clutter that surrounded her as they approached her office space. They'd only been able to find her corner of the department by keeping an eye out for her causality board, a renowned hot mess.

Most agents had busy causality boards, but Amarynth took it to a new level. And this new level was busy even by her standards. While most causality boards told cohesive stories when you looked at them, Amarynth's didn't even come close. Hers didn't make any sense to the casual observer. Her causality board was less like a movie storyboard and more like an abstract collage of magazine clippings that didn't look like anything until you stepped far enough away.

And even then, you weren't exactly sure what you were seeing.

It was the Magic Eye poster of intuition.

Penny had been certain the first time she met Amarynth that she was looking upon a spirit and not a real live person. This was because Amarynth had the same kind of checked out uber madness that was standard issue in the spirit world, where life and death no longer mattered. It was only with time that Penny came to realize that Amarynth's idiosyncrasies stemmed from a life marked by seeing what other people couldn't and frustration from her complete inability to convey that to another person. Amarynth warned people repeatedly about what would happen, and no one listened. The Cassandra of PsyOps.

This was a common affliction among connection agents. But poor Amarynth seemed to have it worse than most. She was able to see even more disparate links than any other connector working for PsyOps. This could have been a *huge* boon if she'd been better at connecting the dots for others, but unfortunately she was tragically terrible at explaining things. Even the highest quality causality board, normally a great help for connection agents, failed Amarynth. She couldn't seem to use it properly.

However, over the years, Viv, Penny, and Karen had come to trust that Amarynth was on to something. No matter how crazy it sounded.

They learned to follow her advice even if it sounded completely illogical. Which it often did.

Well, mostly. Viv still struggled with it sometimes. There had always been something about Amarynth that gave her the creeps. Something that made it especially hard for her to trust the agent.

"Hey Amarynth," Viv said.

"You need to go to jail," Amarynth replied.

"Excuse me?" Viv said.

Amarynth rolled her eyes. "Do I have to spell everything out for you?"

"It's okay, Amarynth," Karen said. "We know you can't." She had meant for it to sound sympathetic, a kind of reassurance, but Penny burst out in laughter.

"Oh man, that's a good one. Sometimes you really surprise me, Karen," Penny said.

"Not me," Amarynth said, clearly not amused. But then again, none of them had ever seen her laugh, come to think of it.

"Okay, well, we need to go to jail. Which jail?" Viv said. Getting information out of Amarynth often required asking very specific questions. And she'd learned early on not to ask too many questions at once because Amarynth found this infinitely more frustrating than answering questions one at a time. The last thing you wanted to do was overload Amarynth. More than one consultation had ended with her becoming overwhelmed and storming out of her office space to go hide in one of the many unmarked closets scattered throughout headquarters.

For some cases, they had time to spare, and they could afford to mess around with a meltdown or two from Amarynth. But something about this case felt different to Viv. More serious. Closer to home. Not that she could explain why. *Is this how Amarynth feels all the time?* Viv wondered. *No wonder she's such a mess.*

"Which jail? The East Watson Correctional Center," Amarynth replied. She wrote down the jail's address on a piece of paper seemingly from memory and handed it to Viv.

"I just know the address," Amarynth said, answering the question that no one was asking aloud.

"And why are we going to the jail?" Viv said.

"Because of a case," Amarynth said.

Viv sighed in frustration.

"She means," Karen said. "What should we do once we get there?"

Viv shot Karen a sharp glance, irritated at the interjection.

"You're going to ask the prison guards about Neia Stavropolous and Stephanie Mack," Amarynth replied.

"Who?" Penny said.

"Oh! Right! Okay, I can explain *that*," Amarynth replied. She spun around to face her causality board. "Those were the two women you found earlier, when you called in the newest case."

She pointed to a headshot that looked like it had come from an employee ID. "This is Stephanie Mack, the deceased victim. She worked at East Watson."

Karen felt a cold chill run through her, remembering the state of the woman's body. The blood. The demon with its wings outstretched. Or was it two women sitting back to back? She'd been unsure in the moment and was even less sure now.

"Yep, that's her," Penny said. "That's the spirit I was talking to."

"We'll have to take your word for it," Viv said. "Her face wasn't identifiable at the scene. It was... altered."

"Mmm," Amarynth said. "Unpleasant stuff." She pointed to another picture. "And this is Neia Stavropolous. She also worked at East Watson. Hopefully still will, once she recovers."

"Snow White!" Viv said.

Amarynth turned to face her with an incredulous look. "What?"

"Sorry. The victim who was comatose. I call her Snow White because she was lying there like Snow White did when she was poisoned by the apple."

Amarynth stared at Viv, not seeming to understand.

"In the cartoon? The movie? You know, the old one where she sings 'Someday My Prince Will Come.'"

Amarynth frowned. "Um okay, whatever you say." She paused. "And you say *I'm* bad at explaining things."

Penny laughed. "...Did you just tell a joke?"

Amarynth smiled. "Did I?"

"How is she anyway? Snow W—I mean, Neia," Karen said.

"She's stable. They took her the hospital. Funny thing, too. She woke up and promptly confessed," Amarynth said.

"What? Why are we going to the prison then? This is an easy case," Viv said. "Killer confessed. Case closed." But even as she said it, she had a feeling it wasn't true. That inexplicable intuition again.

"You'd think so, wouldn't you?" Amarynth said. "Only one problem. They physical evidence doesn't support it at all. This isn't a credible confession."

"Okay, so the physical evidence isn't there... allegedly," Viv said.

"Oh c'mon, Viv," Penny said.

"What?" Viv snapped.

"You know Amarynth wouldn't just *say* that it doesn't match if it did. She's never led us astray before," Penny said.

"Maybe not astray *per se*, but she's led us on a wild goose chase or two," Viv said.

"Wild goose chase?" Amarynth muttered, clearly unimpressed. "Geese are sociopaths. Pure avian evil."

"Well, maybe," Penny said to Viv, ignoring what Amarynth was saying. "Maybe sometimes she takes the long way around the barn sometimes –"

"The barn?" Amarynth grumbled, in an identical underwhelmed tone of voice.

Karen stifled a giggle.

"But she always gets us there, to where we need to be," Penny finished. "She's never sent us down the wrong path. Sometimes it seems that way, at first, but ultimately? She's our girl."

"Alright," Viv said. "So Amarynth?"

"Yeah?"

"You said Neia confessed to the crime. Have the truth evaluators been by?" Viv said. It was standard procedure to deploy a team every time a suspect confessed. This team was made up of tueys that specialized in detecting active deception, and that was pretty much it. A simple binary: Deception detected versus no deception detected. Nothing like the loud cacophony of emotions that Karen experienced every time she used her powers. Or more accurately, every time her powers used her, because that's always how it felt to her during a feel.

"They have," Amarynth said. "And they detected no deception. She clearly believes what she's saying."

Viv nodded. "Well, we all know that doesn't mean shit. And you know... Karen read her emotions at the scene, and well, let's just say it wasn't pretty."

"Really?" Amarynth said. "Wasn't pretty how?" She looked directly at Karen. "What did you feel from her?"

"She was..." Karen said, "I don't know how to describe it." She paused for a moment before adding, "She was completely deranged."

"Well, working at a prison can be a high-stress job," Penny said. "Maybe there's something to it, maybe it has to do with her job. Occupational stress. That kind of thing."

"Maybe," Amarynth said. "Well, not maybe. I *know* there's something to it. Just not sure what. Not yet. But if you go there, you should get a head start on things. The prison is important. The fact that she worked as a guard. That they both did."

"Right," Viv said. "We'll get right on it."

"Oh!" Amarynth said. "One more thing. I almost forgot to tell you the most important part."

The team waited while Amarynth fished a notepad out of the leaning tower of objects on her desk, steadying it with one hand like a person braces a Jenga game.

The tower shimmied disconcertingly but didn't topple over.

"Both of the victims are, or were, tueys. Demotivators, actually," Amarynth.

"Well holy shit," Viv said. "How the hell did someone kill and maim a demotivator like that with another one close by? Deranged or not. How is that even possible?"

Demotivators

Demotivators are a very specialized type of intuitive. Their main power is the ability to make everyone around them extremely lazy.

As a power, demotivation can be quite subtle, and many demotivators are not fully cognizant of their power until well into young adulthood, when the tendencies are detected by a routine precollege intuitive aptitude battery.

Part of this delay in detection might be because demotivators are found primarily in underachieving families who live in underperforming school districts. While they don't possess any special scholastic abilities themselves and are quite average performers, as children they will excel at virtually every task relative to everyone who surrounds them, who simply will not try or apply themselves.

In adulthood, many demotivators find work as guards in prisons or mental institutions, anywhere that their powers of pacification will be advantageous in preventing riots or escape attempts. But their abilities aren't simply useful in this one particular context.

Perhaps the most famous demotivator of all is the world renown mononymous demotivational speaker Mallow, author of *Why Worry?*, and many high-end spas and resorts will employ at least one demotivator to help their clients to relax and more quickly go on "island time."

from Insecta Psychica: Towards an Intuitive
Taxonomy by Cloche Macomber

A Very Important Prisoner

Viv sighed as they filled out the visitor's forms. "Of all the prisons in the world, why did they have to work at this one?" she wondered aloud grimly.

Prisons in general weren't exactly user friendly for visitors, but East Watson Correctional Center was a paragon of bureaucracy. And to enter, you basically had to sign your life away not once, not twice, but in triplicate.

The intake worker scowled. "You try getting steady work as a demotivator," she said. "You work where you can."

"Oh," Karen said, "Are you....?"

The worker shook her head. "No, I'm not a tuey. But I've been friendly with a lot of demotivators. They hire a lot of them in this facility. Good for keeping high-profile prisoners in line. Our escape rate is statistically insignificant. Essentially zero."

"Essentially?" Viv asked.

The worker frowned and didn't answer.

Karen tried a change of topic. "And you knew Neia and Stephanie, didn't you?"

"Sure," the worker said. "Not that I worked with them much. They work their own beat. Demotivators are usually paired with each other. Being too close to them isn't good for morale, you know. But over the years, you do spend a bit of time with them, especially on breaks. Super relaxing breaks." She said the last bit wistfully, looking off into space, before catching herself and returning to a professional, unemotional posture.

"I'm sorry for your loss," Penny said.

"Sure you are," the worker said. She handed them another stack of forms.

"She is," Karen said. "We all are."

"Look, I know it's what you're supposed to say. But you're here today because you're doing your job. Just like I'm doing mine. You're homicide detectives. Without a stack of dead bodies, you can't pay your rent."

"Well, I'm sorry you knew someone in our stack then," Viv said.

The worker looked Viv in the eyes, considered her face briefly. "Thanks," she said. "I appreciate that."

Viv had learned long ago that there are certain people in this world who aren't used to kindness. Especially big gestures or grandiose general purpose statements of comfort. Such things always rang hollow to people like that, who were accustomed to a difficult life and being kicked on their ass. It was easy for them to tell themselves you didn't mean it, that it was something you said to everyone, that you were placating or flattering them.

Sometimes you could still get to them though, if you made the kindness small enough, specific enough. Only when you'd broken the kindness down into its smallest components could you reach them. Tiny particles that worked their way through the giant barriers they constructed to keep others out.

"Sorry you knew someone in our stack" did the trick this time. The worker loosened up considerably. She relaxed, shuffling the parade of increasingly more specific, pessimistic, and downright morbid forms over the desk.

As the detectives initialed boxes to indicate to the prison that they wouldn't sue if they were electrocuted, disemboweled, or flung into an alternate dimension (that last one was just a rumor, but prison officials weren't taking any chances with litigation, the damages could be astronomical — literally), the worker actually smiled a few times. And even more tellingly she laughed at a few of Penny's stupid jokes.

"Neia and Stephanie worked deep in the prison," the worker explained once the forms were filled out, leading them through a series of corridors that even to Viv, with her keen visual powers, looked nearly identical.

Even the overhead lights seemed to blink in a similar pattern. Like they all had loose connections. "Prison disco balls," their guide joked in the first corridor.

"Staying alive," she remarked in the second. It was clear though to them that this was a rehearsed joke. Something she had said many times to many groups of visitors before them.

There was a slight visual variant in the third corridor. Viv noted a quarter second delay between overhead light blinks as they headed through the area. She concentrated on this difference, making a mental note, not sure if it were important.

"Aaaaand disco inferno," their guide said in the third hallway standing underneath that blinking light, before opening a locked door that spilled out into an open area.

A conspicuously empty and silent open area. There was another desk, where a few guards sat deeply engrossed at their computers. One was typing furiously on their keyboard. The other looked much more relaxed as they smiled and clicked their mouse every few seconds.

On the back wall were a series of doors that appeared to lead to janitor's closets.

"This isn't your normal cellblock," Penny thought aloud.

"Of course not," the worker said. "This is where we keep VIPs. Very important prisoners." She gestured to the janitor closets. "Those are actually cells, but we wanted them to look as non-descript as possible. It's possible to clear out this entire room in 10 minutes if you need to. Make it look like an empty room."

"Why would you need to?" Karen asked.

Their guide didn't answer the question.

"Who's staying here now?" Viv asked, trying a different tack.

They walked towards the desk together as a group. As they came closer to it, Viv suddenly felt tired.

She wasn't the only one. "Do you have chairs?" Penny asked their guide.

Their guide frowned. "We do." She gestured over to a stack of folding chairs leaning against one of the walls.

"I saw those," Karen said. "But they're over there. Do you have any that are closer?"

Their guide shook her head no.

Viv abruptly sat down on the floor.

"You can't sit on the floor," their guide said. "It's against prison regulations."

Viv vaguely remembered that rule being somewhere in the stack of papers she'd signed but wasn't exactly sure. Thinking hurt her head. She could do with a nap. "Then bring me a chair," Viv replied.

"But they're way over there," the worker said.

"*Penny. Karen,*" Viv said, making the most menacing eye contact with the worker that she could.

Penny and Karen sighed. They were suddenly exhausted, too, but knew better than to challenge Viv when she was at the end of her rope. And judging by her expression, she was. Together Penny and Karen made the arduous 12-foot journey to the folding chairs.

This is waaaay harder than it should be, Karen thought. *I feel like I'm blazing the Oregon Trail.*

 Karen, always looking for a way to impress Viv, grabbed two chairs. Penny picked up just one for her.

"Hey, what about me? Where am I supposed to sit?" their guide asked Penny, upon seeing this.

Penny sighed and grabbed a second one, not wanting to anger their guide and risk getting kicked out of the prison.

Groaning from exertion, Penny and Karen set up the folding chairs so that all four of them could sit down. Viv insisted on getting a boost from their guide up off where she was sitting on the floor because standing up from a seated position was so difficult. It was the least the guide could do, Viv argued, after Penny had gone all that way and gotten a seat for her.

"Glad we didn't have much further to go," their guide remarked. "I might have had to give you all piggyback rides."

"So which one of you is the demotivator?" Viv asked the two guards behind the desk, raising her voice and waving her hand in their direction. Because she sure as heck wasn't about to get up and get their attention in a more conventional way. Too much effort.

"The one who *isn't* sitting there playing computer games instead of you know... actually working," one guard replied.

"I'm working as hard as I can, given the circumstances," the other replied.

"Sure you are," the demotivator guard replied.

It must be difficult spending your whole life killing other people's work ethic just by existing, Karen realized in that instant. Everywhere you went, you'd be followed by the curse of competence. Surrounded by lazy people. Left to do everything on your own.

Forget being part of a team. Unless you happened to be in the company of other demotivators.

You'd be condemned to an existence where no matter where you went, you'd be set up to have to do more than your fair share.

That had to be depressing.

"Whatever," the second guard said.

"This is why they usually station us in pairs," the demotivator explained. "But we've been shorthanded ever since... the incident. A bunch of us are working solo."

"You are *not* working solo," the second guard said, clearly offended.

"Okay," the demotivator said. "Well, we're not working with other demotivators. We're paired with normals. Or different kinds of tueys. But as you can see, we aren't actually working very efficiently."

"It's fine," Viv said. "We know what you mean."

"Do you have any idea why anyone would have wanted to hurt Neia and Stephanie?" Penny asked the demotivator.

"Other than the obvious, no," the demotivator replied.

"The obvious?" Karen asked.

"Well, prisoners want to get out. Demotivators make that nearly impossible. Kill or derange a demotivator, you upset the natural balance of things. Our staffing situation is a mess at the moment. Maybe you can escape during a time like this. Or if you can't escape, maybe you can use the short staffing to pull some strings. Get paroled. Early release. Easier to convince a prison that's shorthanded to let people out. Especially if you have friends in high places," the demotivator said.

"Friends in high places?" Viv said. "Anybody come to mind?"

The demotivator rose from her desk, bringing a clipboard to the circle where they sat in their folding chairs.

"Here's a list of our current high-profile inmates," the demotivator said, handing it to Viv.

One name leapt out instantly to her. "Oh my God," Viv said. "You have Bronson Eck locked up here?"

The demotivator nodded.

"An Eck?" Karen said. "How is this not all over the news?"

"Beats me," the demotivator. "When you have enough friends and enough money, I guess news stories don't have to happen."

The Ecks were one of the Four Noble Families who made things run. The Families that everyone knew and no one dared to cross. Their earliest members were researchers that had been responsible for a great many important scientific discoveries, something they would never let society forget.

Each of the Four Families had given their names to many institutions and important places. Notably, the Skinners had founded the city of Skinner, the epicenter for intuitive activity in the world, also known as the Psychic City. B.F. Skinner had been their patriarch, the father of operant conditioning. He was responsible for showing how people's responses could be shaped and strengthened based on training.

While no one knew exactly how the intuitives came to be and certainly couldn't trace their existence to any one founding event, many did suspect that Skinner was somehow involved in the sudden emergence of psychic activity. There was no evidence of this, but it frankly seemed like something he would do. He liked playing God.

The very building they were sitting in was named for another one of the Families: The Watsons.

Skinner's sister city of Watson also bore the researcher's name. Together the two cities and their exhaustive networks of suburbs encompassed an impressive swath of urban — and suburban sprawl. Although only one part of the larger Psychic State, Skinner-Watson itself was the size of a small state all on its own.

John Watson had been a behaviorist who had insisted that a child could be shaped to follow any particular path depending on their nurture, regardless of nature.

Some people suspected Watson of creating the intuitives. But people largely agreed that if it had been Watson who created the intuitives, it would have had to have been by accident. He just wasn't like that, they argued, wasn't someone that would have wanted to unleash such a major experiment without safeguards in place. Although he *was* prone to accidents, so one had to admit it was *possible* that he slipped up somewhere and had done something that led to a bunch of people having psychic powers.

Maybe he'd done it and didn't even realize what he'd done. Accidentally changed society forever. Stranger things had happened... and were still happening.

The final two Noble Families, the Ecks and the Macombers, had originally been part of the same Noble Family (they were all called Ecks then), a research team devoted to charting and cataloguing personality and how it changes over the course of one's lifespan, but they had been cleft left apart a generation ago by a particularly nasty divorce and the family feud that followed, demonstrating an important truism: We reserve our most violent hatred not for those who are completely different than us but for those who are nearly identical to us and only diverge from us in tiny ways.

What unfolded between the two Families was spectacular tabloid fodder. Following the divorce, the Ecks publicly announced that they were glad to be rid of the Macombers, an eclectic crew who seemed obsessed with alchemy and other vaguely magical pursuits like Neo-Freudianism. But privately and through their actions, the Ecks seemed to remain fixated on the Family that was once a part of theirs, even if that fixation often looked like hate and violence.

The Ecks were pioneers in the research surrounding decision-making, game theory, and economics. The older generation had become very wealthy due to this work, but the Family's younger members kept getting into trouble. It was as if the very qualities that drove them to succeed as a Family in the first place — a seeming inability to ever be satisfied, a tendency to take risks others wouldn't, a very weak moral compass, and a tireless desire to amass as much wealth as possible, no matter the means — had come back to haunt them, particularly as the bloodline thinned.

They had begun to focus more overtly on amassing power, on building up a superior reputation... and strangely, on appearing on reality TV programs. But lately even that hadn't seemed to be enough. There were whisperings all around the Eck Family that they were being consumed by vices. Further, a socially sadistic stripe was seen throughout the younger members; they didn't just want to control others but to humiliate them. This sadism, too, was a form of addiction, just as potentially dangerous to their longevity as a clan as other more conventional bad habits.

Bronson Eck was a clear case of this. A young man with an incredible mind for numbers, he struggled with sociopathy and a gambling addiction. His powerful family had been able to shield him from the consequences of his actions for many years, but once he murdered a Macomber over a high-stakes game of poker, that shield of protection had quickly dissipated.

There were simply some places too far out.

A Family member could get away with almost anything. But murdering a member of another Family? That was unforgivable.

Still, incarceration was enough. No one wanted to make a fuss. Or cause a media spectacle.

They all had their reputations to consider. Victim and victimizer alike. It made them all look bad when people paid too much negative attention to any of the Families.

 The detectives left the prison about 20 minutes later. "You know," Penny said. "We spent more time filling out forms than we did actually investigating."

"That's detective work for you," Viv replied.

"Speak for yourself," Penny said.

"I was," Viv said.

Penny rolled her eyes, but it was a soft roll, the one you do when you genuinely like someone, but you're not terribly impressed by what they just said.

"It's too bad we couldn't interview Bronson Eck today," Penny said.

"I know, right?" Viv agreed.

Karen just sighed. That was frequently her way of adding her own opinion to the mix. Sometimes when she did this, Viv would call her a moody teenager, and there wasn't much she could do to defend herself against the allegation, especially as she never went anywhere without her trusty hoodie. It was convenient, a bit like a shell to a turtle. If things got to be too much — which they often did in their line of work — she could retract for however long she wanted, hide under the massive hood.

True, turtles are physically incapable of leaving their shells, at least leaving their shells and surviving afterwards. Shells are built into their skeletons. If you took a turtle out of its shell, you'd basically be ripping its body in half.

To be fair to Karen, no one had really tested out what would happen if you took Karen's favorite hoodie away from her permanently, although said hoodie was often spotted on the bathroom floor for brief periods of time when she was showering.

"Don't worry, Karen," Penny said, knowing as soon as the words left her mouth that it was a tall order. Karen's anxiety seemed to thrive on such challenges. Rise up in response to them. Penny quickly added, "We'll go through the proper channels and come back."

The proper channels presented yet another bureaucratic maze, but hopefully Martin could throw his weight around or appeal to his own supervisors to do so and get them a sit-down. Martin was good like that.

As they drove away from the prison, they talked over the case. It seemed very likely that this crime had something to do with the Families. *Maybe that's why I've felt so troubled by this*, Viv thought. *Why I felt like it wasn't a normal case. Because if it involves the Families, it isn't.*

"We have to be careful if it's the Families we're dealing with," Penny said aloud. "They could end us just like that." She snapped her fingers.

"Oh please," Karen said. "They wouldn't even have to snap. They're rich enough to get someone else to snap for them."

"And pay them to like it," Viv said.

They laughed, but it was a joyless laugh, one that relieved tension and filled space but didn't reflect true happiness.

"I really hope it's not the Families," Karen said. "But I don't see anything else here that even comes close to explaining why someone would have wanted to come after those women. Pretty standard prisoner load, especially in the cellblocks they typically worked. According to their personnel file, they haven't even worked in the prison system that long."

"Oh?" Penny said. "Where'd they work before?"

"On a locked mental ward," Karen said. "Funny coincidence there though."

"Coincidence?" Viv said.

"Well, they worked at Nirvana Heights," Karen said.

"Now, *that's* a name I haven't heard for a long time," Penny said.

"And I'm glad, too," Viv said. "It's not something I want to talk about. Especially not now."

Because they had pulled into the driveway in front of Viv's mother's house, finally making it to the visit they'd had to cancel on account of rushing to the scene of the crime.

And all three of them knew that Nirvana Heights would be the last thing in the world Viv's mother would want to talk about.

"Wait here," Viv told Penny and Karen as she left the car to enter her mother's house. "I'll come get you in a minute, I mean... if..."

Karen nodded. "We know."

Penny said, "If the currents are right."

Viv nodded, got up, and left the car.

After Viv had vanished into the house, Karen turned to Penny and said, "I think I have just enough range to keep an eye on her without the feelings coming back."

Penny smiled. "I think you do," she agreed.

"I'm going to stick close," Karen said. "Just in case things go pear shaped."

Penny nodded. "Don't blame you. With that family, you're pretty much guaranteed it'll go pear shaped. You're lucky when the pear doesn't rot."

Karen nodded.

"If Tenny weren't a wax fruit, she'd have gone off thirty times by now," Penny added.

Karen laughed and left the car, being careful to shut the door quietly. Treading as lightly as she could, she made her way to the front hallway, closing the door slowly behind her. Pressing herself against the mud room wall, she listened.

Love Me, Tender

Euphemia "Tender" Lee – or "Tenny" as her gentlemen callers had nicknamed her – was a lady of indeterminate age who was... well preserved, you might say. If you were being tactful.

If you weren't being tactful, you'd say she looked like a Texas trophy wife. Skin improbably tanned. Tight facial expressions that never quite moved naturally through the full range, stopping just short, like a batter who pretends to swing but stops themselves before they inadvertently strike out.

Tenny dressed like a corporate lawyer except her necklines were always a few inches lower and her stilettos a few inches higher than would be tolerated in most boardrooms.

Not that she'd ever worked a day in her life.

Unless you counted raising her brat daughters and pretending whatever man she was talking to was the most fascinating person on the planet as work.

If you didn't know her well, you'd assume that Tenny adored men. She spent enough time with them after all. Had been married nine times. Languished attention on them.

But her daughters knew differently. Having little respect for her daughters and little regard for what they might think of her, Tenny always spoke to them without a filter.

"Men have two purposes," Tenny had told her daughter Viv when she was still in elementary school. "To disappoint us and to feed us."

"All men?" Viv had asked when she was a little girl, wide eyed.

Tenny nodded. "The disappointments never get any better," she continued. "But if you find a good man, the meals do."

The same exact woman sat before Viv now. Tender Lee hadn't aged a day in the time that Viv had aged 20. Well, not physically anyway. Mentally, her mother could be a bit here and there, especially over the last few years. But Tender Lee covered over the gaps in her memory with finesse. Confabulating with the best of them. Making up new details to explain any discrepancies.

She was good at making everything make sense, even when nothing did.

It had taken her daughters a while to notice her mental decline because Tenny had always had a tenuous relationship with the truth. Some kind of psychiatric diagnosis, probably a personality disorder. She'd been treated in the past, even spent some time inpatient on a locked ward at Nirvana Heights, but wouldn't tell anyone what for.

"Oh, you know," she'd say, tossing her hair with a dramatic flourish as if expecting it to distract the questioner like a cascade of scintillating lights, "Stress. Exhaustion. Your standard risks of being a society lady."

Typical of her. She kept her true cards close to her chest and flung false ones in every direction to distract onlookers, just like a magician performing a misdirection. Viv's mother had always lied. The reasons why just changed over the years. It had always been about survival. In the beginning, survival hinged on the manipulation of others. These days, survival was about maintaining a coherent plotline even as she fell into emotional sinkholes that her deteriorating memory created. No matter the cost.

And yet… there was something different about her today. "Why, Mom," Viv said. "You're having a good day, aren't you?"

Viv's sister Love popped her head into the living room. "Of course she is, you twat, Mama has a good day every day."

Tender nodded. "Your sister is right, Viv."

"Why, *of course* I am," Love said. "Every day's a good day on God's green earth when you're alive, Mama. For you, for me, for everyone. Some of us are just more grateful than others." Love shot Viv a dirty look.

Huddled out of sight in the mud room, Karen stifled a laugh. It was a real trip anytime she hung out with Viv's family. The first time had been jarring as for some reason Viv didn't have the thick Southern accent that her sister and mother spoke in.

Later she'd asked Viv if she'd trained herself out of it.

"No," Viv had replied. "It just went away when we moved West." She explained that her mother and her sister had kept theirs on purpose "to honor the General."

"The General? General Lee?" Karen had asked. "Robert E. Lee?"

"Oh, Bobby?" Viv had said, doing a spot-on imitation of her mother, along with her mother's affected giggle. "You know, honey, Bobby was *family*. Too bad about that nasty old Northern war. We really had them in the first half."

It was amusing to Karen, knowing that the accent Love and Tender still used was on purpose. But not surprising.

Because so much about Viv's mother was on purpose. Or, if one were so inclined, you could call her *contrived*.

It was a sharp contrast from Viv, who while definitely having some deep-seated control issues was about as genuine as they came. Love her or hate her, Viv was who she was. You never had to wonder where she stood.

Whereas her mother was more of a blank canvas. The real woman, had she ever truly existed in the first place, had been stripped away years ago, like a house undergoing a radical renovation. Everything had been knocked out, rebuilt, to satisfy each new occupants' whims. Every new man's desires.

And it was a mystery what original structures lay underneath – if anything.

Sometimes Viv thought there might be nothing there, nothing underneath her mother's façade except for a box ready to be filled up with other people's desires. She noted that was what her mother thought the ideal woman should be, after all – a blank space ready to accommodate everyone she met but especially rich eligible bachelors.

There was certainly no love in this woman. No commitment. Nor even any genuine affection. Her relationships with men were transactional, and she had always viewed her children not as fully-fledged individuals but as accomplishments, expensive possessions, or at best human pets.

Anything her children did that didn't bring her prestige was of little interest to her. And anything they did that could potentially bring her shame or dishonor... well, that was just insufferable, wasn't it?

Like having your dog shit on the floor while you had company over.

It was no good.

Couldn't have the neighbors talking about her, could she?
Unless that talk were bitter envy of how their own lives
couldn't measure up to how the Lees were living.

So it had come as little surprise to Viv that her mother hadn't
approved when Penny had moved in with Viv and started
picking out new furniture. Nor was it surprising when Viv's
mother had approved even less when a few years later Karen
joined them.

That just wasn't how things were done. Who ever heard of
a bunch of women living together? They should all have
husbands. Children. Big diamond rings.

Not traipsing around who-knew-where as homicide
detectives.

Homicide. Hardly a concern for a lady. Certainly not
something Tenny Lee could brag about, that her daughter
was stalking around dark alleys poking at dead bodies and
guessing at how they ended up there.

Viv sat on the plastic-covered couch holding a chipped
teacup in her hand, one of "the Regency dishes" that
her mother practically worshipped but were clearly
reproductions. This tea set had been through a tough time,
brutalized by various moves from home to home, the
inexorable U-Haul shuffle that had marked her adolescence
as her mother met a new "soulmate" every other week.

Holding it in her hand, Viv felt herself relating to the little
cup. She had been quite brutalized herself by all those moves,
dented and dropped like the rest of her mother's possessions.
As she reflected on this and sipped tea, Viv braced herself for
the talk that she got every time she visited. The one she knew
would be coming.

But instead her mother said, "You know, I wasn't so sure when these ladies moved in with you, Viv, but now I'm glad."

Viv cocked her head. What was her mom on about? She had never said anything remotely like that ever before. She sounded... supportive.

Tenny Lee smiled broadly. "I had big dreams for you," she said. "My dreams. Regular dreams."

Viv winced. *Alright*, she thought. *If that's the worst of it, it's not so bad. I know we're different and that Mom centers everything around herself.*

"But you're chasing your own dreams now," Tenny continued. "And that's a good thing."

Who was this woman? Viv wondered. This was completely unlike her mother.

"Thanks, Mom," Viv said aloud. "I appreciate that."

Tenny smiled broadly. Took a long lingering sip from her own teacup. "Besides," Tenny said. "I wasn't sure how someone like you would ever find someone decent. Now I know."

Viv frowned. "What do you mean... someone like me?"

"Oh honey, you're a smart girl," Tenny replied. "I don't have to spell it out for you."

"Are you sure about that?" Viv said.

"Dear, you *know* what I mean," Tenny said.

"I know what you *could* mean, Mom. That's not the same thing."

Her mother sighed. "Fine. You've always been stubborn. That's the first thing, really. The first strike against you."

"Stubborn?" Viv said. "Really? You think anyone's stubborn that you can't just lead around by the neck."

"By the neck?" Tenny sad, smirking. "I suppose that's one way to do. Not exactly the body part I usually have in mind."

"Mom, that's gross," Viv said, suddenly thinking of other body parts her mother could have used as a leash in all her liaisons with wealthy men.

"Whatever could you be talking about?" her mother said, affecting a coquettish smile. Or trying to. Her face didn't move these days as much as it used to, although Viv could tell when her mother was trying.

Viv frowned.

"Anyway," Tenny continued. "You're stubborn. You curse. Dress like a house painter. And a sloppy one at that. It's like it'd kill you to show some skin or let anyone know there's a body under there."

Viv rolled her eyes.

"And your visions, honey…" Tenny said, letting her voice trail off.

"What about my visions?" Viv said.

"Well, it's not the kind of thing most people want to put up with. That most people understand. To be a tuey on top of the rest of that, well… let's just say you aren't an easy girl to set up with eligible bachelors."

"Not that you didn't try," Viv remarked.

"Not that I didn't try," Tenny agreed. "As any good mother would."

Viv snorted. The notion that her mother had been a good one was the funniest thing she'd heard in quite some time.

"Ungrateful, too. Which is a death knell to being a successful woman, to landing a good man, a good provider. That's what most providers want, gratitude. A thank you. They want you to make them feel big and powerful. Indispensable."

"I can take care of myself," Viv said.

"In a fashion," Tenny said. She didn't elaborate.

Which was fine with Viv since Viv didn't really want her to.

"Anyway," Tenny continued, "If you can't be grateful to your dear old mother, who literally gave you life, then how ever will you butter up a man the way that he needs? It's no wonder you became a lesbian."

Normally Viv didn't mind that word – *lesbian* – nor even mind the strange notion that it was something she'd become and not something she'd always been, but when her mother said the word *lesbian*, with an uncomfortable emphasis and clear disdain, it sounded like a different word altogether.

It sounded like a slur. Viv winced.

"Was it difficult for me? Yes. Embarrassing? For sure. But you know, that part of you made sense. You weren't quite right, couldn't give men what they needed. So you found another woman who can't give men what they need... well, it's a bit tacky and weird, but that makes sense to me," her mother continued. "And besides, Penny is a real lady. The kind of woman I'm surprised couldn't make it work with men."

Viv felt herself freezing in place, the blood beginning to boil in her ears.

"Karen though? That was a bit of a shock, I'll admit it. It was hard enough when you took up with Penny," Tenny continued, "but Karen, too? Really, Viv?"

"What about Karen?" Viv grumbled, feeling positively masochistic even asking. It was a weird sensation, to be so suddenly robbed of her power. As her mother sneered at her (or tried to, working against the natural paralysis of too many anti-wrinkle injections) from behind her teacup, Viv felt herself becoming a small child again. Stuck in the driver's seat as her mom soliloquized odiously.

Viv had never quite understood why, but her mother had a way of rendering her helpless and passive, even as her mother said things that infuriated her. Once again, Viv found herself unable to speak in a situation where she would have let someone else have it.

"*Whaaaat about Kaaaaren?*" Tenny repeated, stretching out the words and laughing. "My dear, you let a crazy girl into your life. One who could very well steal your common law wife from you, the moment you drop your guard. How does that make any sense?"

Viv swallowed. This was not something she wanted to discuss with her mother. Not now. Not ever.

In the hallway, Karen fumed silently. None of what Viv's mother was saying was true. Well, maybe the bit about Karen being crazy had some merit. Okay, there might be some truth there. She *was* different than other people emotionally. That said, "crazy" wasn't a nice way of describing someone else. But then again, when was Viv's mother ever nice when she didn't want something in return? And it was true that Karen had struggled with her mental health. Not that Viv's mother were one to talk, as she'd spent time herself on an inpatient psych ward.

So the "crazy" charge was mean and a bit of an odd allegation coming from Tender Lee (pot, kettle anyone?) but true enough.

But the rest of it was way off base. They weren't just a bunch of failed heterosexuals. Women who couldn't hack it at the one true goal in life of being transactional puppeteers of hapless rich men. Not everyone wanted to live like Tenny.

And Karen would never try to break Viv and Penny up. She'd never wanted to. She wasn't a homewrecker. Karen loved their dynamic the way things were, with both of them in picture. It was an unconventional life, sure, living with two lovers who were also involved with one another, but it made her happy.

She thought for sure it made Viv happy, too.

But if that was the case, why wasn't Viv defending her?

"Everyone blames me for the way you turned out," Tenny continued. "A one-woman home for wayward girls."

"*Mom*," Viv said. It was her darkest, sternest tone. And it was all she said. It was a kind of warning.

"Ah," Tenny said. "It would seem I've stepped way out of line." She batted her eyelashes. "Forgive me." She waved her right arm in an intricate pattern in the air.

A servant arrived carrying a plate of tea cookies. "Here, dear," Tenny said. "Have a few. You're practically wasting away."

"Thanks," Viv said, reaching for one.

"I can't believe you waste a body like that on a couple of women," Tenny said.

"Mom," Viv said in that same tone.

"Oh dear, what came over me?" Tenny said. "So... how's the detective life going? Any exciting cases lately? It seems like every time I talk to you, you're working or about to."

Viv smiled. Leaned forward. And started to talk about their current caseload. She wound up by talking about a case they'd just wrapped up, one where a man had accidentally locked himself in his own freezer but for a while had seemed like it might be foul play. And a few more cases that were seeming like they were domestic disputes that had gone horribly wrong.

Viv made sure to save their biggest case, the Snow White incident, until the end. She did her best to be a compelling storyteller, painting the scene of both her vision of the scene beforehand and the crime for her mother in vivid detail.

Tenny, who had been slouching and gazing idly up until that point as if her daughter was not talking about grisly murders but reading the phone book, came to life then.

"Really?" Tenny said. "The victims were tueys? That's unusual, isn't it?"

Viv nodded. "Very. Especially a pair of demotivators." Viv recounted her own experience at the prison. The way she'd felt suddenly as though she were incapable of doing *anything*. It was as though she'd been up for days *and* had 100-lb weights strapped to each leg.

"Ah, so you became lazy all of a sudden?" Tenny said.

Viv nodded.

"Reminds me of when you were a teenager," Tenny joked.

"Mom!" Viv said, but it was a light protest, like a joke between old friends.

Karen seethed in the entryway. She was glad Viv wasn't being pummeled by her mom anymore but irritated that Viv hadn't come to her defense when her mother had attacked her. And now it was as if everything were okay between the two of them. Like they were old pals.

Gross.

Karen briefly considered bringing it up later with her, but she knew how that would go. How it had gone the other times that Karen had questioned Viv's relationship with her mother.

"You don't know what you're talking about," Viv had said in the past, when Karen had expressed concerns about Tenny's effect on Viv's psychological health.

"Well, I can't say that I know what it was like to be raised by Tenny," Karen had said, "but you know I didn't have an easy time with my father."

Viv had nodded.

"So maybe I have a bit of insight into what I'm talking about," Karen had said.

Viv had rolled her eyes.

"And I know you hate when I play 'the Empath Card' –"

"I do," Viv had interjected.

"But… Viv. I'm probably the only other person in the world who really understands how you feel when she treats you like that. I don't just feel for you, I've felt it *with* you. And I'm not sure that relationship is *worth* it."

Viv had frowned. "What do you know? You're a fine one to give advice."

"What do you mean?" Karen had said.

"I'm not going to listen to a *quitter*," Viv had said, putting as much weight as possible on that final word.

If Viv's intention had been to shut Karen up by any means possible, it had worked. It had stung. Karen had glared at her, combing her mind for something to say back. Karen had wanted to scream at Viv, but nothing had seemed profane enough. A simple "fuck you" or "go to Hell" could never convey the depth of the violation of being judged like that. It had almost seemed like it would take violence to communicate such a thing.

It was true that Karen had cut her father out of her life. That she didn't talk to her him anymore. But to characterize that as quitting… well, that was a complete mischaracterization. Quitting implied something was easy. That something was a concession. A form of surrender.

Cutting her father out hadn't been surrender; it had been an amputation. The hardest thing Karen had ever done. Painful, but necessary. Like sawing off an infected leg to save her own life.

"I didn't quit," Karen had said to Viv. "I amputated something that was killing me."

Viv had rolled her eyes. "My mother isn't killing me."

"No," Karen had said. "But she drains you. She empties you. She does that to everyone. You're not any different."

It had been Viv's turn to feel profoundly wounded. "Look, Karen, you don't have to be cruel. I get it. I know I'm not special to my mother," Viv had said in a tired voice. "That's a hope I gave up a long time ago."

"That's not what I meant," Karen had said.

"Sure," Viv had said. In a tone that meant that she didn't really want to agree but wanted to end the conversation.

"I didn't," Karen had said again, deliberately.

"Oh for fuck's sake," Viv had said.

"What?"

"You and Penny are always doing this," Viv had said, her voice weary.

"Doing what?"

"Saying mean shit and then adding on 'that's not what I meant,' when you realize you've hurt me. You don't get to decide what should hurt me and what shouldn't. Your intent is one thing, but your impact is another. And one isn't more important than another. They can co-exist. You can mean well but still hurt me," Viv had said.

"I know that," Karen had said.

"Do you?" Viv had challenged her.

"Of course I do," Karen had said. She'd experienced it. "I've actually felt it before," she had explained. "I've said something in good faith and actually *felt* the other person take it the wrong way. I've felt their pain."

"I find that hard to believe," Viv had said.

"Why? You know how my powers work," Karen had said.

"I just don't understand how someone who could really *feel* another person's pain could ever cause it," Viv had said. "You'd think you'd stop, knowing how it felt. And knowing you'd have to feel that pain with them."

"That's just the thing," Karen had said.

"What?"

"If you don't intend to do something, if you aren't doing it on purpose, it's hard to stop doing it. It's literally an accident. And just because my toes hurt, too, when I accidentally step on yours, it doesn't mean that I can just will myself to be less clumsy," Karen had said.

Viv hadn't known what to say, so she had stayed quiet.

"There's a certain point where you just have to forgive someone," Karen had said. "Let them be human."

"Or psychic," Viv had said.

"Or both," Karen had said.

Karen thought about that conversation again as she seethed in the mudroom, waiting for Viv's visit with Tenny to be over.

Finally, Tenny began to talk about her plans for later in the evening in that tone of voice that politely signals to a guest that they maybe should head out.

Karen took that as her cue to leave and quietly headed back out to the car to sit with Penny.

"Good visit?" Penny asked perkily.

"As good as could be expected," Karen replied. This was, after all, Viv and her mother.

"I was kind of hoping she'd invite us in for once," Penny replied.

"Viv would have to grow a spine for that to happen," Karen said.

"That's not very nice," Penny said. "But I get it," she added, after a pause.

The front door swung open, and Viv appeared. As Viv climbed into the car, neither Penny nor Karen asked her how the conversation had gone.

Instead Penny asked if either of them needed her to pick up anything on the drive home.

Karen proposed a series of snack options, while Viv shot each one of them down. Penny mentally prepared a driving route that would take them near a grocery store but not set them back too far if they couldn't figure out what they wanted.

Viv and Karen never did come to an agreement. They were home without ever coming to a consensus.

Penny lingered in the car for a moment as Viv and Karen tore into the house, heading in opposite directions.

"I guess it's up to me," she said to the empty car.

The Interloper

Neither Karen nor Viv were up to making dinner after the visit at Viv's mother's house, so it was up to Penny to pick up the slack.

"Like usual," Penny said to herself, when she was certain they were out of earshot. Passive-aggressive, but she didn't particularly care. Something had to give, even if it had to give in private.

Being the perky, positive one was a role she mostly relished. She liked being the one with the even keel.

The one who was always unruffled. Resilient. But on certain days, it was a tough ruse to keep up.

Because of her powers, Karen had seen under her veneer many times. Karen knew the truth. And yet, Karen was happy to let Penny keep up the façade. In more positive moments, Penny attributed this to Karen being on her team and supporting her. "She doesn't want to blow my cover," Penny would tell herself.

Other times, it just seemed like an awfully convenient way for Karen to take advantage of her. To ignore the secret truth and just act as though Penny was as unflappable as she pretended to be. Act like Penny was always game to do chores. Like Penny never had down times or bad spells.

Today was one of those times. Penny grumbled as she rifled through the cabinets looking for a pot. Karen had of course just haphazardly put away the dishes –*again*—with no rhyme or reason.

"Viv would kill her... if Viv ever bothered to open the cupboard," Penny said to herself. Because she couldn't remember the last time Viv had cooked dinner.

"She's been sick. New medicine," a voice in Penny's head said.

Except... the voice *wasn't in her head.*

Penny spun around. Standing next to the sink was a stranger.

She felt a tight braid of fear in her chest. Who could this be? Who the hell was in her house? How had she missed the sound of the door closing, footsteps?

But then she saw the dirty fork sitting next to the drain directly behind her guest, and it dawned on her what was going on.

Ah yes, Penny told herself. *It's a spirit. Not a living person.*

"I don't think I know a single person who hasn't been sick lately," Penny said to the spirit. "Everyone's working harder every day. Especially in this neighborhood... am I right?"

"Evoking pity's an interesting strategy," the spirit said.

"Strategy?" Penny asked.

"You use strategies when interacting with the undead. Gambits. I don't know what you call them in your private thoughts, but that's what they seem like to me anyway. I've seen you talk before to some of my friends."

"Did you?" Penny asked. In her own head, she wondered if this were even possible. Spirits traveled of course, but she'd never heard of them engaging in this form of metacognition. As far as she knew, they weren't capable of observing other scenes between the living and dead and reporting in on them later. This was the first she'd ever heard of such a thing. But she supposed anything were possible.

"There's a lot you don't know about us," the spirit continued. "Even after all this time."

"Like what?" Penny said.

"Why bother explaining?" the spirit said. "You're clearly not a great listener."

"That's unfair," Penny said.

"Really?" the spirit replied.

"Yes," Penny said. "I listen just fine."

"You might hear the words," the spirit said, "but the ideas, well..."

"Well what?"

"Your mind is too full of your own beliefs. You're too set in your ways to really learn from us is what I'm saying. Typical arrogance of the living. Like a child explaining to her parents how the real world works. Although I guess that analogy doesn't work so well on someone without parents, does it?"

Penny winced in spite of herself. How did the spirit know about that? She rolled her shoulders, conjured her most unfazed expression. Then Penny frowned as pointed a frown as she could muster. "I suppose you're just going to stand there and waste my time with riddles all night."

"Tsk tsk," the spirit said. "That's a horrible tactic, too. I have all the time in the world. What do I care if you waste yours? You're not going to motivate me that way, you're not going to compel me to do anything with an argument like that. Sloppy, really, as an approach. You're slipping. I do believe I've gotten under your skin, Penny Dreadful." And then the spirit went a step further and said her *other* name, the one she'd been given when she was born. What some might call her "real name" if they were conventional thinkers, but Penny considered her fake name. Her dead name bestowed at birth and changed at the soonest possible opportunity.

Penny's eyes opened wide. She couldn't remember the last time a spirit had called her by her first name, let alone her full name. And she couldn't remember the last time *anyone* had called her that *other* name. What in the world…

"Ah, maybe you're listening now," the spirit continued. "I have your attention, as you fleshy types like to say."

Penny waited.

"That's a funny premise, too, attention. You walk through life thinking that you're perceiving each and every thing exactly as it is – especially you psychics –"

"Intuitives," Penny corrected. Usually she didn't bother, but this spirit was annoying her.

"Oh please," the spirit said. "No one calls you intuitives. Outside of a few echo chambers online. You're psychics. Or tueys."

Penny sighed. Language had a way of evolving. After the word "psychic" became a slur, governmental forces had rebranded their classification system. "Psychic" was now fine for systems, institutions, and powers – why PsyOps was able to retain its name as the Department of Psychic Operations – but offensive as a label when applied to actual people.

Their proposed solution was to call individuals with psychic powers "intuitives." Quickly, however, people began to call them "tueys," which turned into an even better slur on account of it sounding an awful lot like a person spitting on the ground. Ever so occasionally, the most anti-tuey person would actually spit on the ground when saying it.

Penny expected a new culturally sensitive label to emerge any day now. It was only a matter of when. Language seemed to function that way. Anything could be weaponized. And with enough time and enough discrimination against people of the outgroup by people who were far too comfortable in their ingroup, well... it would be.

Every word would end up as a weapon. Bouncing to a new word didn't fix anything; it simply delayed the inevitable.

The spirit didn't spit when saying "tuey," but this was just as likely on account of the fact that the spirit presumably lacked salivary glands as anything else.

"As I was saying before I was so unnecessarily interrupted," the spirit continued, "you psychics are thin-slicing perception just as much as anyone else. Do you see more than normals? Sure. Different things? Sure. But you're far from being able to see the whole picture. Which you won't admit. There's an arrogance about you that won't let you ever admit that."

"An arrogance?" Penny said.

The spirit nodded. "I'd wager it's a protective arrogance. Like defensive narcissism. Where you've been attacked so long and you've spent yourself puffing your ego up so large as a result that you completely lose perspective. On your limitations. Your weaknesses."

"Interesting theory," Penny said in a bored tone of voice that indicated that she actually felt the opposite way.

The spirit sighed. It was a curious sound. It sounded strangely real, like the spirit were breathing. If Penny didn't know any better, she would have sworn the spirit had lungs. "Look, all I'm saying is that you'd do better if you didn't interfere with the Families or anything they're doing. Even if it means walking away from a murder case, leaving it unsolved."

Penny cocked her head. And just how did the spirit know about *that*? The list of things this spirit shouldn't know was getting uncomfortably long.

The spirit smiled.

"Are you threatening me?" Penny asked.

"No," the spirit said. "I'm doing you a favor. People much more important than you have regretted running afoul of the Families. Or vanished. I just thought you should know."

"Well, thanks for the information," Penny replied, coldly.

"Suit yourself," the spirit said.

At that moment, the kitchen light turned on spontaneously and flared to a brightness Penny didn't know it was capable of, blinding her. The glass in the fixture promptly broke a split second later, spraying slivers down on the kitchen floor.

When Penny's vision finally cleared from the flash and she could once again see, the spirit was gone.

Again, no footsteps, no sound of doors opening or closing. No indication that her visitor had left by conventional means.

Penny grumbled and went to the closet to get a broom and dustpan.

It occurred to Penny only after she'd finished sweeping up the shards of glass that there was no corpse in her kitchen. No body for the spirit to have come from.

Although there was a dirty fork in the sink... and she did spy what appeared to be a business card dropped on the floor where the spirit had stood only moments before.

"What kind of spirit leaves their contact information?" Penny wondered aloud as she bent over and picked it up.

The card was cheaply made, looked less like something professionally printed and more like something that had been spit off a bubble jet running out of one or more colors of ink. She recognized the cardstock from the office supply store. The cheapest grade.

Looking for a Change? The card read. *Try Change Patterson!*

"Is this ghost running for local government?" Penny asked herself, giggling. "A personal injury lawyer maybe."

She studied the grainy image on the card, ostensibly of this Change Patterson fellow. It didn't quite look like the spirit who had accosted her in the kitchen, although... there was a little something familiar around the eyes. But it was tough to be sure in such a low-quality image.

She flipped over the cheap card in her hand. Printed on the other side were two words printed in a calligraphied font. *Shapeshifting Services.*

Well, that explained it. You never knew who – or what – you were going to run into in the Psychic City. A literal shapeshifter seemed a little farfetched even for Psychic City, but Penny suspected whoever, or whatever, had spoken with her was at least passable with the art of disguise.

A figurative shapeshifter? Now, that was possible.

They'd made themselves *look* like a spirit, after all. Rather convincingly.

There was a number on the card, too, accompanying this implausible offer of shapeshifting services. Penny doubted she'd ever call it, but she tucked the card into her pocket for later just in case.

Approaches to Taxonomy

So far, most efforts to comprehensively classify intuitives have failed. The problem lies in the numerous new discoveries being made every day. And not just of specific subtypes but entirely new realms of psychic power. It's impossible to say whether these "new" types are powers of recent onset or ones that have existed for quite some time and are only just now being known among the general population.

To date, hundreds of intuitives types and subtypes have been discovered, but given that many intuitives eschew mandatory government registration requirements and instead keep the fact that they possess powers a closely guarded secret, the current list is likely quite incomplete.

This makes a taxonomist's job particularly difficult. This volume's author has tried their best but forges ahead knowing that this best effort will likely be quite insufficient.

Perhaps one day it will be possible to recruit an intuitive to aid in this area of scientific discovery. To date, however, it seems that the intuitives are opposed to being fully known or censused, let alone properly catalogued.

from Insecta Psychica: Towards an Intuitive Taxonomy by Cloche Macomber

"I don't like labels," Viv said between bites of dinner.

"That's beside the point," Penny replied. "This isn't about you. Which labels you're comfortable with and which you aren't. This is about what just happened. What the hell we'd even call the *thing* that was in this very room."

"Well, why does it matter whether your guest was a spirit or an intuitive or...?" Viv's voice trailed off.

"Right, or an 'or.' You don't get it, Viv. The existence of 'or' is scary as hell. Beings with powers we haven't heard of. There might be psychics that make psychics like us look like normals. Super-psychics. You don't know. No one does."

"Geez, Penny," Karen said. "You just said the P word *and* the N word. We're *intuitives*."

"Oh shut up, Karen. No one actually says 'intuitives' offline," Penny snapped. "And all that N word, P word crap is a cop-out. You're not brave enough to say the actual word so you hint at it and make the other person say it mentally in their head. Like a damn coward. Just say the offensive words. Don't make other people say it for you."

Both Viv and Karen were suddenly quite concerned. This was very unlike Penny. She always held it together. Neither of them could remember the last time she was cranky at all, let alone this cranky.

It was Viv who spoke first. "Are you okay, Penny?"

"No, I am not okay. *Honestly*," Penny said. "I don't know how either one of you can eat." Her own plate sat untouched.

"Well, it'd be rude not to after you went to all the trouble of making dinner," Karen said softly, conjuring up her warmest smile. "Thank you by the way."

That gratitude chipped away a small piece of Penny's icy demeanor. "You're welcome," Penny replied, but it was an automatic reply, something she said without thinking, and she still felt mostly cold.

"You said that thing knew all about you?" Viv said. "Including stuff it shouldn't know?"

Penny nodded.

"Like what?"

"My full name. Both of them. It knew my other name... and the fact that I don't... have any parents," Penny said. She took a second to compose herself again. She didn't like to talk about her parents, or the lack of them, at all. That was part of why that part of the conversation with "Change" had been so unsettling. Penny never talked about the fact that she was an orphan. It wasn't exactly public knowledge beyond the few people she'd talked to about it and a handful of forms where it had to be filled in. Pretty much no one else knew but the foster families she'd lived with when she was a ward of the state.

And lord knew she didn't talk to anyone from her time in foster care anymore.

Penny had snipped those past connections clean like a stray thread the very first moment that she could. And built herself a new future from the ground up. A shiny custom-built future where *she* was in control of her own destiny. Not at the mercy of others. Not being forced to shuffle from place to place hauling all of her possessions behind her in a garbage bag.

Any connection to her past messed that up, ruined her chance at a fresh start, so they all had to go.

Her new name was chosen, too, at that time, the time of self-resurrection. She christened this new self Penny Dreadful – the last name chosen strictly as an homage to her love of puns. Her new first name, "Penny," had long been a nickname of hers, inspired by a teacher who had greeted her by saying "a bad penny always turns up."

The nickname had been meant as an insult, but Penny rather liked it. Maybe she was cursed by her condition, her destiny to see things that made others think she was crazy. Maybe she was a bad penny, but you couldn't get rid of her. No matter what you did, she always turned up, and that was something.

So when other children had taunted her by calling her "Bad Penny" and then eventually "Penny," she'd welcomed it. Wore it like a badge of honor.

"What?" Viv said. "Your other name? You won't even tell me that name."

Penny nodded solemnly.

"Or me," Karen added.

"And that thing knew all about the fact that we're looking into the Families as part of a murder case. It didn't really get more specific than that, but still... how would it know that?" Penny said. "It's not like we've talked with anyone else about our caseload."

Viv frowned. "How indeed."

Karen shot a suspicious glance at Viv. Viv had been talking to her mother about all their cases just an hour prior. With her sister Love and whatever servants were working comfortably within earshot. Surely, Viv would say something. Surely Viv would alert Penny to this possibility.

But Viv didn't. She kept quiet.

Karen bit her lip in frustration, wrestling with conflict. She could volunteer the information, that Viv had been yakking to her mother about work, but then Viv would know Karen had been hiding in the hallway listening the entire time. And Karen wasn't eager for a lecture from Viv for invading her privacy.

"The spirit, or whatever it was, actually threatened me," Penny said.

"Threatened you?" Viv said.

"Said more important people than us have disappeared going down this path," Penny said.

"Uh oh," Viv said. She had a good idea what was coming next.

"So it's settled," Penny said. "We're expediting this investigation. We're going to dive deeper into the Families. Do what you have to, Viv. Call Martin as soon as possible. Get him to call in a couple of favors. Send my regards. We're going to interview Bronson Eck first thing in the morning no matter what. Even if we have to break into the prison ourselves."

Threatening Penny had backfired. The last thing you ever wanted to do was to tell Penny she couldn't do something. It was guaranteed to make her want to do it even more.

Viv smiled. "You got it."

"Now," Penny said forcefully.

"Geez, Penny, can't I finish my dinner first?" Viv complained.

"No," Penny said.

Sighing, Viv picked up her phone and called Martin.

Reactance

This theory states that individuals have certain freedoms with regard to their behavior. If these behavioral freedoms are reduced or threatened with reduction, the individual will be motivationally aroused to regain them. This is psychological reactance.

-Jack W. Brehm

Citation: Brehm, J. W. (1966). A theory of psychological reactance. Oxford, England: Academic Press.

Tarnation Hall Transcript

All kidding aside, is there any force greater than reactance? Any power more impressive than rebellion? Than defiance?

If you want to see truly superhuman feats, you shouldn't ask someone to accomplish them.

No amount of cajoling or pleading, no size of threat or bribe can possibly compare to what you can get out of the person that you tell, "It can't be done."

"Do not do it."

"Whatever you do, don't –"

Ah, dear friends, even as I tell you this now, even as we all agree that this is speculative, hypothetical, not for "realsies," I can see you leaning forward in those chairs, awaiting my challenge. Ready to hear whatever it is that I will say you can't do.

You are so eager for your opportunity to prove me wrong.

And with that, I would like to tell you that whatever you do, don't take a deep breath and relax.

[crowd laughter]

Mallow, Tarnation Hall Demotivational Lecture Series

The sun hadn't even fully risen yet when they arrived back at the prison. Only high enough for the light to chuck daggers into Viv's skull.

The last thing I need right now is a migraine, Viv thought to herself, feeling like solar pincushion. She suspected that dealing with Bronson Eck would be headache enough. No need for the genuine article to show up as well.

Plus, there had been far too many times in the past when a traditional migraine had bloomed into a vision. And typically, *these* visions weren't work related or terribly helpful in any other way. Instead, they were like bad trips. Less like flashes of the future (or a present happening somewhere distantly) and more like what would happen if you painted a portrait of reality and left it unattended in a place where a cat could walk across it.

Logic was invariably off in these migraine-induced visions. They swam in an uncanny valley. Mundane scenes but with always something askew. The pawprints in this reality were people's body parts in unsettling configurations. The sky the wrong color.

It was as though her mind were repeatedly answering the prompt "What does anxiety look like?"

No, not today. Not happening. There was simply too much to do to mess around with pawprints.

So Viv covered her eyes and whipped her sunglasses onto her face as quickly as she could as they walked into the prison.

Martin was already there, flanked by three rather tall piles of paperwork. He spun around quickly. "Ah, perfect timing. I just finished the intake forms."

"In record time, really," the guard manning the front door commented.

Viv didn't ask how long that time was but had a feeling from the bags under Martin's eyes that his tenure filling out forms was considerably longer than their previous intake process. Made sense. Very important prisoner and all. More hoops to jump through.

Martin pointed to the bottom of the piece of paper before him. "I need you all to sign this one, and we're good to go," he said.

Karen quickly signed, as did Penny. Viv hesitated.

"What?" Martin said.

"My mother told me never to sign anything without reading it," Viv said.

Martin frowned. "You really want to read all *that*?" he said, gesturing around him at what appeared to be at least two or three novels' worth of reading material.

Viv frowned. "Well no, but…"

Martin sighed sharply. A sigh loud enough to drown out whatever she was going to say next. The breath equivalent of "la la la la, can't hear you." Except less juvenile and more disappointed.

Viv felt stuck. To the others, it was such a minor sticking point. A mere bureaucratic formality. But Viv knew how easy it was for manipulation – for outright evil – to hide among the mundane. The everyday.

Viv thought about it every time she went to cash her tiny paycheck, shrunken down to miniscule amounts due to extra law and order taxes imposed on her simply because she was a psychic citizen. Money she wouldn't have had to pay if she were a normal.

No matter how hard she pushed herself, no matter how many hours she, Penny, and Karen worked, it seemed impossible to get much more than poverty wages.

Her job for PsyOps sometimes felt like indentured servitude. A normal in the same position would be taking home far more money. It hardly seemed fair.

And Viv was willing to bet that these inequalities weren't the cause of overt changes but instead came about because someone somewhere along the line had stopped paying attention and allowed it to happen.

Clutter could be dangerous that way. And so could distraction. They provided camouflage for evil deeds, which easily got lost in them.

Penny spoke then, pulling a suitably distracted Viv from her thoughts. "I bet your mom was talking about prenups when she said that, Viv," Penny said. "Not getting access to a prisoner for a murder investigation."

Viv nodded. "You're probably right." She signed and quickly looked away from the contract. Best not to dwell on it.

"Good morning ladies," Bronson Eck greeted them warmly.

Viv shuddered. *Ladies.* One of her least favorite words. It was the verbal equivalent of sanitary napkins. Utilitarian perhaps. But uncomfortable and artificial and never quite able to contain everything it was supposed to. And irrevocably linked with fifth grade health class. The week where the boys and girls were split up and a misleadingly titled film "The Miracle of Birth" dramatized the horrors of childbirth.

"Good morning, Mr. Eck," Penny said.

A more down-to-earth person may have replied, "Oh please, Bronson is fine." But Bronson Eck was not a down-to-earth person. He was, in fact, quite enamored with himself and his elevated station in life. It's sometimes said that kids with trust funds are prone to being born on third base and because of this subsequently laboring under the false impression that they've hit a triple. Bronson Eck was thrilled about having been essentially born between third base and home, able to steal a run whenever the mood struck him. He thought it made him a Major Leaguer.

"Madam," Eck said, tipping his head to Penny and winking at her.

Penny blushed and felt sick to her stomach.

Viv turned her head and pretended to cough as she involuntarily rolled her eyes.

This guy is cheesy as hell, Karen thought to herself. *It's like he thinks he's in a movie.*

Karen was right. Bronson Eck did in fact think he was in a movie. What remained to be seen was what kind of movie he thought he was in. That would soon become evident, however, as Eck spoke again.

"So ladies," Eck said, sending another chill up Viv's spine, "To what do I owe the pleasure of this visit? Did my father arrange something... conjugal for me? I must say. I would have been thrilled with one lady friend. Three really is a rare spat of generosity. Even if only one of you – " his gaze lingered uncomfortably on Penny – "would normally be something I'd pick up for myself. I'm sure I can find a supporting role for all of you. Buy one get the other two free, right?"

He waggled his eyes in true *chicka bow wow* fashion. All he was missing was the porno stache.

Viv glared at him.

"Just a little reference for you bargain hunters. I mean, I'm sure you've clipped a coupon or two, haven't you, darling? A psychic salary isn't everything it's cracked up to be."

He pretty much only directed his gaze at Penny. Looking her up and down with overt elevator eyes. Pausing self-indulgently at certain "floors."

"I have a few ways for you to make a bit of extra money, if you know what I mean. What do you say?" Eck said.

"I say," Viv said, "that I don't give a shit who your father is. I'm not going to take this kind of disrespect."

"*Viv*," Penny said.

"What?" Viv snapped.

"We have a case to solve," Penny said.

"I'm not going to stand here and let him treat me – treat *you* – like a piece of meat. Like we're presents sent here to be his own personal playthings," Viv said.

"It doesn't matter what he thinks though," Penny said.

"I'm sitting right here. I can hear you," Eck said.

"I know," Penny said.

Viv laughed.

"He's locked up here. You know how prisoners are. He's escaping into a world of make-believe just like anyone else. His fantasies are just a little... more entitled than the average person. And he's more likely to voice them," Penny said.

Viv nodded. "Because he hasn't really been taught about 'no.'"

"Not properly anyway," Penny said.

"So you're saying it's a 'no?'" Eck chimed in. "You ladies are missing out." Viv twitched again.

"Honestly?" Penny said. "Unless you have a portal to Hell hidden in those pants, then I've probably seen everything you have to offer."

"Ah," Eck said, sounding wounded. "I left the portal to Hell in my other pants. The ones I use to plane shift." He cracked a smile. He studied their faces curiously. "You don't know whether I'm kidding or not, do you?"

In truth, it was hard to tell. Not only were the Families incredibly wealthy, but they were rumored to also be privy to technology that didn't officially exist, artifacts that weren't supposed to be real, cutting-edge scientific (and experimental) tools. A pair of plane-shifting pants wasn't out of the question.

"No," Viv said. "But we're going to pass on checking."

"Pity," Eck said. "You would have at the very least found a retractable ladder to heaven."

Penny groaned, losing her composure for the first time during the encounter.

"You mentioned a case," Eck said. "Are you talking about that game of cards I was in? That sore loser Macomber?"

Karen's jaw dropped. Was this how he was going to refer to his murder charge? "That game of cards I was in?"

Viv wasn't having it. "If you mean your murder of Jack Macomber, yes."

Eck rolled his eyes. "Maybe you live under a rock, but I'm *innocent*. Well... sort of. I'm innocent of the murder anyway. I've had a lot of fun in my life."

Penny sighed. "Yes, yes, I'm sure you're a virile playboy. Gallivanting around the globe. That's not what we're concerned with today."

"Unfortunately," Eck said.

"Poor you," Viv said.

Eck glared at her. "I'd be careful if I were you," he said, his voice growing colder. "You should try not to offend me. I'm a very important person. And I'm rather *connected*. Sure, *I'm* locked up here. But my friends are not. And a psychic's life... well, you have your powers, but what else do you really have? Certainly not resources. Or important friends."

"Is that how you killed your guards?" Penny said.

"Excuse me?" Eck said.

"Your guards here at the prison. Did you have your important friends kill them?" Penny said.

"I don't know what you're talking about," Eck said. "Are there not guards out there? Could I just walk out of here? If so, that's news to me."

Viv shook her head. "There are guards out there, just different ones."

Eck shrugged. "I hadn't noticed. I'm stuck in here in any event."

Penny looked at Karen. "Feel him out," Penny said to Karen. "I'm gonna go for a walk."

"Oooo, feel me out? That sounds fun. Except maybe you could do it?" Eck said.

Penny signaled to the guards that she wanted to be let out of the interrogation room. As she left and put distance between herself and Karen, Karen began to feel painfully aroused, like half the blood in her body had rushed precipitously to her groin.

Of course, how obvious, Karen thought. And how disgusting given the current circumstances.

Karen did her best to push down her own personal disgust, however, so it wouldn't interfere with her feeling Bronson Eck's emotions.

"So about your guards," Viv said.

"I told you. I have no idea what you're talking about," Eck said.

Karen noted he felt defensiveness – that was hardly surprising. Another murder charge wouldn't exactly be a welcome development.

But there was something else underneath that defensiveness. Eck was confused. Surprised.

If this murder had anything to do with the Eck Family, Bronson wasn't involved.

"I've got it, Viv. I've felt it," Karen said.

"Felt it?" Eck said. "Felt what?"

"She felt the earth move," Viv said sarcastically.

Eck looked at her. Karen felt another spike of confusion emanating from him.

"Have a nice day, Mr. Eck," Viv said, in a flat tone.

"So he doesn't know anything?" Penny asked.

Karen shook her head no. "He's clueless."

Penny sighed. "Ugh. A dead end."

"Well maybe not," Viv said.

"What do you mean?" said Penny.

"Well, it's possible that he's protecting someone," Viv said.

Karen shook her head. "Not to his knowledge. He felt defensive, sure, but that was probably for his own sake."

"Do you know that for sure?" Viv said.

"Well, I guess not," Karen said.

"He could have no idea what happened *and* also be protecting someone else. Someone he could feasibly *suspect* of doing the crime. Even if the crime itself were news to him," Viv said.

"I guess," Karen said. She wasn't sold, however.

"Look, if you don't like my theories, maybe you could come up with one of your own," Viv snapped, sensing that Karen wasn't exactly on board. In this case, you didn't have to be an empath to get that impression.

"I'm sorry, Viv. I don't have an alternate theory. I just know that he wasn't directly involved. That the fact that his guards were attacked was news to him. And he genuinely didn't view the attack as beneficial to him," Karen said.

"Anything else?" Penny asked.

"He was really turned on," Karen offered.

"Ugh," Penny and Viv said in unison.

"That was the strongest emotion he was feeling, truth be told," Karen said. "Even more than defensiveness or confusion. Arousal."

Viv frowned. "I'm really kicking myself right now."

"Why?" Karen asked.

"I'm thinking we should have brought a telepath in with us," Viv said.

Ouch. Karen felt that statement right in the chest. *Well, maybe if you wanted to be 100% sure about the wrong thing,* she fought back in her own head.

But she couldn't bring herself to say that – or something similar – aloud. Because she often wondered herself if Penny and Viv wouldn't be better served teaming up with a telepath or even a precog. A more common – and potentially more useful? – team member.

Karen stood there frozen in place as tears filled her eyes. She quickly yanked the hood on her sweatshirt forward to make it less obvious.

Differentiation of Common Types

While hundreds of varieties of intuitive have been unearthed, it is worth noting that some types are far more common than others. Two of the earliest discovered types of psychic practitioners have continued to be among the most numerous: Precogs and telepaths.

Precogs, short for precognitionists, are masters of the future. They can see future events with profound clarity. Some precogs do so involuntarily, assaulted by uncontrollable glimpses of things that have not yet come to pass. Other precogs have more control of their visions and with considerable effort can look into a question and see what the future holds.

Predictably, many precogs work for government agencies and most commonly in law enforcement.

However, their findings aren't admissible in court – and for good reason. Precogs only see *possible* futures. Things that *may* happen. There are many false positives (but many accurate readings as well) in even the most disciplined precog's life.

Precog findings, however, are used to guide investigations.

In law enforcement precogs also often work alongside telepaths, another very common type of psychic practitioner.

Most commonly, telepaths hear the thoughts of others. This can be a very handy skill in detective work. Notably, however, while telepaths are privy to the *content* of a person's thoughts, they do not have access to the *context* of those messages. Telepaths do not sense the emotional state of the thinker and are unable to look back in a thinker's mind to see what thoughts preceded the current message.

Empaths, conversely, have the ability to feel another person's feelings but do not have access to the verbal component of thoughts. This can lead to less precision about the actual message but better sense of the context of their thoughts – and importantly some insight into what possibly preceded the current feeling, as emotions – or "hot cognition" – tend to dissipate more gradually than a cold thought (or a "cold cognition").

Empaths are believed to be generalists. Further reports of empathic specialists are widespread but at the present time, unverified. Rumors persist, however, that empaths exist whose skills are limited to a certain single emotion.

However, these specialists aren't simply able to detect that particular emotion. Instead, they have a full range of control over the emotion in question, that they can cause it in others or remove it from someone currently experiencing it.

Empaths in general, however, are exceedingly rare. This is believed to be due to the incredibly high rate of suicide for empaths. The leading explanation is that this suicide rate is linked with empathic burnout and intense compassion fatigue. It is incredibly stressful feeling other people's emotions all the time. Many empaths do not survive into adulthood, the age of majority when they can be successfully employed by government agencies, in either a Green Star or Blue River capacity.

Telepaths, however, have a lower rate of suicide than the general non-psychic population.

Telepathy is also found prominently in individuals who are very concrete thinkers. Telepaths tend to be people with a high belief in a just world and who view things as primarily black or white, zero or one, and/or binary.

Telepaths are often very certain of the accuracy of their findings, while they are often very much off the mark.

Two main categories of telepath exist: Receptive and expressive.

Receptive telepaths can hear the thought messages of others.

Expressive telepaths can send thought messages into the minds of others.

Of the two, receptive telepaths are far more common than expressive. Even rarer is a telepath who has both powers, receptive and expressive.

from Insecta Psychica: Towards an Intuitive Taxonomy by Cloche Macomber

"Short meeting," Martin said as the final two detectives walked out of the interrogation room to join him where he was waiting with Penny.

"Is Roscoe around?" Viv asked.

Karen's heart sank. Telepathic boy wunderkind. He had joined PsyOps a few weeks after his eighteenth birthday. It had only been a couple of months since then, and he was already making waves around the department.

At this rate, he'd be running the department in three years, some said. Karen wasn't sure exactly why, but the idea made her feel miserable.

It probably didn't help that he bore a striking resemblance to someone in her past. Someone she'd rather forget. A cruel co-resident at the ranch for troubled teens Karen's parents had sent her to, thinking it would correct her "behavioral problems."

It had taken quite some time for anyone to realize that Karen was an empath, far longer than it probably would have in other households. Unfortunately, empathic powers weren't routinely screened for the way that other more common psychic talents were. And Karen's parents hadn't been exactly keen to get her generally tested for psychic intuition in the first place, fearing a positive result. Their neighbors had a child who had tested positive for psychic abilities, and they'd seen how that had gone. All their dreams as parents had been destroyed. The neighbor kid would never have a normal life. Kids. A normal career.

So they'd done the best they could to get Karen exempted from testing. Cited religious beliefs. Karen's father, Augustus Cross, even went so far as to invent an entire religion and register it with the government. The Grounded Temple. The church's main belief structure was based in the avoidance of negativity and the power of positive thinking.

Psychic powers could be overcome and switched off if everyone would just believe a little harder, the church said. All you had to do was kick in a few more thoughts and prayers.

The church believed that psychic powers were a collective delusion, a test sent from God. And it was important for believers to do everything they could to pass that test.

Grounded Temple members were accordingly forbidden from testing their own children for psychic abilities. To do so was to simply invite temptation. It was exactly what the Devil wanted them to do.

"The Devil? Surely, that's a typo," the clerk handling Mr. Cross's application had inquired.

"No, that's correct," Mr. Cross had said.

"Capitalized?"

"Are you a Christian, sir?" Mr. Cross had asked, his voice growing quiet and his gaze becoming more intense.

The clerk had nodded.

"And as a Christian you capitalize God, don't you?" Mr. Cross had asked.

The clerk had nodded again.

"In the Grounded Temple, we acknowledge the Devil as a real threat, sir. We take the Devil seriously. And we demonstrate that we take the Devil seriously that way. It is not a typo. There are no mistakes on this form," Mr. Cross had said.

When Karen had been a little girl, her father Augustus had tried very hard to impress upon her the ideals of avoidance.

Whenever Karen was overwhelmed by the constant cacophony of other people's emotions, Augustus Cross would simply look at his daughter and say, "Calm down."

When she would ask him how, he would helpfully instruct her, "Just don't think about it."

And when she would scowl reflexively at this utterly useless advice, he'd snap at her. "You look like a monk with that giant hood over your face. Only your religion is self-pity. Honestly, Karen, you disappoint me. I had hoped any daughter of mine would be above petty teen angst."

For someone who was so adamant that she needed to calm down, Karen mused, her father's actions said something entirely different. He seemed hellbent on agitating her by sticking guilt daggers into her and twisting them.

Perhaps if it had been only him she would have survived her adolescence unscathed. However, he had a whole Temple behind him who seemed just as happy to oblige. There was an entire community ready and willing to reinforce his parenting choices.

It was through the Temple that Mr. Cross had met Karen's stepmother Celia Banks, the first woman he'd dated since the morning Karen's mother had left on a long drive and never came back.

Mr. Cross called his new bride "Sissy," and despite Karen's psychic abilities, even *she* wasn't exactly sure whether it was out of affection or disdain.

But Karen knew one thing for sure: There wasn't any of what she'd personally call love in this marriage. Commitment? Sure. Trust? Fine. But no affection – and certainly no passion.

Ms. Banks and her father focused more on Temple precepts than on one another, on feeling as little as possible, pleasant or unpleasant. It was all a form of unnecessary distraction from the purest essence of being, which as far as Karen could discern (having never mastered the art of Temple ritual herself) involved a state of completely thoughtless, emotionless meditation.

Or at least this was what the Temple followers *claimed*.

As a young empath, Karen had noted all too well the disparity between what they reported went on inside of them and what seemed to be happening. Practitioners who were bored, hungry, tired, or even lustful during their ritual meditations would tell her father afterwards how calm they were, how centered, how delightfully empty. These testimonies were lies, but they were ones her father happily believed.

Karen learned through those sessions that there was a big difference between how people actually felt and how they *wanted* to feel – and in a wrestling match between the two, it was often the latter that won out. She'd note an absence of the remorse that people often felt with deception when the practitioners told falsehoods. This meant that they weren't consciously lying – instead, they'd managed to engage in self-deception, to get themselves into the mental state where lies felt like the truth.

It was based on these observations that Karen was first shipped off to the ranch. She'd come to her father in earnest, feeling as though he should know of his followers' hypocrisy.

Instead of thanking her for the intel, he'd become enraged, an intensity of emotion from a man who most of the time had the disposition of a buoy in calm seas. Bobbing slightly at times but never straying too far from a state of perfect equilibrium.

"I'm just telling the truth. That's how they really feel. They're lying to you," Karen said.

Augustus scowled. "You've put me in a terrible place, I'll have you know."

"I know," Karen said. "And for that, I'm sorry." But she had misunderstood what he meant by that, a fact that would soon become clear.

"There are three possibilities here. And none of them are easy," he said.

"Three?" Karen asked.

"The first is that you're telling the truth, you can feel these other people's emotions," her father said.

"That's what it is. I'm telling the truth," Karen interjected.

"Don't interrupt," he said.

Karen frowned.

"I highly doubt that you're telling the truth. But if you are, it's bad news. Because that means that my only daughter is defective... a psychic." He shuddered at this thought.

Karen sighed.

"The second possibility is that you're lying to me and acting out in order to get more attention. Probably because you're upset that your mother left. You've never really warmed to Sissy, you know," Mr. Cross said. He sighed deeply, getting a faraway look in his eyes.

"It's only been a few months. I haven't really gotten to know Celia," Karen replied, after a few seconds.

"Don't interrupt," her father said.

Karen chewed on her lip, puzzled. Interrupting? It had certainly seemed to her like he had completed his thought, seeing as he managed to get carried away on another silent train of other ones before she began to speak. But Karen had noticed over the years that whether someone else felt interrupted was an entirely subjective phenomenon.

Pauses in conversation were often ambiguous.

Karen had noted that laidback people rarely seemed to complain of being interrupted, even when they clearly were. And control freaks constantly claimed they were being interrupted, even after quite luxurious pauses.

The whole interruption issue seemed less based on clear-cut behavioral cues and more based on the subjective belief of a given speaker that they should still be *in control* of the discussion.

But she didn't tell her father that. Of course. Instead, she waited. And hoped he wouldn't expect her to beg him to continue, as jaded interrupted people often did.

("What were you going to say?"

"No, it's too late now."

"Seriously, I want to hear what you have to say. I'm listening."

"We'll see about that."

"Seriously."

"Okay, so – ")

Karen knew that when an interruptee came to this particular emotional point, they would typically glower and brood until begged to resume sharing their previous thought.

Mr. Cross did indulge in a bit of glowering and brooding on occasion but thankfully broke into the next phase of conversation *this time* without the need for supplication.

"The third and final possibility," he continued, "is that you're emotionally lazy. You lack emotional control. Those feelings you thought you felt from my followers were always your own, and you're simply projecting them onto others."

Karen sighed, not daring to speak, lest she be accused of interrupting yet again.

"I'm inclined to believe it's not the first possibility. Because I love you, and I'm not giving up on you. You're not a psychic. You're redeemable. *My daughter* is redeemable. You are a normal girl. You are," he said, making intense eye contact that made her deeply uncomfortable.

Karen felt panic from her father, the same sensation one gets when they're being chased in a dream by some unseen force.

In a moment, however, that panic in him switched over to his usual sense of calm – perhaps laced with a bit more self-righteousness than normal.

"No, nothing's fundamentally wrong with *you*. Something's wrong with your behavior. Or your attitude. Probably both," he said. "And I know just the thing to help."

It was that very day she was shipped off to the ranch.

Meanwhile, Back at the Ranch

One Eighty Acres on its most basic level was a reform school for troubled teens. It was, however, also a reform school that was trying awfully hard to be a charming ranch.

Residents were treated to a beautiful view as they drove down the long, dusty road that separated the ranch from the rest of civilization. In the distance, mountains loomed like sleeping gods. Conspicuously perfect prairie grass waved hello with each gust of breeze.

Ornate windmills dotted the range, not the spartan windmills you find on public land installed to produce renewable energy but smaller decorative ones that would look completely natural as a whirligig thrust into someone's front yard.

Or perhaps as a weathervane, Karen mused on that first day, as her parents drove her there against her will.

In any event, One Eighty was a contrived setting. Almost like a cowboy-themed amusement park that had been erected in the middle of the desert. One that claimed it could turn your child right around. Send them in the other direction. The good one.

Karen seriously doubted that her new home for the next however long could simultaneously be Ranch World *and* an agent of revolutionary personality transformation. A workshop for mending "broken" young people like her.

While her parents oohed and ahhed at this idyllic setting, it was instantly clear to Karen that everything at her new home was artificial. The farm. The brick façade on the dorm. The smiles on the instructors' faces.

From the very beginning, life at One Eighty was a nightmare. She found herself in the midst of a chaotic soup of emotions, hormones, anger, and attitude. She was surrounded on all sides by teenagers who were angrier than her and had extreme problems with their own emotional control.

The very worst had been a younger boy with piercing blue eyes and bowl-cut black hair. A boy who thought he had all the answers but in fact had none of the patience to fully understand the *questions*.

Karen had sworn his name was... Mike? Matt? Something like that. They'd lived together on that same ranch for three years. But like many things in her past, she'd managed to forget about him.

And then Ryan Roscoe had walked into his first day at PsyOps to a row of high fives, an eerie doppelganger of the little boy who had once tormented her, and it had all come flooding back to Karen with such a force she was almost knocked off her feet.

It didn't help that Roscoe generally rubbed her the wrong way. He had the same arrogant air as Mike-Matt. An eagerness to respond, a disdain for listening. They even had a similar walk.

Something about Roscoe really bothered Karen. But she wasn't sure exactly what. *Is this just transference?* She found herself wondering.

Empathic Transference

Transference was initially defined rather narrowly, as a process that simply occurred between therapist and patient. Transference emerged as a term for the phenomenon whereby a patient would project emotions associated with other past figures in their life (most prominently, people from their early childhood) onto their psychotherapist. In essence, a patient would begin to feel for their therapist and treat them as though they were another authority figure or valued person, for example, interacting with their therapist as though their therapist was their mother or father.

Countertransference was a similar process but moving in the opposite direction – from therapist to patient. In response to patient transference, a therapist would respond emotionally to that transference with countertransference, perhaps guided by prominent figures in their own psyche. A client could just as easily become emotionally indistinguishable from their own children.

As understanding of the field of transference has progressed and particularly as taxonomists have devoted more study to the dynamics of empaths and empathy, it's become evident that transference and countertransference are much more ubiquitous in interpersonal relations than anyone previously knew. Transference is not simply something that happens in therapy – but something that happens everywhere.

Beings of all stripes – whether intuitive or not – head into new acquaintanceships carrying the impressions of every other person they've known up until that time.

However, due to the high degree of involuntary social connectivity that comes with automatically feeling the feelings of others and the consequent difficulty in forming normal emotional boundaries, empaths are particularly vulnerable to transference effects and plagued by them.

In layman's terms, it is nearly impossible to get a blank slate when meeting an empath. They have a strong impression of you before you even say a word. Emotionally speaking, they almost always begin your acquaintanceship by mixing you up with someone else.

from Insecta Psychica: Towards an Intuitive Taxonomy by Cloche Macomber

Where in certain ways living at the ranch felt very much like a prison sentence, it wasn't all wasted time. After all, even when behind bars one can get ripped pumping iron or pursue a college degree. Similarly, Karen decided to spend her years living in the desert compound focusing on emotional control.

It was a natural choice. Emotional control was part of the basic curriculum of the program her father had enrolled her in. Now, the classes weren't intended to help psychic empaths improve their powers. In fact, the program was in general predisposed to extreme levels of psychophobia. But the syllabus invariably focused on the residents building up self-control, emotional intelligence, and other forms of social restraint.

Karen took these lessons a step further and began to work on what she came to think of as emotional discernment. She wasn't sure what else to call it, lacking any sort of empath in her life to guide her and unable to even talk of her psychic abilities without fear of retribution.

Emotional discernment. It became the focus of her life, the activity that kept her sane.

When Karen had first become aware of her empathic abilities, it had been deeply confusing. The emotions were in her brain, but they felt distant, foreign, muffled. A bit like the sounds of a person moving about in an adjacent room with moderately thick walls in the way.

With time, she'd figured out how to better discern what exactly those feelings were, but her sense of them was still fuzzy, imprecise. At the ranch, she practiced homing in on more specific shades of the emotions of others. And she worked on becoming better at discerning between the feelings of multiple people. Got better at making sure she wasn't rolling her own feelings up into her reads of other people.

It wasn't always easy. In the beginning especially, the feelings around her mixed together into one large cacophony of emotions. It was a bit like standing at a crowded cocktail party with her eyes closed, the many voices all sounding like nonsensical noise when heard at the same time. But with time and practice, she became rather adept at singling one feeling out from the rest, much the way a person can listen intently to one speaker in a crowd of voices if they are determined enough and pay the right kind of attention to the task.

While she sat with peers talking about the day's lesson – rewriting sender and receiver language – "I feel X when you do Y" instead of "You make me feel so X," she'd nod as though she were deeply engaged but instead try to pinpoint exactly who in the room was super hungry. Who was sad. And who was bored.

That last emotional state was pretty easy to find, boredom. During lectures, usually everyone there was at least a little bored.

The hidden mission statement of the ranch seemed to be teaching all of them to tolerate boredom a little better.

Most days even the teachers were a little bored.

Everyone seemed to feel a little trapped there. While the teachers hadn't been dragged there against their will *per se*, it wasn't exactly a dream job. It was no one's first choice to be there.

One Eighty was a place they'd all simply ended up.

It had been rare in the din of other people's emotions for Karen to ever be able to let her mind drift, but the sheer amount of boredom at One Eighty made this occasionally possible.

Because boredom, emotionally speaking, functioned almost as white noise. She could certainly sense it, as anyone else could hear static, but it didn't exactly captivate her attention or provoke any emotional response.

And it was on one such occasion, when everyone else in the room was bored, that Karen heard words that she was certain hadn't been spoken aloud.

"Emotions will time travel to pursue you."

She heard it quite clearly. Well, she sort of heard it and sort of saw it. The words jumped out to her as effortlessly as the headline in a newspaper.

However, it came to her through a different channel than any other sense she had. It wasn't her vision, her hearing, her empathic sense, touch, taste, smell.

It was like thinking but not really. If thinking were writing, this was reading.

Did I just think someone else's thoughts? Karen wondered, looking around the room suspiciously, focusing on the emotions of all who surrounded her.

But all she continued to sense was boredom. If she'd been sent some kind of message, the sender wasn't in the room.

"Emotions will time travel to pursue you."

Once she sensed those words, she found it impossible to stop thinking about them. Running them over and over in her head, inspecting them from every angle.

Were they a warning? A threat? A form of reassurance?

And where had they come from?

If this was a telepathic message, then who in the world had sent it?

It wasn't until several days later that she'd have the answers to any of these questions.

Emotion is a process, a particular kind of automatic appraisal influenced by our evolutionary and personal past, in which we sense that something important to our welfare is occurring, and a set of physiological changes and emotional behaviors begins to deal with the situation.

Paul Ekman, Emotions Revealed

"Is she sleeping?"

Karen heard the voice, but kept her eyes closed.

She'd found in her time at One Eighty that the best defense frequently involved deception. When another resident wanted to mess with her, the best way to prevent getting seriously hurt was to play dumb, not let on that she knew that there was a trap waiting for her.

And when the attack came, she'd have her own element of surprise: The fact that she'd known the attack was coming all along.

This voice wasn't familiar. But the speaker surely could be up to no good. After all, why would someone be sneaking into her bedroom in the middle of the night if not to prank her?

Karen wondered idly if they'd be trying to write on her face with a Sharpie or stick her hand in a glass of ice water to try to make her pee.

Maybe they had come in looking to steal something from her.

You never really knew with an intruder. Only that it wouldn't be good.

And that's when it hit her. She couldn't sense the intruder's emotions. She felt nothing from them.

Normally, a would-be prankster had a certain vibe emanating off them. Inevitably, they were some mixture of excited and nervous. Really, the only thing that usually changed was the ratios.

But this time, Karen sensed nothing.

Nothing?

No, nothing. Not even white noise like boredom. It was as though no one at all were in the room with her.

Karen opened her eyes.

And before her stood not one but two of the strangest people she'd ever laid eyes on.

"Ah, I guess not," the voice said again. Karen noted that it belonged to a thin woman who had to be over six feet tall. Every angle on her body was sharp, kinked. It looked as though you cuddled with her that you'd end up drawing your own blood. She was the human equivalent of a red pen that slashes lines through a student paper.

She stood bolt upright with her chin slightly lifted, just enough so that she could look down on the person she was viewing. Her face was drawn into a sharp scowl.

The planes of her face were deliberate and bold, almost as if they'd been sketched with charcoal. Karen had seen plenty of resting bitch faces in her life, but this intruder's angry default was a taken to a whole new level. She looked as though at any minute she might start shouting.

But she didn't. This first intruder stood there rather quietly with that enraged expression on her face.

Standing next to her was a very small, slight man. Hunched over and wizened, he barely made eye contact with Karen as she surveyed his face. He seemed to be staring intently at something on the ground. But when Karen looked at this apparently fascinating spot, she noted a completely unremarkable square of carpet.

This short man sighed at regular intervals. Deep labored sighs that made Karen wonder if he had a respiratory problem. His eyes were rimmed with pink tinges that made her wonder if he'd been crying recently or just had an extreme allergy to something found on the ranch.

What in the world?

"Right," the incensed-looking woman said. "You must be wondering why we're here." Oddly she didn't *sound* mad – or even peeved. Her tone was level and completely at odds with her facial expression and body language.

The man beside her sighed again. Loudly. With one of his hands, he covered his face and groaned. He said nothing.

Karen wondered, however, why she didn't sense anything from him either. Why no sadness? Exhaustion? Illness?

He *looked* severely depressed. Defeated, even. But she felt nothing coming from him. Strange.

"It's a pleasure to meet you," the knife-like woman said, extending her hand. "I'm Anger."

Spurred on by a tendency to reciprocate social niceties, Karen automatically took Anger's hand and shook it. A few seconds passed before she processed what the strange woman had said.

"What?"

Anger looked at her companion. "This is how it always goes, isn't it?"

"It is," he replied. Again, the tone of his voice was a departure from his appearance. He sounded calm, even emotionless, even as he looked distraught beyond words.

"How *what* always goes?" Karen asked.

"We should really just hire some trainees," Anger said to her companion. "Put an ad up online. Apprentice – Grief and Anger."

"The job duties would scare them away though," the man replied.

"Good Grief," Anger said. "You really do take yourself too seriously."

"I think that could be one of the job duties," Grief replied. "Takes self seriously. Takes everything very seriously."

Anger laughed.

"Although it really depends," Grief said.

"It really does, doesn't it?" Anger replied.

"Maybe that's why it would be so hard to replace me with a stand-in," Grief mused. "I can be really dynamic and unpredictable, can't I?"

"I suppose you can," Anger replied.

Karen felt deeply unsettled that even as they laughed or joked neither of them smiled. And again, she sensed nothing at all emotionally.

It was, she realized, exactly how she'd feel if there were no one else in her room at all.

"Ah," she said aloud. "I must be dreaming this."

Grief shook his head. "Like a broken record."

"And not even one I particularly enjoying listening to," Anger replied. "Something more like 'Grandma Got Run Over by a Reindeer.'"

"Ah, that's a classic," Grief said.

"I'm sorry," Karen said. "But if this isn't actually a dream, and you're going to barge into my room in the middle of the night and kick up a fuss, the least you could do is include me in your conversation."

"Right," Anger said. "I'm being rude." She stuck out her hand again. "I'm Anger."

Karen pressed her lips into a tight frown. "You did that already."

"Sorry," Anger said. "You get into habits in our line of work, you see."

"And what line of work would that be exactly?" Karen replied.

"You don't know?" Anger said. "Isn't it obvious?"

"You look as if you've escaped from some costume party," Karen said.

"I wish," Grief said.

"Karen," Anger said, "We're emotions."

"Oh great," Karen said. "Now I'm hallucinating emotional projections. Why can't I just feel my emotions like a normal person?"

"Karen," Anger said sternly. "We're not *your* emotions. We're emotions. We don't belong to anyone. In a sense, we belong to *everyone*."

Grief nodded as if to reinforce Anger's point.

Karen felt sick. "This. This is a first."

"Well for you maybe," Anger replied. "As we were saying, we've visited lots of empaths in our time. And we've visited you before, just not in this form."

"Think of it this way," Grief said. "Isn't it about time we were properly introduced?"

"Okay," Karen said, still reeling from the strangeness of it all, "if you're emotions, then why can't I feel anything?"

"Oh, that's rather straightforward actually," Anger said. "We have no heft for you in this form. No weight. You only sense when people are *feeling* us. And right now, neither of us is feeling Anger or Grief. We *are* Anger and Grief. We don't *feel* Anger and Grief."

Grief nodded. "It's a key difference."

Karen stayed silent.

Anger asked, "Do you understand?"

Karen shook her head no.

"Well, think of it this way," Grief explained. "Isn't it different when someone else touches your arm and when you touch your own arm?"

"Yes," Karen said, "But I don't see how that applies."

"An experience is different from the outside than it is from the inside," Grief said. "I know it's not a perfect analogy, but it's the best we have unfortunately. As you know all too well, emotions are often very hard to explain."

"Okay, fine," Karen said. "Let's say that I accept your premise, that you're actual emotions, and that you've showed up in some obvious, overstated human form, that you're here to properly introduce yourselves... that still doesn't explain why. It doesn't explain why you didn't do it sooner. And it doesn't explain why now is the time to do it."

"Ah," Anger said. "That one's a great deal easier to explain. Would you care to, Grief?"

Grief shook his head. "No, you can do the honors for once."

Anger nodded in appreciation at Grief. "The reason we're here is simple. This is the first time you've ever run away from us, Karen."

"Run away from you?" Karen asked. "I've been spending hours trying to refine my powers. To better distinguish between different shades of emotions. I'd hardly call that running away from you. If anything, that seems like I'm pursuing you more than ever."

"Ah," Anger said. "You're so close, dear."

"She is, isn't she?" Grief added.

"You're being rude again," Karen said.

"Right," Anger said. "That's something you have to understand about emotions. We're not always bound by the rules of politeness, of courtesy."

"We just kind of do our own thing," Grief added.

"Clearly," Karen said.

Anger ignored the frustration in Karen's voice. "You've been so busy trying to focus in on other people's emotions that you neglected your own, Karen. That's why we're here."

"Anger and Grief?" Karen asked.

"Yes," Grief said. "You've been running from us for a very long time."

"Really?" Karen said.

"Yes," Anger said. "Ever since your parents brought you here."

"We've come an awfully long way to find you," Grief said.

"Months," Anger said.

"It's odd to judge distances using time, isn't it?" Karen said.

"Is it really though?" Anger said.

"Yeah, you'd think you'd talk about it in terms of miles," Karen said.

"How many times have you told someone something was a half hour away?" Anger asked.

Karen said nothing. She didn't have a good answer to that.

"We've traveled months to see you, Karen," Anger said.

"Why?" Karen asked.

"Because that's what we *do*," Anger said. "We'll time travel if we have to, but you can't get away from us. Eventually, we'll find you."

"You haven't let yourself mourn, haven't let yourself grieve," Grief said.

"And you haven't let yourself admit how unfair it is. How wrong. You haven't let yourself be angry."

In that moment, Karen burst into tears, squeezing both of her eyes shut. Anger looked at Grief knowingly, and they descended upon Karen, pulling her into a tight group hug.

When Karen once again opened her eyes, her visitors were both gone.

She sensed the familiar disembodied message again the next morning. "Emotions will time travel to pursue you," it said again. Only once. Just as before.

Karen didn't recognize its voice as belonging to either Anger or Grief. But she knew that the message was identical in every way to the first time she'd heard it, only this time it sounded less like a warning and more like a bookend. Closure. An echo.

"I know," she replied aloud. "And thank goodness for that."

That wasn't the last time Karen would be visited by emotional travelers in her time at the ranch. Oh no.

From time to time, one of them would drop by. Anger and Grief returned. As did Sadness, who really was a lot to manage. High maintenance. Draining. Bit of an attention whore. A small doses avatar, if you will.

And a carousel of other emotional avatars, each with their own story and purpose.

Rather than sapping her, their visits predictably revitalized Karen whenever she was drained. She also found that she started to see glimpses of them whenever she focused on channeling her empathic powers.

It wasn't as if they were there exactly. Nothing quite as tidy as that. They moved far too quickly for that, jumping from person to person, everywhere and nowhere all at once. But if she focused really hard, she could see vestiges of where they'd been. Tracer trails. Shadows of a sort.

At first, they manifested as amorphous blobs, ones that Karen would have been hard pressed to describe to another soul, even if her life had depended on it. But as she got quicker and more precise about tuning into their movements, Karen found she could associate the faces of her visitors with the emotions themselves.

When another person felt something in her presence, Karen would essentially see a playing card being dealt from a deck, and on its face was the emotion in question.

At that point, emotional discernment became quite a bit easier – much akin to standing while a group of people played cards but with everyone's hand face up.

Once she learned to account for the background haze of resignation and frustration that came from being around so many people who felt like they had settled, Karen got very good at emotional discernment at the ranch. But one thing she never got a hang of? Confidence.

Everything felt like a guess to her still.

Which made it particularly devastating even many years later whenever either one of her partners would doubt her intuition.

Had Viv understood this, perhaps she never would have made the offhand comment about using a telepath instead of relying on her.

She certainly wouldn't have consulted one.

And had Viv known that Karen felt hinky about Ryan Roscoe, she absolutely would not have arranged for a consult with his investigative team.

But Viv knew none of this, and so she set up such a consult quickly, all the while completely oblivious to how much pain she was causing Karen by doing so.

"The brain is designed with blind spots, optical and psychological, and one of its cleverest tricks is to confer on us the comforting illusion that we, personally, do not have any...'naive realism' [is] the inescapable conviction that we perceive objects and events clearly, 'as they really are.' We assume that other reasonable people see things the same way we do. If they disagree with us, they obviously aren't seeing clearly. Naive realism creates a logical labyrinth because it presupposes two things: One, people who are openminded and fair ought to agree with a reasonable opinion. And two, any opinion I hold must be reasonable; if it weren't, I wouldn't hold it. Therefore, if I can just get my opponents to sit down and listen to me, so I can tell them how things really are, they will agree with me. And if they don't, it must be because they are biased."

-Tavris & Aronson, Mistakes Were Made (But Not by Me)

Ryan Roscoe strode out of the holding cell, his head raised high. He had a regal bearing, Viv noted. There was something different about him. The way he held himself. The way he spoke.

Something that made others defer to him.

In spite of herself, and despite promises she'd made to herself long ago not to kowtow to anyone, Viv felt herself deferring to him as well.

Well, she thought. *He certainly has a way with people.*

And a fabulous tailor, too, come to think of it. Always dressed to the nines in bespoke digs.

That was another mystery all its own, how Roscoe afforded to dress like that on a psychic detective's salary. Some suspected he knew someone, had a connection to the fashion industry. Others theorized that Roscoe himself were responsible for creating them. He could be a closet fiend with a sewing machine for all anyone knew.

Whatever the case, Roscoe inevitably looked like he strolled off the pages of *GQ*.

Even his strangely cut hair had a way of looking chic and in the moment. No one else could have made a bowl cut look like it belonged on a Milan runway. But there he was, doing just that.

"So?" Viv prompted him.

"I don't have anything substantive to add, I'm afraid," Roscoe replied.

"Nothing?" Viv said. "You were in there for nearly an hour."

"Well, you may have noted that Eck's a bit of a talker," Roscoe said.

"I did," Viv said.

"Sometimes people who talk that much have correspondingly empty heads," Roscoe said. "But not Eck. He had a very active mind. Just most of it wasn't terribly relevant to the case." He tipped his chin down and smiled. "And most of it wasn't terribly safe for work, I have to say."

Viv groaned.

"He's filthy. Truly."

"I believe you," Viv said.

"I mean, if you'd like, I could write down some of it, but I hardly think it's what you're interested in."

"You'd be correct," Viv replied.

"As far as the case itself," Roscoe said, "Detective Cross seemed to be dead on. "

"Ah," Viv said.

"And do forgive me for being so bold, but I can't figure out why I was called in to check out this suspect. Have you lost confidence in your partner, Detective Lee?"

Viv frowned. "That's not it."

"Then what is it then?" Roscoe said.

Viv said nothing. But he didn't need to. It was an easy matter for Roscoe to retrieve the thoughts in question.

"Ah, I see," he replied to her unspoken sentiments.

Viv rolled her eyes. Telepaths could be so rude. So invasive.

"Well, I suppose I can't blame you, worrying about what other people think. It's difficult enough working with someone you're also dating. Let alone *two* people you're dating at once. It only makes sense that you'd be sensitive to that," Roscoe said.

His voice was tender enough, but Viv was having none of it. She felt invaded and annoyed.

"Don't you have better things to be doing?" Viv replied.

"Yes, ma'am," Roscoe replied. "Good luck with the case."

How Did You All Meet?

Any time you pursue an unconventional path in life, there will be no shortage of people ready and willing to enthusiastically warn you against it.

This was the case for Viv and Penny when Karen moved in with them.

"A three-person marriage? I could never do that," a PsyOps clerk with pancake makeup had unhelpfully offered when Viv had filed the domestic cohabitation forms at the office.

"Well, it's a good thing you're not," Viv had snapped back.

It wasn't necessarily the most prudent decision, being short with someone she needed something from. Her curtness did cause the clerk to hesitate and idly wonder if she could come up with some reason to deny the request. But whatever, the clerk finally decided, before stamping and certifying the documents. No need to punish Viv for her insolence. Surely, she reasoned, Viv's home life would soon become punishing enough.

Even Martin, usually quite supportive, had echoed that sentiment when he'd first learned of their arrangement. "Three women in one house? That's an awful lot of hormones."

"What do you know about hormones?" Viv had snapped at him. "I don't believe I've ever seen your wife. I imagine you don't see her much either. Maybe that's by design."

Martin frowned. "Ouch, Viv."

"Ouch right back at you," she said.

Penny typically took a different tack whenever anyone said something like that to her. She'd channel her best Mona Lisa smile and shrug, throwing whoever was admonishing or challenging her off guard. Did it convince them? Probably not. But that wasn't the point for her. She just wanted these tedious conversations to be as short as possible.

Karen wasn't one to punch back like Viv, but she couldn't seem to affect the same flippant distance that came so easily to Penny. Karen had to say something – and typically what came out of her mouth was defensive or apologetic.

"Don't you feel like the other woman?"

"Well, I suppose I technically am," Karen would say. "Penny one's woman to Viv. I'm another. Viv's one woman to Penny. I'm the other. I'm the other woman. But the trouble isn't that I'm the other woman, it's what that role typically means: Deception, betrayal, lies. There's none of that in our relationship. It's all above board. We're all honest. We tell each other the truth."

"That sounds exhausting."

"It's not so bad," Karen said, before adding, "I'm not here to break up anyone's relationship, so don't you worry." She suspected that was the cause of most suspicion, people's worry that monogamy could easily be vanquished by a solitary example of something else that was working just fine.

People weren't exactly eager to admit it, but it did seem that a lot of them implicitly viewed monogamy as particularly fragile, and a lot of people did seem to nurse a private worry that the only thing keeping monogamy going was a lack of competing alternative relationship styles – ones that were considered to be viable or healthy in any event.

As a result, they were prone to viewing a non-monogamous setup with suspicion, not only more conflicted than they might have otherwise been but also largely unaware of those conflicts.

Because of this, Viv, Penny, and Karen found they were all warned repeatedly that monogamy was a safer, more reasonable bet.

As much as everyone had tried to warn each of them about the perils of having two serious long-term lovers, they really hadn't experienced much in the way of drama, especially after they got together and decided formally they wanted to move Karen in, to make a serious go of it.

Karen had been worried about the innate power imbalance of joining a home that had been shared by two other people for many years – and to which she was added on as more of an extension or afterthought – but that had gone rather smoothly. She fit in well.

The most gut-wrenching dilemma Karen encountered in her early weeks at their little house on Bell Avenue was whether she should be throwing away the tissues on the left nightstand.

The nightstand in question was directly adjacent to Viv's third of the sprawling emperor size bed they shared. It was covered with small wadded up tissues.

Viv's sinuses seemed to flare up rather easily, something she attributed to the medicines she took to prevent the headaches and seizures that had plagued her since she was a little girl. She'd often wake up in the middle of the night to blow her nose.

This was difficult for Karen to get used to, even sleeping on the far right of the bed, with Penny in between them as a buffer. Karen had a hard time adapting to how restless that Viv could be as a sleeper. How loudly she blew her nose.

But with time, Karen mastered sleeping through these late-night vigils. And the only evidence of them was the used tissues sitting on the nightstand.

Her first instinct was to clean them up. After all, they weren't hygienic, and frankly it was kind of gross how Viv just let them sit there.

But would doing so cause Viv to resent her? Perhaps the close placement of these tissues, used or not, were important for convenience's sake. Viv might need something within close reach to blow her nose. Maybe she should use fresh tissues every time, but maybe that wasn't so easy in the middle of the night (when getting up and going to get new tissues could disturb Penny and Karen).

But if that were the case, why didn't Viv simply keep a box of fresh tissues on her nightstand with a small trashcan within her throwing radius?

Was she being eco-friendly? Trying to save money?

Karen batted this line of thinking back and forth, afraid to speak up and ask Viv, which was absurd, really, with how many more delicate things they'd been forced to be frank about in the course of moving in together.

This issue, however, sat right at the nexus of Worth Bringing Up versus Not Worth Bringing Up. It never quite seemed to meet the threshold of being a topic of conversation. But it still wouldn't leave Karen's mind entirely.

One day Karen screwed up her courage and threw away the dirty tissues on Viv's nightstand.

Viv didn't seem to notice and didn't say anything. But the next morning, new tissues appeared.

Karen threw those away as well. Viv still didn't say anything.

The next morning, new dirty tissues appeared.

Karen then didn't pick up the nightstand for three days. Viv didn't say anything.

At that point, Karen realized then that Viv didn't seem to notice or care about the tissues on the nightstand nearly as much as Karen had worried she might care. It seemed the best course of action was to ignore the tissues entirely.

This was an attitude that would serve her well as the months and eventually years unfolded with the three of them living as a triad. Face the demons if they approach, but don't go demon hunting.

Do the work needed to keep the relationships healthy and strong, but don't invent more work just for the sake of work.

And Karen would also learn that it was often easier just to speak up and ask about something than to perform little experiments and try to test her partners.

But that last lesson would take time.

Still, Penny and Viv had to admit that Karen had come a long way from when they met her.

Now that was an *awkward* question they got asked a lot: How did you all meet?

When it was just Penny and Viv, it had been a much more comfortable question. An easier answer.

"In college," they'd say, in unison.

Viv would smile, remembering the spooky girl dressed head to toe in pink, sitting on a park bench, seemingly talking to herself.

Viv had been warned about Penny, by people she trusted.

"That girl's fucking psycho."

"What a weirdo."

"No one's *that* crazy," one friend had said to Viv. "I think that poor girl's faking it for attention."

Maybe so. Maybe not. Viv wasn't big on reputation as a guiding force. She'd heard plenty of smack talked about Penny Dreadful. I mean, her name was enough of a red flag all by itself, wasn't it?

Girl either had parents who wanted to torture her, or she was a show business type who was attention hungry. About to start an all-girl punk band or something.

Penny Dreadful. What kind of name was that?

But Viv had seen her that one day, in the purple half-light of twilight. Penny's hair was almost glowing, and something about the lambent light brought out the lines of her face in a way that was really striking, as though she weren't a flesh and blood person but had been sketched by a comic artist.

In that moment, with the lights whispering over Penny's face, Viv felt a warmth in her chest that took her by surprise. Viv decided to discreetly listen to Penny's "conversation."

"You don't have to worry, you know," Penny said, to what appeared to be no one, as she sat beneath a tree. "I'll be here for you. I won't give up on you."

Penny paused. She leaned forward as though she were listening intently to someone.

But all Viv could hear were the rustling of the leaves as a gust of wind swept through them.

Penny nodded her head. "Well, those other people weren't me. It doesn't matter what you say. What your doubts try to tell you. I'll be the exception to the rule. You can count on me. Even if you don't realize it yet, you can count on me."

Another pause.

And then Penny said, "No, it's not. It's not weak to need other people. I pity the person who told you that. They must have a deep emptiness inside themselves to feel like all they have to offer the world is being as little of a burden as possible. It must be lonely to view other people that way. As boon or burden. Nothing in between. That's not how it works, Kip. Not really. It's a give and a take. Always. It's just more comfortable for people to round up or round down. Try to artificially split everyone into two groups: Villain or saint."

Viv listened as Penny continued. "Ever heard the myth of Procrustes, Kip?" A beat.

"Well, that's okay. It's not one of the greatest hits. Not like Icarus and his wax wings. Medusa and her gaze of stone. Procrustes isn't one of the biggies. But it's a good one, I promise."

Penny paused. Then continued.

"Sure. Procrustes was one of Poseidon's sons, a blacksmith. He lived along the Sacred Way, a road from Athens to Eleusis that cultists traveled to make their pilgrimage. Procrustes would invite each one who passed by his home to spend the night there in his bed. The only problem was that the bed never fit anyone exactly. Instead of leaving well enough alone, Procrustes would amputate the travelers' legs if they were too tall for the bed. If they were too short, he would beat their legs with his smith's hammer to stretch them."

Penny waited.

"Yes, I know it's grisly. But don't miss the point."

A beat.

"The point is that forcing things to fit a paradigm usually takes violence, whether physical or psychic, and nearly always ends in unpleasantness. So you'd do well not to try to force me into the same box as those who hurt you."

Viv stepped forward. "Who's Kip?"

Penny started. "I... uh... how long have you been listening?"

"Does it matter?" Viv replied.

Penny started to gather her things.

"You don't have to go," Viv said.

"Don't I?" Penny said.

"No," Viv said. She spoke the word with as soft edges as she could, letting it fade away slowly like a puff of exhaled smoke.

Penny sighed.

"You're so suspicious," Viv said. "So guarded. Maybe you should try taking your own advice."

"How so?"

"Maybe you could trust someone for once," Viv said.

Penny stared at her. As she met Viv's silver eyes, she felt as though Viv were looking through her. That Viv could see Penny's past as clearly as she could the tree that loomed above them or the sky. There was something intense about those eyes. And the way they looked at her.

Penny also noted something else peculiar about Viv's eyes: They were silver the first time she looked at her, but they didn't *stay* silver. Each time she looked into Viv's eyes, they seemed to change color.

"What color are your eyes?" Penny asked.

"What color do you think they are?" Viv said.

"I don't know," Penny admitted. "It seems like they change color every time I look at them. How are you doing that? Are they changing with your mood?"

"Not my mood," Viv said. "Probably yours. They look different based on what their observer is thinking or feeling… or at least that's how it seems to me on my end."

"What color are your eyes when you look in the mirror?" Penny asked.

"Green," Viv replied.

Strange, Penny thought. Green was the only color that Viv's eyes didn't seem to be to Penny. She watched as they flashed into molten metal. Then Viv's eyes were cerulean blue. Finally, they were muddy and flecked with gold.

"Have you ever seen things that other people didn't?" Penny ventured watching Viv's eyes shift through more shades.

"All the time," Viv replied.

Without realizing what she was even doing, Viv brushed a stray hair away from Penny's face and touched her cheek. An energy began to hum between them, like two simultaneous tones playing. They both felt it, nearly heard it. A dyad sounding. A resonance. Harmonious or dissonant? It was too intense at first for either of them to know which. Only that they had the potential to greatly impact one another.

Startled at the touch, Penny froze in place but didn't pull away. "You do?"

"Mm…" Viv said. "It gets exhausting. I can never really explain it to other people. What I see. They always think I'm crazy."

Penny sighed. "Me, too."

"You know," Viv said. "Everyone warned me you were crazy. They told me to stay away. That you'd be nothing but trouble."

Penny nodded sadly. She'd heard people say that about her plenty of times when they thought she couldn't hear them (and a few times brazenly when they knew she could).

"But I'm starting to think," Viv said. "That you're the most sane person I've ever met. I'm starting to think *they're* the crazy ones."

Penny smiled and took Viv's hand in hers. And in that moment, they both felt and heard the two tones sounding together once again, this time more clearly: They weren't the same notes but not entirely different. The interval between them was just right. A perfectly harmonious dyad.

Their relationship was easy. Whenever Viv crashed at her barebones student apartment, Penny would wake up early the morning after to pack Viv sandwiches cut into the shape

of different animals in a bagged lunch. This was because
Viv found it difficult to eat when she spent time with Penny,
especially in the beginning. There was something about
Penny that was so radiant. It was a little distracting.

Eating seemed like such a waste of time. Viv would much
rather spend hours in deep conversation or wrapped up in
the sheets, kissing every square inch of her girlfriend. There
was nothing quite as beautiful in this world, or the next,
as Penny's naked form. It reminded Viv of the sumptuous
lines of the women in Renaissance paintings, especially at
moments when Penny was unguarded, unaware that Viv was
watching her. When she didn't have time to whip herself into
one of her stock camera-ready vanity poses.

Viv loved those times the most, the moments when Penny
wouldn't have been considered by people who didn't know
her as photogenic. And Viv found herself snapping *those*
images more than any other in her eidetic memory for
safekeeping.

She treasured her mental images in which Penny looked
imperfect. Natural. Unaware that anyone was looking at her.

In the first few years they were together, Viv and Penny rarely
fought. Whenever they did fight, it was inevitably quite civil
and quickly resolved.

And it was Viv who convinced Penny to finally get tested for
psychic powers. To take a comprehensive perceptive battery
(CPB). Because while Penny hadn't come up as positive on
the routine testing she and everyone else had been subjected
to in public school, it was a well-known fact that the routine
testing only picked up 80% of cases.

The remaining 20% of cases currently able to be confirmed
required a much more thorough process to unearth.

The standard battery was required for all high school sophomores (and administered *ad hoc* based on teacher recommendation at any time during the school experience). Typically, so long as you stayed out of prison and didn't request to be given one, you didn't ever have to take the CPB.

But Viv had a sneaking suspicion that what Penny dismissed as "just the way she'd always been" and had slipped by on routine examination would come up on the longer test immediately.

"Look at it this way, Penny. You're either psychic or not. Wouldn't you rather know the truth either way?"

Penny frowned. "I'm not so sure. I don't know if I'm ready to be part of the... system."

Viv shrugged. "It's not so bad. They're paying for my school. And I'll have a job when I graduate."

Penny sighed. The State had provided for her until she became 18. But she'd been on her own the last few years. Her good grades had earned her a scholarship for tuition, but she wasn't sure how she'd ever pay off the debt she'd amassed for living expenses. The job market wasn't looking so great either. True, tueys were underpaid – and sometimes it looked like slave labor from her vantage point – but bringing home *something* had to be better than what she'd seen her peers struggle with.

The economy was bleak and getting bleaker every day. Like everyone else she'd grown up with, she'd been told that education was what would save her life. That she only had to pick something, study hard, and that she would forge a successful way forward. She was told repeatedly that talent and hard work were rewarded.

But life had taught her different lessons. And she'd come to realize that an awful lot of successful people had arbitrary connections that weren't factored into this overly rosy equation of Talent Plus Hard Work Equals Success.

Nepotism made the world go round. Bad news for an orphan.

"Alright," Penny said. "I'll take the test."

It was a testing morning that dragged into afternoon. Then afternoon lingered so long twilight began to descend. The test took Penny twelve hours, all told.

Phase 1 was your standard Ganzfeld experiment. Or at least Penny thought it was standard since this was her first time doing one. The test was at the very least consistent with what she'd been told to expect by Viv. The examiner escorted Penny to a comfy chair, where she was instructed to sit down.

Penny was given a pair of headphones that fit snugly around her ears and played continuous static at a volume that made it so she could hear nothing else. She also donned a pair of goggles that blocked out all light.

For the next half hour, Penny sat as the examiner, a normal, presumably focused on a series of images and "sent" them telepathically to Penny. As this happened, Penny was instructed to speak aloud what, if anything, she was receiving. What she was experiencing as far as thoughts, feelings, emotions.

"I'm really glad I went to the bathroom before this test," Penny said aloud. She knew it wasn't the right answer, but it was the first thing that popped into her mind. The static on her sensory deprivation headphones sounded very much like a roaring river, and even now she could feel her bladder twitch if she thought for too long about water.

She cleared her throat. "I'm thinking of water," she said. "A waterfall."

"I'm trying not to think about water because it's a bad idea. They show you in those movies, don't they? What happens if you think about water too long. Or try not to think about water. Don't think of an elephant. Don't think of having to pee. And certainly not a waterfall."

Penny failed this phase. It was a disaster. "That was one of the worst performances I think I've ever seen," the examiner noted.

If that isn't a bit of extra credit communication I could have lived forever without, Penny thought but kept to herself.

It's at times like these when I'm glad I can't send thoughts, Penny mused, as her examiner prepped for the second portion, which also was slated to take hours. *It's bad enough worrying about an errant email. A "reply all" by mistakes that goes to just the wrong person. Could you imagine if you could accidentally click send on a stray thought? No, thank you.*

In the second phase, the examiner tested Penny with a deck of Zener cards. The deck had twenty cards, all told. Five symbols appearing four times. Penny already knew what they were: Yellow circle, red cross, blue wavy lines, black square, green star.

Not only were these symbols part of the standard abbreviated battery, they'd taken on a life of their own outside of psychometrics. In the early days, when everything was more underground, psychics had peppered them throughout their fashion choices. Putting one on a ring served as an easy way to alert others nearby that you were intuitive. Later, someone had arranged them into a kind of psychic flag, although few were bold enough to wave such a flag openly, let alone permanently hang it outside their home.

Penny's favorite band growing up used the green star extensively in their imagery: On stage, on their albums, on their band-themed T-shirts.

Eventually, the State got on board, too, and these five symbols came to represent the all-important psychic "classification."

On Governmental Classifications

Even though psychic taxonomy was (and still is) in its infancy, the State has roughly sorted psychics into discrete custodial statuses based on the nature of their respective powers.

That's how it's purported to be organized, although the available facts fail to bear this assertion out. Independent meta-analyses conducted on the State's psychic classification of individual citizens have yielded some glaring statistical irregularities. It has been, to date, impossible to fit the data to a slope that doesn't have something else wrapped into it. The most historically common cause in experimental designs such as these has been bias.

When statisticians have attempted to explain this poor correlational fit, they have come up with a few possibilities. While it's impossible to say definitively a more apt undiscovered "third variable" doesn't exist, the one that is currently the most mathematically sound relates to a cross-product of how potentially economically useful a State examiner would rate a psychic's powers to be and how high that subject scores in personality scores of agreeableness.

Or, in other words, the best way to reliably achieve a green star regardless of psychic power, is to be nice to the person testing you and convince the State you can make it some money.

[Editorial note: The preceding paragraph is not present in the second edition or any subsequent original editions. It has been left in this reproduction for historical accuracy.]

Here are the current State Classifications:

Black Square: Detention/Imprisonment. Deemed too dangerous to have any traditional civil liberties. Property of the State.

Red Cross: Heavy Monitoring. Residents at an intensive outpatient center. If they are allowed to leave the facility, it is rare and never without the supervision of a State-qualified guardian.

Yellow Circle: Light Monitoring. Bound by an intricate reporting system whereby they must make regular visits to a State Sponsor, who will certify that they are obeying all relevant rules and regulations and that they pose no danger to themselves or others.

Blue River: Allowed to live on their own terms with monitoring only as needed with cause.

Green Star: Allowed to live on their own terms with monitoring only as needed with cause. Work in the employ of the State. Afforded additional privileges.

It's worth noting that these additional Green Star privileges aren't specified in the State Code and are subject to change at any time, based on officer discretion and the interpretation of the laws of the Psychic State.

However, some general patterns have been observed and maintained for over two decades. For example, while Blue Rivers need to check in with authorities any time they go on a long road trip, Green Stars are allowed to travel out of the immediate area without telling anyone – provided they aren't missing a scheduled shift at work to do so.

While many abide by this system of classification and find it sufficient to describe the range of psychic experience, others are less convinced. The Psychic State's decision to adopt the Zener symbols as such important differentiators was looked on with much disdain by psychic taxonomists in the early days of its adoption.

Formerly, taxonomists omitted all mentions of this classification in their handbooks, and it took several waves of reemployment before this material was grandfathered in as legacy theory and the body's convention moved from exclusion to inclusion.

Early critics of the State Classification Method pointed out its overly simple categories and replicability/ reliability problems. They also expressed concern about the difficulty posed to the State by using symbols formerly used for self-identification and counterculture liberation to adorn tools intended to catalog that same population in order to keep the peace but in doing so also depriving some people of the liberties those symbols had originally celebrated and hoped to preserve.

The response from the State to these voiced concerns was quite clear: That was the whole point.

It was theorized in the early years of the Psychic Phenomenon that State control would soon be in jeopardy. After all, how would it be possible for a State to maintain control over an entire class of citizens who possessed exceptional powers?

However, theory would turn out to be far off the mark. In reality, it would turn out to be quite easy to keep psychic citizens under State control. And the reason is simple: Psychic citizens are still human beings and as such possess all the normal failings and biases that most people struggle with.

While some psychic citizens do rebel against the State, to date they have done so as lone actors. Anti-State resistance has yet to be launched in an organized and coordinated manner. Therefore, those efforts have little effect.

Instead, it's much more common to see psychic citizens fighting amongst themselves and blaming one another for their problems, displacing their frustration upon their peers instead of working to dismantle the systems that are actually oppressing them.

In plainer terms: The hold that the State has over its psychic citizens is only possible because intuitives don't cooperate with one another. If intuitives across the State threw down their zero sum mentality and collaborated, they could easily overthrow the government.

Unfortunately, like many other oppressed peoples, they look to each other first as primary obstacles, and enmity towards the government (their true oppressors) has always been more of an afterthought.

from Insecta Psychica: Towards an Intuitive Taxonomy by Cloche Macomber

Penny found the second phase of the comprehensive perceptive battery just as confounding.

Try as she might, she couldn't guess the cards the examiner held in his hand.

At the conclusion of the battery, she was informed of her score: 20%.

Precisely what one would expect due chance, if a subject with no psychic powers were simply guessing.

Penny knew it was a bad sign when the examiner moved her to the third phase exam room and didn't sit down right away, retiring instead to an undisclosed location.

She was showing no promise. Of course. It would be a waste of a day. What would she tell Viv?

"Hello," she greeted the person sitting in the room's other chair, a preppy boy with neatly combed hair wearing a blue V-necked sweater with a designer logo on it and a pair of newly pressed khaki pants. "Are you being tested today, too?"

"Aren't we all being tested? Isn't that how it works?"

Penny cocked her head. "Are you majoring in philosophy?"

The boy laughed, throwing back his head with wild abandon.

Penny spoke to the boy for several minutes. He was irritating, she decided. Full of himself. Withholding. What was his deal?

Hopefully, the next task wasn't a cooperative one. She couldn't fathom how she'd make it through it without murdering him.

The examiner returned, attended by a colleague.

When they got to the door, they stopped and stared.

"Who in the world is she talking to?"

"Herself?"

"If that's the case, it's the most animated case of 'private speech' I've ever seen."

The examiner and his colleague walked back around the corner into a private office. From there, they could access the audio from Exam Room 3.

"...so how many times have *you* taken this test?"

A pause.

Then Penny spoke the examiner's address and wife's name aloud, tentatively and slowly, as though she were repeating it without really absorbing it. "Why should I say that to him?" she seemingly asked the air. "You think that'll get his attention? Make him think I'm psychic? I don't know about that. I don't think it's fair to cheat on a test like that."

The two examiners walked back to Exam Room 3 and opened the door.

"Ms. Penelope Dreadful."

"Yes?" Penny said.

"Who are you talking to?"

"Why, him of course," she said, gesturing to what to them looked like an empty chair.

The examiner and colleague exchanged confused looks.

"Oh no, not again," Penny said.

"You see someone sitting there?" the examiner said gently.

Penny hesitated and nodded.

"I regret to inform you, young lady, there is no one there," the examiner said.

"Oh." Penny frowned and looked away.

"Is this the first time you've seen someone that others couldn't?" the examiner said, trying to keep his voice as calm and level as possible.

Penny sighed. She nodded.

"Have you been worked up by mental health professionals?"

"Plenty of times," Penny said. "I'm not crazy."

"I didn't say you were," the examiner said.

"There's another possibility," his colleague said.

The examiner and Penny both looked at him expectantly. "These... people... you see... do they have anything in common?"

"Not a lot," Penny said. "Well, except for one thing."

"And that is?"

"They all tell me that they're dead," Penny replied. "Well eventually. When they get around to it. It's not always the first thing that comes up in conversation."

The colleague smiled broadly. "If you'll excuse us," he told Penny.

"Sure," she said.

The examiner and colleague stepped into the hallway. "We've been trying to keep the matter quiet, but another subject died in that exam room just a few days ago."

"Died? What exactly were you doing to them?" his colleague asked.

The examiner rolled his eyes. "It was a freak death. Natural causes. A ruptured aneurysm."

"Of course," the colleague said. "I'm sure that's what was on the record."

"Yes," the examiner said.

They exchanged a knowing gaze during a rather pregnant pause.

"Anyway," the examiner continued, "I'm not sure she's actually talking with that... expired subject. But it's possible."

"Get the Medium Module," the colleague instructed the examiner.

"Yes, sir," the examiner replied.

As his colleague walked away, and the examiner reentered the examination room, he grumbled, "A medium. Just my luck. That's gonna drag my average down."

"What a shmuck," the spirit said to Penny.

"Totally," she agreed with her dead companion.

"Totally what?" the examiner asked.

"Totally radical, dude," Penny replied. It didn't make much sense, but it was the first thing that popped into her mind.

The examiner rolled his eyes but proceeded with the next phase.

Penny blitzed through the Medium Module, which basically consisted of her traveling with the examiner to several different locations until she found spirits and interviewing them about things she couldn't possibly know.

It was after dark by the time she met his criteria. Therefore, it was well after dark by the time she returned home to Viv.

"How'd it go?" Viv asked.

Penny plunked down her newly minted State-issued intuitive identification. A temporary issue designed to be good enough until the permanent one arrived in the mail.

"A Green Star!" Viv exclaimed. "Just like me. Good job."

Penny beamed.

"I knew you'd make it happen," Viv said, which made Penny beam even more.

"Oh yeah?" Penny said. "See it in one of your visions?"

Viv winced a little at the word 'vision.' It was a bit woo-woo for her tastes, something Penny typically knew and steered clear of. But Viv she didn't push back this time and gathered herself quickly, ignoring it.

"Mmhmm," Viv said instead. "Something like that."

When people asked how they had met Karen... well, that was a little more difficult to explain.

Viv and Penny had been together for four years when they encountered their first major bump in the road. It's telling that this inaugural bump had really nothing to do with them or their core relationship but a relative.

Because it was in their fourth year together that Viv's mother, Tender Lee, was admitted to Nirvana Heights.

As far as mental health hospitalization, Tenny could have done a lot worse. Nirvana Heights was a 54-bed psychiatric facility, the best in the Skinner-Watson area. True, only about half of those were open to the public – the other half already spoken for and at any given time inhabited by the area's most important people. Members of the Four Families down on their luck. Celebrities who needed to dry out for the weekend. Famous researchers who were going through hard times. Generally speaking, the facility often housed people with connections.

For the most part, the patients at Nirvana Heights were there for a very short time. Very few residents of Nirvana Heights stayed for more than a week or two, with the vast majority gracing the hospital staff with their presence via a 72-hour hold.

Still, Viv knew her mother had truly taken a turn for the worse when Love had called her up in the wee hours of the morning to let her know about the hospitalization.

"I regret to inform you that Mother will be indisposed for a while," Love had said.

Viv had no idea what the hell that meant. "Could you speak in English please?"

"Look, it's not my fault you're a barbarian," Love had countered.

"Just tell me what's going on," Viv had replied.

"Certain things need to be handled delicately," Love had said.

"*Love*," Viv had said, drawing the one syllable out so long and lacing it with such annoyance that she might as well be saying hate.

"Mom's been committed to Nirvana Heights," Love had said.

In that moment, Viv felt her knees go weak. The world could have slipped out from underneath her, and she hardly would have noticed.

As Love began to explain the logistics of Tender Lee's psychiatric admission, visiting hours, regulations, and Love's own plans for dropping in, bright spots cropped up in Viv's vision and her view of the room she was in blurred.

She suddenly saw another room before her. A common area. Her mother was sitting there, surrounded by a motley band of characters. The carpet was dinghy, the furniture basic, battered, and dated. Think a jury duty holding room if everyone was not quite in their right mind.

Actually, still think jury duty in many cases.

A man sat in a rocking chair and popped his tongue in and out of his mouth rhythmically, as though he were a toad catching flies.

Several young adults gathered around a table with a partially finished puzzle on it.

Viv's mother Tender was there, too, sitting on the couch next to a sullen figure with a hoodie drawn tightly over her head.

"You know what I like about you?" Tenny said to the figure next to her.

The hooded figure said nothing.

"It's that you don't talk my ear off. You don't say anything at all, so you never say anything annoying."

No response.

"That's the thing, you know," Tender continued. "Most people are really shit at dealing with others. Even when they try to relate to what you're going through, when they try to be supportive, they turn it around and recenter themselves as the focus of the conversation. They make it all about them. I can't stand that."

Still no response.

"So thank you for that," Tenny said. "You're the best roommate I've ever had."

Viv blinked and the common room vanished. She was once again standing in her own kitchen, listening to her sister Love rant about the conditions at Nirvana Heights that their mother had reported. There were no paleo meal plans. And don't get her started on the thread count on the sheets, wasn't that just a travesty? How could they subject her mother to such threadbare accoutrements?

Since things had been so smooth between them for years, Viv wasn't at all sure how Penny would take the news. After all, Penny didn't have any relationship with her own parents.

She'd never even known them, had grown up as a ward of the state, moving from foster home to foster home.

Would she be able to understand what Viv was going through? Viv didn't know. And Viv also didn't know if it'd be gauche of her to complain about the stress she felt from her mother's psychiatric commitment. Because compared to what Penny had gone through, it wasn't nearly as bad. Viv at least *had* a mother.

But Penny had truly surprised her. Penny had never gone there for a minute, hadn't jumped to comparing tragedies and minimizing Viv's struggles.

Instead, Penny's first words had been. "Oh no, that's awful. I'm so sorry. When are we going to visit?'

Just as it had been when she'd been initially visited by emotional avatars, the first time Karen Cross met Viv Lee and Penny Dreadful, she wasn't completely awake.

Instead, she was sleeping fitfully in her bed at Nirvana Heights. She'd been inpatient at that point for about two days. It wasn't her first psychiatric admission, not by a long shot.

Her time at the One Eighty Acres had failed to deliver on its grandiose promises. Her parents' aim in sending her away had been to set her on the straight and narrow.

Her parents weren't exactly sure if Karen were psychic or simply pretending to be. But either way, One Eighty promised it would do the trick.

If she were faking being psychic, then surely the courses in attitude adjustment, behavioral therapy, and emotional self-regulation would dissuade her from this ill-fated dishonesty.

And in the unlikely event that she did have empathic powers, One Eighty pledged that Karen's stay would result in conversion therapy.

Instead, Karen had emerged from the program with an empathic sense that was more developed and more powerful than ever.

Unfortunately, this didn't come without cost.

Rather than empathy being something Karen could opt in and out of, her heightened powers instead meant that people's emotions constantly bombarded her. Karen found herself frequently exhausted.

And in that exhaustion, she began to go slowly mad.

She hopped in and out of inpatient psychiatric hospitalization, medicated to the gills, trying any possible treatment that the doctors offered, looking for peace of mind.

Her latest stint at Nirvana Heights had up until this point been largely unremarkable. Her roommate Tender Lee was a real trip, to be sure, like someone who had escaped from a low-budget production of *Gone with the Wind*. A vain woman with big hair and an even bigger ego. An incessant talker, clingy, seemingly hellbent on being her friend while they were both committed here.

Karen had coped so far with just being as quiet as possible, thinking that it might drive her away. But no dice.

If anything, the silence made Tender even more eager to be dear friends. The spotlight could always be on her any time they hung out.

Karen had recently resorted to a new tactic, pretending to sleep extra long hours in order to get some kind of break, solitude.

So far Tender had respected that. She hadn't yet yakked at Karen while she was sleeping, although Karen wasn't entirely sure that she might not try it, given enough time and boredom.

Karen was used to not getting any visitors, so she knew instantly that the strangers in her room were here to see Tender. Karen opened her eyes. She saw a tall redhead with copper-colored eyes who was wearing a pair of paint-stained overalls. Beside her stood a shorter blonde woman in an immaculate pink business suit. And of course there was Tender, because it wasn't going to be easy to get rid of that woman. Not by a long shot. She seemed to enjoy the inpatient stay, all of the attention the staff paid to her incessant requests, and the indulgently long therapy sessions she insisted on undergoing.

Karen sat up and prepared as usual to feel Tender's normal cyclone of emotional highs and lows.

And yet, she felt nothing.

She also felt nothing from the visitors.

What in the world…?

"And that's my roommate Karen," Tenny said. "She's emo," she said in a fake whisper – but one that was clearly loud enough for everyone else to hear it.

"Karen Cross," Karen said, leaping to her feet and offering her hand. Her sudden extroversion shocked her just as much as it shocked Tender Lee.

"This is my daughter Viv," Tenny said, gesturing to the tall redhead. Karen noted that Viv's eyes seemed to be shifting color every few moments. Well, that was something she hadn't seen before.

"And this is my partner Penny," Viv said, pointing to the blonde woman standing next to her.

Tenny scowled at the word *partner*.

Ah, Karen thought. *It's THAT kind of partner.* Without that scowl, there would have been more ambiguity, but Tenny's expression gave it away. In her rambling, self-indulgent rants, Tenny had let it be known that she didn't have much respect for same sex relationships. To her they didn't even really seem to be actual relationships.

Karen had intentionally refrained from talking about her own sexual orientation, or arguably lack thereof, the fact that gender didn't matter nearly as much to her as how she felt about the person in question, their character, their values, how well they meshed – or didn't. Or the fact that while she found sex enjoyable physically that it was something that took a backseat to emotional connection.

It was an interesting twist to find out that Tender's own daughter were gay, or bisexual at the very least.

Anyway, her daughter was seriously romantically involved with a woman. A beautiful woman, too.

Actually, they were both really attractive, Karen realized, albeit in different ways. There was something stoic and strong about Viv. Rugged. And those eyes were otherworldly.

Penny, conversely, was a paragon of glossy bubble gum femininity. She was also... sparkly. Radiant anyway. Karen found it hard not to smile whenever she looked at Penny.

And more importantly, Karen felt a sense of peace and calm the moment she met them that she couldn't remember ever having.

For as long as Karen could remember, she'd been flooded with the emotions of others. But now, with them in the room, her mind was quiet. Far less crowded.

All she sensed were her own emotions. For once.

Penny and Viv didn't spend long in her room before moving on to tour the rest of the facility. In spite of herself, Karen began to tail them at a safe distance.

She noted that if she fell too far behind that the emotions of others returned, flooded into her mind.

It was painful watching Penny and Viv say goodbye to Tenny at the locked exit to the ward. Karen knew what would happen next. That the calm would be gone.

And she was right. When Penny and Viv left, so did the calm.

In the days that followed, Karen waited for her roommate's daughter to visit again. But no luck.

"Viv's got a busy life. She's a detective, and she works a lot," Tender had explained, visibly taken aback when Karen asked about another visit. After all, the reason Tender liked Karen so much was because she wasn't much of a talker. She wasn't used to Karen asking followup questions. Or questions apropos of nothing, as this one seemed to be.

Karen grumbled. Felt despondent.

One afternoon sitting outside the nurse's station, observing their feelings to pass the time, Karen got an idea. She'd wait until the nurses were clearly distracted. Once that happened, she'd have her chance.

She didn't have to wait too long. It seemed that there was a love triangle underway between the staff at Nirvana Heights. Or perhaps a quadrangle. Or a hexagon? Karen wasn't too sure.

In any event, there were an awful lot of people working at the hospital trying to be monogamous and failing miserably because they were partnered to people who were trying to be slyly non-monogamous and failing miserably by getting caught.

Which opened a wide window of opportunity for her.

During an intense standoff in a back staff room between a cheater and a jilted lover, Karen crept into the nurses' station and looked up the information in the visitors' log.

Viv Lee and Penny Dreadful, 26 Bell Avenue, Skinner.

Of course they'd live there, Karen thought. Not just in the Psychic City but in one of the most intuitive-dense neighborhoods.

An unrelenting rain practically pressure blasted the street the night Karen was discharged from the hospital, but for all she cared it could have been sunny out.

The entire ten miles that she walked, she was only vaguely aware of how heavy her clothes became. Largely oblivious to how the weight from the water made her body feel as though even gravity had changed and that she very well could have been walking on the surface of an alien planet.

She was fixated solely on the directions, the mess of turns that would take her to 26 Bell Avenue. She recited them over and over again in her head so she wouldn't mess them up.

The weather didn't matter. She only cared about navigating, first through the dense city streets, then through the mixed-use downtown, and finally through the haphazardly zoned suburbs that led to the house where Tender Lee's daughter Viv and her partner Penny lived.

Karen didn't have to check the number on the door. She knew precisely when she arrived. And that they were quite close, judging by the immediate wave of calm that hit her stepping onto the doormat, which she noted read GO AWAY in italics rather than your standard WELCOME.

Drenched to the bone, Karen raised one heavy rain-soaked arm and pounded on the front door.

Even with a door between them, Karen heard a syncopated polyrhythm, the patter of feet bounding towards her. A few seconds later, the door flung open, revealing Penny, wrapped in a fluffy pink bathrobe, her blonde hair tightly wound in curlers.

"Oh... Oh!" Penny said.

Karen shrugged.

"Oh," Penny said again.

The tone was a bit different each time, communicating a different emotion. Karen followed along quite well. In that moment, even as she stood weighed down by dripping clothes, her wet hair shellacked to her face hooded beneath her sweatshirt, with her powers comparably dampened, she felt she could have followed Penny's meaning indefinitely even if all she said was "oh."

"Do they know that you're gone?" Penny said.

Karen winced.

"Oh dear, I... uh... that sounded terrible. I don't mean to imply that you escaped," Penny blurted out. "Oh," she said again. This time the syllable sounded pinched and nervous and even a bit embarrassed.

"It's okay," Karen replied. Because it was. She couldn't explain how, but she knew already that everything was okay now. And that it would continue to be okay for quite some time.

"Um. But... Did you?" Penny said, in spite of herself.

"Did I what?" Karen asked.

"Did you escape?" Penny said. "Oh. Oh gosh, I'm so rude."

Karen cracked a smile. "No, I didn't escape. I was discharged."

"Ah," Penny said. And this particular syllable had a life of its own, one quite distinct from the spectrum of "ohs." "Ah" seemed more solid somehow. A release of tension, but one that wasn't like venting or a hiss of steam but more manifested as a safe fall from a great height would.

"Ah" was a safety net, there to catch you. The denouement after a spectacular drama. This "ah" anyway.

"Well come in then," Penny said, as she was becoming quite uncomfortable watching Karen get rained on. And as Karen was hopefully not an escapee from the mental hospital, provided she were telling the truth.

Karen plodded wetly into the foyer, careful not to go too far, lest she track mud all over what seemed to be a perfectly nice hardwood floor. Karen stopped where she stood and began to take off her shoes.

"A nice gesture," Penny said. "But I'm not sure your shoes will do it."

"I know I'm a mess," Karen said.

Penny nodded.

"But I don't have any other clothes," Karen said.

"Wait here," Penny replied.

A few seconds later, Penny returned carrying an armful of clothes. They were all pink. A baby pink track suit. Fleece socks with bunnies on them. A fluffy pink towel perched atop of this pile of clothes. It was an awkward position, as it was the largest item Penny carried, but somehow she kept it balanced.

Impressive, Karen thought.

"Let's get you out of these wet things," Penny said as she handed the outfit to Karen. Then she laughed. "They say that in movies, you know. I've always wanted to say it to someone. Never had a chance to."

"Thank you," Karen said. She began to pull off her wet clothes, which seemed practically suctioned onto her skin at this point.

It dawned on Penny that this strange woman she'd only met once was about to strip down naked in front of her. When you're in this position, you have a few choices:

Stand there and watch and enjoy the show. Something you can do openly or perhaps you can attempt to do a bit more slyly, acting blasé about the nudity or pretending to not be looking directly when you are in fact sneaking glimpses.

Give the person some privacy.

Insist the person go somewhere where they will have privacy.

As Penny wasn't about to have Karen track mud all over the house, that knocked off the request for Karen to relocate. So she realistically was going to watch or go away.

In all honesty, Penny was quite curious about Karen's physique. It was a real mystery to her given how Karen dressed, hiding her body under so many layers of clothes. Even completely drenched, nothing even close to resembling a wet T-shirt contest was underway.

However, as Penny suspected that Viv wouldn't exactly approve of her gawking over this naked woman, Penny chose to set the stack of clean laundry down where Karen could reach it and go away.

Viv, Penny thought suddenly. *Right.*

Penny knew immediately what she had to do. The longer this stranger were in the house without Viv knowing, the more potential trouble Penny could be in when Viv found out.

Viv could be rather unpredictable when it came to her responses to bizarre events... and well, to everything. As far as Penny could tell, Viv was inclined to have a rather moody temperament at baseline. Throw in her attacks (or as Penny liked to call them, her "visions," although this inevitably made Viv sneer when she said it) and her ever-changing medication regimen to control them, you never knew quite which version of Viv you were going to get.

This could be stressful for Penny sometimes, but it was also frankly what made Viv kind of fun. Dating Viv was like dating a kaleidoscope of multiple different people all blended in a complex matrix that defied total comprehension, each component person with their own needs and concerns.

In any event, Viv's inherent unpredictability kept things interesting between them. Fresh.

As Penny walked up to Viv to announce Karen's rather damp arrival on their doorstep, she hoped that she'd be met with one of Viv's more forgiving iterations.

Viv was sitting in the office, quite engrossed with a book she was reading. Penny cleared her voice so as not to startle her.

Viv looked up, her eyes flashing through three shades in quick succession. Penny wasn't sure what that meant but proceeded carefully. "So you know your mother's roommate at Nirvana Heights?" Penny ventured.

"Just barely," Viv replied. "I know that she had one, if that's what you mean."

"Short woman. Dark hair. Wearing a hoodie. Sad, distracted, but nervous energy. Kind of like what would happen if you gave Eeyore a few too many espresso shots in his trough."

Viv frowned. "Well, that's oddly specific." She became suspicious. "Penny, what's going on?"

Penny bit her lip. "What would you say if I told you she was in our house changing into some of my clothes?"

Viv set down her book and considered Penny's face carefully. "I would say, "Maybe we should call the cops.'"

"But we are the cops," Penny replied.

"You know what I mean. The normal cops," Viv said. "The normals. Skinner PD. The guys with the wee-yoo wee-yoo wagon."

"Is that what you really want, Viv? A team of cops showing up here, finding a psychic gay couple and deciding to ask us the wrong questions? They'd probably take one look at us and decide to handcuff the blonde one. And then it'd get *really* nasty. Because they've probably watched too many pornos about women's prisons."

"Too many?" Viv asked. "Do you know this from personal experience, how many films that is? What *is* the recommended serving of women's prison porn, Miss Penny?"

Penny sighed. Her cheeks burned. This was all getting to be too much.

Viv cracked a grin. "Anyway, you'd probably enjoy the handcuffs."

Penny wanted to laugh, but there was a certain edge to Viv's jab that she found a little too sharp. Penny groaned instead, feeling frustration rise from her stomach into her chest.

"Come with me," Penny said, leading Viv out to where Karen now stood fully dressed. *She changes outfits quickly,* Penny mused. *Wonder if she's done any theater.* The efficiency reminded her very much of an actor who must briskly switch costumes.

"Does she look dangerous to you?" Penny said to Viv, as they stood just out of Karen's earshot.

"Define dangerous," Viv replied.

"Look at her," Penny said. "She showed up outside in the middle of the night, soaking wet. What was I supposed to do? Besides, she's so tiny. What's she going to do? Rough us up?"

"You never know," Viv said. "Sometimes it's the small ones you've gotta watch."

Penny frowned.

"Your heart's just too big sometimes," Viv said, sighing. "You're always picking up strays."

Viv had found this out the hard way. A human rescue was a first, but there had been half a zoo's worth of adoptions, rehabilitations, and releases in the years that they had lived together. *Including the incident with the python*, Viv thought in passing, but they'd agreed long ago not to discuss that anymore.

"Well, it's like I always tell you. You were kind enough to take me in when I was wandering around lost. It's the least I can do," Penny said.

"I don't know where we'll put her," Viv said. Theirs wasn't a big house by any means, and the few rooms they did have were small and spare of furniture. They didn't exactly have a second bed kicking around.

"She can sleep on the couch," Penny said.

"And what about food? Utilities? Rent?" Viv asked.

"Does she look like someone we should be asking about rent at the moment?" Penny asked.

She had a point, Viv conceded silently, noting both the state of the pile of wet clothes dropped abruptly at the edge of their home and how little Penny's punchy sartorial influence did to make this tiny woman look any less wretched. Penny wasn't exactly a tall woman or one with broad shoulders, but this visitor for all the world looked like a small child wearing her mother's clothing.

"Anyway, we can probably get her a job Downtown," Penny offered. "We can drop her off on our way to PsyOps."

"Maybe," Viv said. "If she's stable enough to work."

"Viv, we don't have to figure all of that out right now. We don't have to work it all out tonight," Penny said.

"I know I'm going to regret this," Viv said.

"But?" Penny prompted.

Viv said nothing.

"Please, Mommy," Penny said in her best little kid voice, "Can I keep her? Can I keep her, huh?"

Viv rolled her eyes. "On one condition."

"And that is?"

"That you never call me Mommy again," Viv said.

"I make no promises," Penny replied. "Especially if you start talking about handcuffs again."

"Incorrigible," Viv replied. "Simply incorrigible." And after a beat, she added, "You were the one who brought up the handcuffs this time around, don't you remember?"

"Me? I'd *never* do something like that," Penny said, affecting her best innocent face.

They exchanged a knowing smile before stepping forward together to welcome the soggy visitor into their home.

In a few hours they would know that Karen had psychic powers of her own when she finally came clean about what had drawn her to them in the first place. The sense of calm – and sheer quiet – that their mere presence offered.

It would be months, however, of living in their house and eventually becoming employed at PsyOps on their investigative team (a highly improper assignment but something Karen insisted upon and got the department's respected health department to sign off on because of its benefit to her mental health) before any of them realized Karen had fallen in love with them both.

And as usual, Karen would be the last to know how she truly felt.

A Cold Slog

The Snow White case was turning out to be a difficult one to solve.

A quick visit to the hospital to visit the other victim, the one that had seemingly been stricken mad, turned over no new evidence.

No new leads.

Nothing.

In fact, Penny thought as the three detectives tromped silently back to their car, *that was one of the most pointless trips I've ever made in my career.*

The interview at the hospital was extraordinary in its lack of new information. Typically, they managed to learn *something* additional by visiting a scene, talking things over with a witness.

Just as Amarynth had conveyed to them, Neia Stavropolous confessed to murdering her partner. But when questioned on the details, she clammed up and couldn't elaborate.

A series of followup questions yielded no answers. "I don't know," Neia said over and over again.

As more questions were asked of her, Neia began to curl into a protective posture, forming a ball with her body, tilting down her head.

The last "I don't know" was rather muffled.

From the doorway, a nurse scowled, throwing them a look that indicated she thought the detectives were bullying the poor girl.

Just as the truth evaluators before her had found, Karen noted a lack of deception. Neia believed that what she was saying were true – even if she had no way to explain her confession or piece together a convincing narrative of how in the world she killed another demotivator.

They left the interview knowing just as little as they had before. Arguably less.

Viv grumbled as she received an email from Martin on the walk out of the hospital. Blood typing at the scene revealed that the bloody inkblot on Stephanie Mack's chest didn't match either victim.

Of course there was no DNA testing done, nor any indication of when or even *if* they'd get that. Psychic State labs didn't have that technology, and the sample would have to be shipped internationally to the United States. A*nd I can't see the department heads wasting one of their diplomatic favors on the murders of two psychics*, Martin had written bluntly.

Of course not, Viv thought. *That would involve treating us like we were actually human. Or important.*

She was disappointed but not exactly surprised. She conveyed the information in the email to Karen and Penny as they walked through the parking lot.

Once they reached the car, sat down, and closed their doors, Penny spoke first. "Could it be that someone implanted a false memory?"

Viv raised an eyebrow. "Sucked out her sanity and implanted a false memory? Never seen anything like that before."

"Doesn't mean it isn't possible," Penny shot back.

"Possible doesn't solve murders," Viv replied.

Penny said nothing in response.

"Anyway," Viv continued. "We can't arrest her. Not with the fact pattern the way it is. The lack of physical evidence. Her inability to connect the dots for us on how she actually did it – *if* she did it."

"I guess there's a reason that Amarynth didn't tell us to come *here*," Karen said.

Viv scowled.

Karen immediately regretted invoking Amarynth's name, since the Connections agent wasn't exactly Viv's favorite subject.

"It would have been bad procedure not to come here," Viv said defensively.

"Yeah, Viv, I know," Karen replied.

"Do you?" Viv's tone was sharp.

Karen exhaled slowly. "Yes. I do."

Viv took a few deep breaths herself. Finally, she said, "Well, there's not much to be done about it. We have other cases to work on."

Penny waited a few moments and then started the car.

There was still a lot Detectives Cross, Lee, and Dreadful didn't know, but one thing was for sure: They had hit a dead end on the Snow White case.

This wasn't all that uncommon, for a case or two to go cold. For the team to be at a loss on how next to investigate a crime.

Sometimes these cold cases would spontaneously reheat after days, weeks, months, or even years under deep freeze. And they'd be back in the game.

But other times, that was the end of the investigation.

Even with a team of psychics working on the case, not every crime would be solved.

This was a very troubling reality for Karen when she'd first joined PsyOps. That not every problem would present as solvable, no matter how hard she worked. Not every wrong could or would be met with justice.

Sometimes working as a detective made her feel as though there was no such thing as closure. Just luck. Chance. A dice roll with your eyes closed.

It wasn't at all like the murder mysteries she'd grown up reading led her to believe. In her beloved books, the detectives found their way through a mass of unrelated clues through the power of deduction. Usually while eating something exotic and cozying about an English country garden. However, real life didn't always hand out *hors d'oeuvres* or even clues. Nor did it always reward your efforts to try to scare them up, clues or snacks.

It was frankly quite rare that a crime scene had catering. Not that you'd be allowed to eat at a crime scene even if there *were* snacks – all those forensic rules and crime scene investigators with bugs up their asses.

And real life's answer to Sherlock Holmes was a wild-haired Connections agent with a city-sized chip on her shoulder. Not the most ideal ringer to be depending on.

Not only did Amarynth not believe in closure, she seemed to be stubbornly opposed to it. "Everything is revealed when it's time," she'd say, when pushed. It didn't seem to bother her that their team had the highest rate of open cases at any given time.

"We've also never charged anyone who was truly innocent," Amarynth would add as a followup observation.

"How do you know that?" Viv would ask.

Which would be met with a glare. "Just come up with an explanation that makes sense to you," Amarynth had countered, "And I'll co-sign it."

Normally, the sting of a case gone cold would quickly fade. The city of Skinner could be busy and admittedly quite unsettled. A new crime would quickly come into the picture, edging out the former case. There wasn't much time to dwell on the past and what was still unsolved.

There was always a new puzzle to work on. And it was far too easy to forget about the rooms and rooms of puzzles that were still incomplete. Puzzles that might never get put together.

This time, however, was quite different. All three detectives found themselves thinking of the Snow White case quite often and at random times. Feeling a sense of sadness that the investigation had ground to a halt as well as a sense of implacable foreboding.

It was a cold slog, working through their normal case load over the next few weeks. The City of Skinner itself seemed to have a sense of humor about it, or at least decided to dress up for the party they were attending, as an unseasonable cold front hit them out of nowhere, confounding meteorologists who had not only not seen it coming but were also hard pressed to explain why it was happening.

People in the neighborhood had begun to comment that it was a bracing cold, one that reminded them more of artificial refrigeration than anything natural or expected.

You know, like a deep freezer.

It was said like an obvious fact in small shops, in fleeting niceties bandied from cashier and customer and back again. Cursory, quick.

And curiously cold in its own right.

It was though a deep freezer permeated their collective psyche. Skinner. Their neighborhood. PsyOps. And of course, Detectives Dreadful, Lee, and Cross.

There was no mistaking it. It had become incredibly cold.

And not only was it cold, it refused to thaw.

Even after the cold front moved out of the area, and temperatures began to rise, Karen found herself shivering at odd moments.

Viv fumbled with fine motor tasks, feeling like the circulation had slowed in her hands.

Cutis anserina sprung up on Penny's arms. *Goosebumps*, she thought. *I haven't had these since I was a child.*

First, they attributed the chilled feeling to a psychosomatic reaction to working a case of the body they had found in a deep freezer. "I can't get warm ever since then," Karen said. "It's so strange."

But as the weeks wound on, the sense of coldness only grew.

I feel it, too, Penny caught herself thinking, although she didn't dare talk about it aloud.

Viv bore it stoically but carried a spare pair of gloves wherever she went. (Never mind what people might think or what they might call her.)

After her initial pronouncement – and Penny and Viv's fittingly chilly responses to it – Karen didn't bring it up the cold weather again. Instead, the three detectives did their best to huddle together for warmth and hope the chill would pass soon.

But it didn't.

Even as they tied up all the loose ends on a case they'd been investigating for months, their standard celebration lacked its usual fire. Even as the weather warmed and people shed the jackets they'd thrown on so quickly in concern.

A different cold persisted, a deep freeze that wasn't so easy to thaw.

Nothing seemed real or satisfying while the Snow White case was unsolved.

It was almost a relief when the next body was found.

The Whisper Street Affair

Viv woke up in the middle of the night, drenched in sweat.

She'd been dreaming that she was walking down Whisper Street, when a soft song began to play off in the distance. Ambient at first, but crescendoing as she focused her attention on it.

Just like when Viv was a little girl, and her mother would turn the music on her stereo down when she went to bed. At first, the soft music would be inaudible. But if she sat and focused on it for long enough, her ears and brain would adjust, and the music would seem as though it was the same volume as before.

A cycle of habituation where she would adjust to the stimulus, and so the stimulus would change in her mind.

As she focused on this soft music, it swelled. Louder and louder. The chords seemed quite familiar. But she couldn't quite piece together the melody. Each note was clear and resonant enough, but it seemed to be slowed down to a tempo where by the time the next note sounded she'd already forgotten the one before.

Could it be a lullaby? Or was every slow song played in the middle of the night easily mistaken for a lullaby? Viv couldn't quite tell.

As she came to the end of Whisper Street, she stood below an apartment with a blue light in the window. Shadows moved across the pane, suggesting activity.

As she approached the door of the building, she knocked twice, and the music stopped.

A moment later, Viv was awake.

She picked up her cell phone from the nightstand. Glanced at the screen. A text from Amarynth: *659 Whisper Street.*

As Viv held the phone in her hand, a second text came in. *You're welcome.*

Viv rolled her eyes and called out to Penny and Karen.

When word of the first verified precognitionists hit the general public, the media couldn't get enough. The whole phenomenon had started rather quietly. A case here, a case there. Strange things happening that were hard to explain.

The earliest intuitives thought they were all going mad. As did people around them.

It wasn't for several years after the emergence of psychic powers that anyone thought to test for them. To study them. And later, to regulate them.

The original confirmed cases of psychic power were found chiefly among university students, volunteers for research experiments who participated in studies for academic extra credit.

The first study, conducted by Janira Watson, a young professor and descendant of the esteemed Watson Research Family, was far from a methodical examination of the issues and actually kind of a fluke.

Scrambling for a hypothesis, she had come up with a basic test design that involved a series of questionnaires asking participants carefully worded questions after a series of meticulously selected semantic primes.

She wanted to test the potential strength of advertising effects on consumer behavior, even in the absence of perceived relevance.

Professor Watson theorized that the simple juxtaposition of positive images next to products would render them more valuable and that being exposed to a brief negative image would conversely prime participants to like a product less. Even if the images were completely irrelevant. (The images had been independently scored by another group on their degrees of positivity and negativity. Participants were surveyed on image relevance as part of the study.)

Janira Watson wasn't optimistic as she set out. She had a feeling that her study design was flawed somehow. While she'd done a literature review, she wasn't fully confident that she'd done it well enough. It was possible that the idea was derivative, that this was a replication at best. And she wasn't sure she had dug up enough sources for a strong introduction to the study, even if she eventually did publish one.

She managed her expectations, telling herself that this would be a pilot study. A way of figuring out if the design even worked. Something she would later refine and shape into a suitable research project.

She'd spent far too long coming up with ideas and rejecting them. She needed to test *something*. If too much more time passed without her conducting a study, she'd likely lose her job, famous name or not.

So it was back to her original discarded idea pile. This one seemed simplest to throw together quickly, so this one it was.

Once the study was underway, Professor Watson's research assistant noticed a curious thing: Certain study participants were coming in and filling out all three questionnaires without waiting for the subsequent primes.

"Well, they're probably half-assing it, trying to get done early. Maybe we should exclude those?" Professor Watson said.

"No, you don't understand," her assistant replied. "They're filling them out *correctly*."

"Correctly?"

Sure enough, when Professor Watson went to examine the forms, the participants had correctly identified the primes in the space provided – before being shown them.

"If I didn't know any better," Janira Watson mused, "I'd say that they could see the future."

They both laughed, but on the walk to give her next lecture, Professor Watson found herself wondering. Could it be?

In the end, Watson's initial experiment *was* a pilot study – but not for an investigation into the role of semantic priming in advertising. No, she realized, it was a pilot study for the presence of precognition among the general college population.

Her colleagues rolled their eyes when she reported her intentions. The department head wrote snarky comments on her form requesting research funding, but checked the box approving it. "Why the heck not?" he said as he handed it to her. "It'll keep you out of trouble."

Janira Watson would think of that moment often when she appeared on TV shows with a chyron below her that read, "Scientist, Discovered First Psychics."

Is this staying out of trouble? she'd ask herself silently as she waited with hot lights on her face, staring at yet another studio audience that seemed to blend in with the last several she'd appeared before.

In these appearances, she was often seated next to some of her first confirmed test cases, perfectly normal-looking young people who could predict future events with accuracy greater than chance.

Not perfectly, mind you. A precog saw potential futures, *likely* futures. And bias was always a powerful form of interference, regardless of any given precog's level of perspicacity otherwise.

For matters as inconsequential as a research semantic prime or the sequence of playing cards to be laid down before them like the Zener test, their accuracy was unparalleled. But when it came to interpersonal relationships, things could get quite a bit murkier.

It was hardest to predict one's own future, precognitionists found. But predicting the future of others wasn't always easy either.

Despite what centuries of cold reading and psychic play-acting had led the public at large to believe, seeing someone's future was quite a bit more difficult than anticipating a series of arbitrary symbols.

Still, that's what that same public wanted. They didn't want parlor tricks. They didn't care about Zener cards. They wanted insights into their own futures. Calls flooded the TV stations where intuitives had appeared on programs. People wanted to know information about their professional futures. What they should invest in financially.

And an awful lot of people –most of them– wanted the newly identified psychics to make predictions about their love lives.

Horoscopes had been quite popular prior to the discovery of psychic powers, but who needed to see what the day held for Sagittarius when you had a real life precog to ask about that hunky fellow who worked down the hall?

It didn't take long for the government to step in. Citing concern for the safety of these first psychics gone public, the precogs Watson had worked with were immediately put into the Black Square Program, in which they were effectively imprisoned. The government claimed this was for their own good, but they also benefited from the study and experimentation on these first psychics, whose participation was *not* voluntary.

Janira Watson seethed. This was not what she'd wanted, but it was out of her hands now.

The timing was impossible anyway, she reminded herself. The Psychic State had just gained independence, and they were thirsty for anything that would allow them to defend and maintain their recent secession.

As the years passed, however, and their knowledge of the psychic phenomenon increased, governmental control did relax somewhat, and subsequent citizens were granted more freedom and lower-security status.

They also employed a series of regulations regarding the use of psychic power, in order to preempt bedlam from breaking loose. The heaviest restrictions surrounded the use of psychic power in legal negotiations, in the financial industry, or in conjunction with sex.

The first two were intended to prevent the erosion of centralized legal powers and the risk of economic collapse due to psychic destabilization.

The latter, however, was mostly a measure taken to square with existing vice laws. Particularly as the public saw the emergence of more varied forms of psychic power than simply precognition and telepathy (the earliest forms, which would continue to be the most common), there was grave concern about love charms and the ability for someone to improperly compel another to have sex.

In general, the laws prohibiting the commercial use of psychic powers in sexual intercourse didn't differentiate between sex and love. It didn't care about consent. Legally, the State believed you couldn't consent to a love charm.

And most importantly, the law didn't differentiate between compelling someone to have sex with you and asking a precog what your love life looked like.

Predictably, however, that didn't stop the public desire for those services.

Savvy businesspeople took full advantage of this unmet need, setting up shop, particularly in seedier neighborhoods, that advertised Fortune-Telling.

In the eyes of the State, Fortune-Telling was considered a For Entertainment Only industry, an entity completely distinct from the verified psychic phenomenon. Legally speaking, it wasn't any different than hiring someone to deliver a candygram. Or having them dress up elaborately and pretend to predict the future at a child's birthday party.

In other words, it was perfectly legal to pay someone who was *pretending* to have psychic powers to give you predictions or advice about your love life. But completely illegal to pay someone who actually *had* psychic powers to do so.

Savvy undocumented precogs who wanted to find a way to earn a living quickly tapped into this phenomenon and began to work at Fortune-Telling houses, pretending to be frauds. This typically meant that they'd have to be wrong often enough to not arouse suspicion. Usually this involved faking wrong answers in addition to their occasionally incorrect predictions.

The "best" Fortune-Telling Houses were rumored to have as much as ten percent of its workforce made up of undocumented precogs pretending to be charlatans. Legally, they couldn't come out and say this of course, not without risking a government raid and on-the-spot psyon testing of all employees – but the rumor mill spread the word plenty well.

Consumers knew where to look.

The Warrens of Persephone

The witness was an extraordinarily beautiful woman. As she sat before them, her long legs were tucked underneath her at an improbable angle, with harrowing flexibility. She was positioned more like a bendy doll than an actual human being. Her long thick hair was piled into an elaborate updo that stayed improbably in place, despite looking soft and not shellacked down with hairspray or even mousse.

As they spoke, she held a pear absentmindedly in her right hand. Fruit baskets were scattered around the room. Gold-painted wicker, judging by the look of it. Made to look more opulent than they were but doing a pretty good job regardless.

Tapestries hung on the walls depicting scenes from Greek mythology.

The myth of Persephone, Penny noted. The princess of the underworld, who had in some myths been abducted by Hades to be his wife in the Underworld and in other versions of the same story ran away from her family to voluntarily pursue a love affair with the Prince of Darkness.

In all tellings of the myth, Persephone did look back on her former life and tried to keep both old and new acquaintances. And the way she split her time between overworld and underworld was responsible for the seasons – because Persephone was spring personified. So when she was underground, winter would descend. Or something like that.

It wasn't Penny's favorite myth, not by a long shot, so that's about as much as she knew.

Their current witness fit in quite well with the ambiance, with the art. Statuesque. And holding a bowl of fruit that would look at home as props for a still life painting.

"Gretchen Mills" is what she gave for a name.

But who knows if that's her actual name? Viv thought. *Sounds like an off brand cereal company.*

Karen also had suspicions about the name but wrote it down anyway.

"I don't have any identification," the witness had told them, turning out the pockets of the satin robe she wore and giving a coquettish shrug.

Even with her empathic powers dulled, Karen recognized that gesture anywhere. Affected helplessness. She imagined it had probably served "Gretchen" quite well in her line of work. A performance that said who are you talking to? Little old me?

Karen suspected that underneath this veneer of waifishness lie a very savvy *grand dame* in the making.

"Ms. Mills, how did you know the victims?" Penny asked.

The witness looked off to the side. "I've been so rude," she said quietly.

"What do you mean, rude?" Viv said.

The witness grimaced and then smiled.

"What my partner means to say--" Karen began.

And it was Viv's turn now to grimace.

"--Is that we don't think you've been rude at all. Two people you know were attacked last night, one was killed, and yet you've agreed to meet with us and to talk about the issues. Before you've had time to really absorb what's happened, really. That doesn't seem rude at all to me. In fact, that seems rather commendable. Not everyone is so open to helping out our investigations."

The witness smiled. "Perhaps. But I've been a terrible hostess."

"How so?" Karen asked.

"I didn't ask you if you wanted any fruit," the witness said.

"Honestly, Ms. Mills," Viv said, "It's not standard procedure for investigative leads to feed us."

"Is that what I am? A lead?" Gretchen said. "How extraordinary."

"I'm not sure if we'd even be allowed to accept food from you," Karen said. "There are rules about gifts. To stave off bribery."

"Five dollars," Penny said.

"Hm?" Karen said.

"We can accept anything under five dollars," Penny said.

Viv nodded. She remembered that regulation clearly as Penny had claimed the value of the python she accepted during one past investigation as $4.99. But Viv stayed silent because she'd promised Penny she wouldn't bring up the python ever again. It had been before Karen was with them, and it was something Karen just didn't need to know about. Something Viv was eager to forget and Penny arguably even more eager.

"Five dollars could get a whole bowl of fruit," Karen said.

"More or less," Viv said, "Depending on what's in season and how big the bowl is."

"I'd like a piece," Penny said.

"Go right ahead," Gretchen replied.

"Does it matter which basket?" Penny asked.

Gretchen shook her head no. "Help yourself."

As Penny walked around the room comparing the baskets, she noticed that while the fruit placement looked haphazard when viewing a single basket that when you compared multiple baskets they all seemed to be completely identical.

There was a particular position to the fruit. One that whoever had set up the room had been careful to replicate over and over again.

She also noted that all the fruit visually seemed to be perfectly ripe. Perhaps even overripe. So much so that she suspected if she were to squeeze the stone fruits too hard that they might explode in her hand.

Seconds away from a mess, really, she thought, before adding. *Delicious.*

After careful consideration, Penny picked up a pomegranate and slipped it into her pocket.

"Oh dear," Gretchen said. "I'm afraid you can't take that one."

"I doubt it's more than five dollars," Penny said.

"Well, no," Gretchen said. "But the pomegranates aren't for guests."

"Why not?" Penny asked.

"Penny, you're wasting time. It doesn't matter. Just put the damn fruit back," Viv replied.

"No, it's okay," Gretchen replied. "It's a good question. A very important one."

Penny kept the fruit in her pocket. She wasn't about to put it back without a good reason.

"The pomegranate is different than other fruits," Gretchen said. "It has a lot of purpose and meaning to us here at the Warrens of Persephone. You may know us for our services to the public..." She let her voice trail off in euphemism, before continuing, "But there's a lot more to us than that."

"Such as?" Viv said.

"Is that related to the crime you're investigating?" Gretchen said. It was a tone she hadn't used in their conversation yet. Wry. Knowing.

Ah there's the savviness, Karen noted.

"No," Viv said. "But a *good hostess* doesn't keep secrets from her guests."

Gretchen smirked. "Or does she?"

Viv frowned.

"I think a good hostess keeps plenty of secrets. Much is made of honesty as a virtue, noble truths – but there are times when discretion takes far more strength. I think refraining from burdening people with trifles can be noble. And times when sharing certain knowledge can put someone else at risk. Keeping someone in the dark can be protective, you know?"

"Like Persephone in the Underworld, under the guidance of Hades," Penny said. It escaped her mouth before she was even aware that she was speaking.

"Precisely," Gretchen said, smiling.

Viv groaned.

"You know, maybe I *can* tell you," Gretchen.

"You can," Penny replied. "And you can let me keep the pomegranate?"

Gretchen considered this. "Maybe," she said.

"So what *is* it that you do here?" Viv asked, irritated with how far off track they'd gotten.

"Well, as you know, and as any cursory search of *public records* would tell you," Gretchen began, "The Warrens of Persephone is a premiere – no, *the* premiere provider of Love Divination Services."

"You're fortunetellers?" Viv said.

"As far as the law is concerned," Gretchen said.

"So as far as *we're* concerned," Viv said. "We're the law. Since we work for the State."

"Do you?" Gretchen asked.

"Uhhh," Viv said. "Yes." She dug her identification out of one of her overall pockets. "Detective Viv Lee. Green Star. Level 3 Investigator, Department of Psychic Operations." She thrust the identification forward for Gretchen to review as she spoke the words on it. While Viv only had to view something one time for it to be forever locked into her permanent memory, she'd spoken those particular words dozens, if not hundreds of times. Basically, any time she needed to offer credentials, whether to a superior, colleague, or an uncooperative witness.

"Viv? What's it short for? Vivian? Vivica? Vivid?" Gretchen said.

"Nothing. It's just Viv," Viv said. "Viv is my entire first name."

"It's *certainly* not short for Vivid," Karen offered.

Viv scowled. It sounded so defensive when Karen put it like that.

"Riiiight," Gretchen said, shaking her head slowly and drawing out the word. "Because a woman who takes herself as seriously as you do wouldn't have a foolish name like Vivid Lee. I can see that vividly. That it's not short for Vivid. Vividly. I see it vividly."

Good thing she doesn't know my relatives are Tender Lee and Love Lee, Viv thought. *She'd have a field day.*

"It really isn't short for anything," Penny offered. "I've seen her birth certificate. Her mom's a character. Trust me."

"You I *do* trust," Gretchen said to Penny. "Anyway," she continued. "You might technically work for the State, but you're far from the law. No, you're something else entirely. Especially you." She fixed her gaze on Penny.

Gretchen rose from her chair, walked over to Viv, and placed the pear she was holding in Viv's hand. Her expression grew serious. She sighed.

"Your crime scene unit was all over this building earlier today, so I suppose there are a lot of basic facts that you either know already or will know shortly. So I'll spare you those," Gretchen said.

"Okay," Viv said. "I appreciate that."

"I run this organization, the Warrens of Persephone. I am, as some might say, the boss. One of the two victims, Heather – the victim who is... no longer living, worked for me here for the past three years. The other victim, the one who seems to have had a psychotic break, is a regular client of hers.

I'm fuzzy on his name. John something? John Johnson?" Gretchen said.

"James Jackson," Viv offered.

"Yeah that's it, I think. Maybe. I'm always surprised when clients give their real names. I don't presume anyone's giving me the correct name anymore. Sorry about that by the way, giving you a hard time. It's a hazard of this business, just assuming that everyone you meet's going by another name."

"It's fine," Viv replied.

"Most people I know have at least three different names. One they go by legally, that they sign to things and maybe hear on the rare occasion they head back to stay with their family. You know, on holidays. Then they have a second one that their friends call them. And finally, there's the work name. I of course mostly know work names when it comes to my employees, unless we are particularly close."

"Were you particularly close to Heather?" Viv asked.

"You could say that," Gretchen said. She paused. "Are any of you eideticists?"

"Yes," Viv said. "I am. Why?"

"You should really try that pear I gave you," Gretchen said.

"I'm not hungry," Viv replied, truthfully.

"It's good for your *vision*," Gretchen said with a peculiar emphasis.

"That's carrots you're thinking of," Viv said.

"Well you can never get too many vitamins, can you?" Gretchen asked.

Viv didn't have an answer to that. This woman was loopy, she decided. Viv frowned, wondering what the easiest way to get this conversation on track would be.

"And while you eat that pear, I think you should look at that tapestry," Gretchen said, pointing to one hanging directly behind Viv's head. This tapestry depicted Demeter, the mother of Persephone, wandering the Earth, clearly distraught, searching for her missing daughter.

Viv cocked her head sideways. "Like I just told you, I'm an eideticist, so I have a photographic memory. I saw that tapestry when I came in. And I can recall it whenever I want."

"Ah," Gretchen said. "But pears always taste better when you're looking at art. The mind's eye is different, you see, when it comes to matter of heightening one's gustatory perception. Trust me."

"Viv," Penny said. "Just do what she says."

"What?" Viv said.

"Just turn around and eat the fruit and look at the tapestry," Penny snapped.

Penny's tone was so intense that Viv found it strange. Viv gawked at Penny for a few seconds, and then it hit her. *Oh,* Viv realized. *I'm a camera. My eyes are a camera. The witness wants to tell me something off the record. She wants to turn off the security camera. Or least to turn it towards the wall.*

In her entire career at PsyOps, Viv had only had her eidetic memory banks subpoenaed twice. It wasn't a common occurrence, being summoned to reproduce her memories for a court proceeding. The process was laborious and quite expensive, requiring not only the services of a skilled thoughtographer to record the images but also two telepaths, one receptive and one expressive to pull the images from Viv's mind and transfer them into the mind of the thoughtographer. It was theoretically possible for one telepath to do both operations, although PsyOps had never retained the services of a telepath capable of both receptive and expressive telepathy, not that Viv could recall anyway.

Regardless of how many telepaths it took to transmit the images, once the thoughtographer received Viv's thoughts, they would then imprint them upon a form of media that could be viewed by normals. Typically, this was either still or video photography.

Thoughtography sessions usually lasted for several hours, and many sessions were taken to completely transfer Viv's memory engrams onto film, a process that physically and mentally exhausted both the eideticist and thoughtographer as well as any telepaths involved.

Given all of that, PsyOps usually left her memories well enough alone, allowing Viv to voluntarily report upon their contents when relevant to an investigation and heavily relying on external evidence to supplement them when going to trial, instead of basing the strength of a case primarily upon them.

But there was something different about this case, which not only involved the murder of one intuitive and the maiming of another but had also now apparently graduated into a serial murder, serial maiming. From the report given to them by crime scene investigators, the killer's *modus operandi* was identical to that of the Snow White murder. One murdered. Another assaulted and driven temporarily mad. All of this was once again followed by a very earnest-sounding confession from one of the victims that just didn't line up with the available physical evidence.

Just like in the first crime, the deceased's body had an intricate pattern of blood spatter on her chests, obscuring most of her breasts and abdomen. Blood spatter that once again looked like a psychological inkblot projection test.

If Gretchen had something to say that she didn't want to say on camera, it was probably important.

Penny was right. Time to go off the record.

"Well, my blood sugar does get a little wonky on the new migraine meds," Viv said.

"That it does," Penny replied.

Karen wasn't sure what they her two partners were on about but decided it was prudent just to let whatever was going to happen, happen.

Viv turned around and stared at the tapestry. As she did, she took the tiniest, most imperceptible bites of the pear, taking great care to make sure that the pear entered her field of vision every so often. The bits of pear flesh were akin to sands in an hourglass, and she wanted to empty the timepiece as slowly as possible.

As Viv stared at the tapestry, she wondered if her own mother would have gone to such great lengths to find her as Demeter had when Perspehone ran away.

Probably not, Viv decided. Not unless there was a man involved. Or a big payday.

Typology of Memory

Properly speaking, a person's eidetic memory is their short-term visual memory. Pretty much everyone, intuitive or normal, has some form of eidetic memory. It's what allows you to briefly still see something in your mind's eye soon after you look away from the object or close your eyes.

Research has revealed that eidetic memory stems primarily from the posterior parietal cortex in the brain's parietal lobe. In most people, the actual eidetic image is present only for a few seconds, at which point it dissipates completely and any relevant information is encoded into short-term memory. Sometimes nothing is encoded, and once the image fades, to our minds it is though we never saw it.

In rare instances, even a normal might find that they have a particularly long-lasting eidetic memory effect. This is sometimes colloquially known as "having a photographic memory." Instead of the image dissipating quickly, they can recall it for a much longer period of time.

Pure photographic memory is exceedingly rare in non-intuitive populations. Even those with arguably photographic memories are subjected to more decay than we would associate with photographs, with the most persistent photographic memory images lasting perhaps a few months at most.

However, there are intuitives called eideticists who possess the power of pure photographic memory, gifted with eidetic memories that are perfect and never seem to fade. Indeed, some eideticists complain miserably of not being able to forget unpleasant experiences; the best they can do is simply move quickly past them as they are recalling other memories close to that period in time. The psychic population is still quite young yet, with the psychic phenomenon emerging only in the past three decades. However, as the first eideticists are aging, a common complaint is the length of time it takes them to pull up specific memories as their overall eidetic archive increases.

To date, no eideticist has simultaneously possessed expressive telepathic powers, so for the most part their photographic memories stay locked within them. However, with the aid of expressive and receptive telepaths and a skilled thoughtographer, it has become possible in recent years to retrieve memories archived within an eideticist.

Eideticists are relatively rare among the psychic population. However, thoughtographers are far less common. As of this writing, there is only a handful of known thoughtographers. They are largely in the employ of the Psychic State, used for mnemonic subpoenas on high-profile cases.

There's some dispute among taxonomists about the classification of thoughtographers. Some prominent subject matter experts advocate that thoughtography belongs in its own category, however small their population might be. Others contend that thoughtography is essentially a specialized form of expressive telepathy, one that manifests the thoughts of others not in transmissible cognitive form but in more concrete, tangible forms, most commonly on either still or moving film. At the present time, the State is working with the most skilled thoughtographer to attempt digital transmission, but efforts up until now have proven futile.

Naysayers of the digital thoughtography program state that it might be a bit too ambitious to move from abstraction to abstraction and that it would be best for society if thoughtographers just stick with what they're good at, etching visual memory upon physical forms. They argue that the greater good would be better served by utilizing every thoughtographer actively in the public interest rather than sacrificing any of them for experimental programs that are unnecessary and may never pan out.

Time will tell whether the State's gamble on digital will pay off.

What is for sure is that the number of eideticists and their ratio to the relative number of thoughtographers is quite reminiscent of the number of photo developing centers to the number of shutterbugs. Or, rather, the ratio as it was in the predigital age, when you had to bring in your film to have it developed commercially, unless you were a whiz with a functioning dark room (something that was out of the reach of most amateur photographers).

This seeming dependency is quite an apt comparison, as eideticists are very much like the film negatives and camera and the thoughtographer very much like the developing process that turns them into photographs. This balance has led some taxonomists to wonder if there's order among the chaos of emerging and/or newly discovered typology.

from Insecta Psychica: Towards an Intuitive Taxonomy by Cloche Macomber

Once Viv was facing squarely away from her, basically turning the camera for State's evidence to the wall, Gretchen opened up considerably.

"As you know, this is a legal operation," Gretchen said. "As legal as any of them are anyway."

"Oh?" Penny said.

"Look, you didn't hear it from me, but there's not a single Fortune-Telling House in Skinner – or the Psychic State, even – that doesn't have a handful of tueys kicking around in it."

Karen flinched reflexively at "tuey."

"I'm sorry," Gretchen said, noting Karen's flinch. "Intuitive. It's a bad habit, I admit. Sometimes it feels like the rules are changing every day. What you can say, what you can't."

"It's fine," Penny said. It mostly was, and beyond that, she *wanted* it to be fine, which was just as important.

"Heather was an intuitive," Gretchen said. "The real deal. A precog. As her boss I wasn't exactly supposed to know, but..."

"You did," Penny said.

Gretchen nodded. "We were close. And it was obvious."

"Obvious?" Karen said. "How so?"

"Heather wasn't good at throwing the predictions. She had a hard time screwing up her readings. And at baseline, she was pretty damn accurate for a precog. She'd focused a lot on mitigating her personal bias, mindfulness work apparently. Meditation," Gretchen explained. "To be fair, we do a lot of that in the Warrens of Persephone. We like to take care of the people who work for us. More than a lot of places do. Sure, we're technically an employer. Registered properly with the State by the way."

"Not going to check, don't care, wrong department," Viv called back over her shoulder through a mouthful of chewed up pear.

"Don't talk with your mouth full," Gretchen said, not quite sure what Viv was saying.

You're not my mother, Viv thought, rolling her eyes, but no one could see it.

"In a way, we're also home for the women who work here. Some of them are really girls, you see. Don't have anywhere else to go. We try to look after their welfare. Physical, emotional, spiritual. We provide classes. Guidance," Gretchen said.

"Are you a cult?" Karen asked.

"Karen!" Penny said, shocked.

"No, I don't mean that as an insult. My dad runs a cult. I don't judge," Karen said.

"Your father runs a cult?" Gretchen asked, clearly amused.

"The Grounded Temple," Karen said.

"Ohhhh," Gretchen said. "Your father's Augustus Cross?"

Karen nodded. "Yup. Unfortunately."

Gretchen laughed. "They'd hate to hear you call it a cult, you know."

"That's how cults are. They don't like for people to think of them as cults. One person's cult is another's religion and vice versa. It's all a matter of perception. Me, I cut to the chase and call them all cults," Karen replied.

"I suppose that's efficient... if insulting. There are an awful lot of religious people out there. More if you count the spiritual ones, the ones who believe in something or a lot of somethings but would blanch if you called them 'religious.'" Gretchen said.

"Sure," Karen said. "But being popular doesn't make something right."

"You know," Gretchen said. "I get it. It's tough to believe in the supernatural."

Karen nodded.

"Although to be fair, before the Psychic Phenomenon exploded, I never would have believed that people existed that could read other people's minds. Feel their emotions. Have perfect photographic memories. And...?" She pointed at Penny.

"Speak with the dead," Penny replied.

"Of course, that makes *so much sense*," Gretchen replied.

Penny cocked her head. Why did that make so much sense? Literally no one had ever had that reaction to the revelation that she was a medium, a relatively rare psychic power and one whose existence many people still doubted. It didn't help, Penny supposed, that there were so many cold readers around pretending they could contact people's loved ones in the beyond. It didn't help at all.

"How did you know I'm an empath?" Karen asked.

"Is that going to help you solve your crime?" Gretchen
replied.

"Don't you know it's rude to answer a question with another
question?" Karen said.

"Then why did you just do it?" Gretchen shot back, smirking.

Karen, Penny, and Viv groaned in unison.

"To answer your original question on my own terms, yes,
the Warrens of Persephone engages in spiritual practice.
We believe in the duality of all people, all things. Just as
Persephone could simultaneously be springtime incarnate
and the queen of the underworld, typically we all have
two, or more, opposing facets. We believe that what makes
an individual happier and healthier, what allows them to
flourish, is not eliminating contradictions but balancing
them appropriately," Gretchen said.

"Huh," Viv said.

"I would expect you three to understand that better than
most," Gretchen said. "Most people limit themselves to a
single lover, after all. Or at least that's what they try to do."

Viv laughed. She was surprised Gretchen had picked up
their dynamic. That, too, was unusual. "You'd make a good
detective," Viv said.

Gretchen smiled.

"Your belief system honestly sounds like a much better
religion than the Grounded Temple," Karen said.

"Thank you," Gretchen replied. "If your detective job ever
doesn't work out, you'd be welcome to apply here."

"Um... thanks," Karen said. "I think."

"Anyway," Gretchen said. "I'm very sorry Heather isn't here with us anymore. Unfortunately, she was very sought after, so the list of suspects is rather long, even when just looking at clients. But here's her book." She handed it to Penny.

"If you need help sorting out aliases, don't hesitate to call," Gretchen said.

"The multiple name problem again," Karen said.

Gretchen nodded. "There's a lot of it going around."

Viv turned around, holding the completely stripped pear core in her hand. "Do you have a place to throw this?"

Gretchen gestured toward a bin that looked like a small pillar sometimes used to display art. She showed Viv the hidden pedal that would flip the top up.

Why do fancy places always feel a need to hide the trash? Viv mused as she chucked the core in the bin. The fancier the place, the more impossible to throw something away. It was a wonder that palatial mansions didn't turn into landfills. *They probably would*, Viv decided, *if they were open to the public. Maybe that's why they're all in gated communities.* She got a brief flash in her mind of a mess of seagulls sitting atop a mound of 17th century furniture.

"Thanks," Viv said aloud. "We'll be in touch if we need anything else."

"Of course," Gretchen said. "Happy to be of help."

Gretchen followed the three detectives, escorting them from the building, guiding them out a different way than how they'd entered. Company headquarters were quite labyrinthine and complicated. Viv noted that even with her normally keen sense of direction, she could easily get lost in this building.

There were living quarters, a shared kitchen, small classrooms, even a space that looked like a chapel. Art decorated virtually every surface, even hallways. Typically, these depictions were of tales from Greek mythology.

Viv noted that a great many of the faces of the gods and goddesses looked strangely familiar, although she couldn't quite place from where. *Perhaps they used local models?* she wondered.

They exited through a large stone door that spilled them out onto Whisper Street. Viv stepped out first followed by Karen. As Penny was about to leave the building, Gretchen said her name.

Not Penny Dreadful. The other name. The one no one knew. Or the one that no one was *supposed* to know.

Penny's blood went cold. She spun around.

"Say hello to Kip for me," Gretchen replied. She reached into the pocket where Penny had stashed the pomegranate and fished it out, before shutting the door in Penny's face.

"Are you coming, Penny?" Viv called from the sidewalk. "This car isn't going to drive itself."

Penny turned to the street. "Of course," she said. "Be right there."

Ghosts Don't Haunt Places

There's a little something most people don't know about ghosts. Something you wouldn't know unless you're either a medium or have one in your life who is comfortable enough to open up to you about how it all works.

Ghosts don't haunt places. The whole haunted house thing? A spirit hopelessly imprisoned in the place where they met their demise? Doomed to lurk a singular location until whatever unresolved issues they have are somehow addressed and they can achieve earthly closure with a clutch of tormented living human beings who just want to use the structure and an exorcist-cum-therapist tasked with throwing some peculiar spiritual intervention like an arcane 12-step program, just with more Latin?

None of that is true. That's the stuff of fiction. A little bit of Victorian fan-waving. A campfire story.

Ghosts aren't stuck anywhere. Ghosts ramble. They're usually quite transient.

In fact – and she wasn't sure exactly why – but if Detective Penny Dreadful had to guess, she'd say that as a medium *she* wasn't going to see ghosts at all but that they were coming to *her*, as though she were some kind of ghost magnet. A beacon for spirits.

Not that she was exactly sure about any of this. Nor did she have a way to be. Penny had grown up without a living person handy who could take her by the hand, teach her about ghosts. Most of what she'd learned about them over the years had observation and a lot of trial and error.

When she was younger, she couldn't differentiate between the dead and the living. They looked pretty much identical to her.

Over time she'd gotten better at distinguishing between the two, but even now, she wasn't always sure when she saw someone if they were a spirit or a human being.

Spirits for the most part acted more erratically, although some human beings rivaled ghosts in their callousness and emotional disorganization. Most of the time that she first saw a particular spirit, she was near one or more dead bodies, or a place where one had been within the past few weeks. In her line of work as a detective, this was typically the crime scene where the victim had been discovered.

But as a young woman, she'd also found hospitals to be particularly easy places to find spirits, and if she wanted peace and quiet, it was essential to give the graveyard and retirement homes a wide berth.

After the first introduction to a ghost, however, Penny found that she could incidentally run into a given spirit at random locations, which told her that they weren't bound to any one place. Not the place they once lived or the place they died. Not the place they first had their heart broken or their fortune squandered.

But any one of these places and usually multiple.

It was what led her to believe that she wasn't finding the ghosts but that they were coming to her. After an initial introduction, they'd somehow learn her frequency and seek her out when the mood struck them. A few times maybe. But not often. Never the same place.

And always on *their* terms, initiated by them. Forget about Penny ever *seeking them* out for a reunion.

Except for Kip.

Kip had been different from the very beginning. Kipper Dante, he called himself when they'd met, but as Penny fumbled to say this, he'd amended it to "Kip." *That* little Penny could say.

Penny's foster family liked to call him "Mr. Nobody" and as a group considered him Penny's imaginary friend.

It was hard to be sure about him, about what exactly he was, since she couldn't distinguish between the living and the dead when she was very young, but Penny suspected Kip was the first ghost she'd ever met. He'd been there from the very beginning, from her earliest years.

He inevitably sat beneath desert willows, waiting for her, ready to discuss whatever she had on her mind.

The first tree was at an early foster home. When she was moved to another residence, she expected to never see Kip again, but there he was, under a different tree.

A desert willow again. Always under a tree. And always under the same kind of tree. Only under desert willows. But it didn't seem to matter which one. Kip lived, or perhaps dwelled is a better word, under all of them.

Kip had a lot in common with the tree. A desert willow generally prefers full sun. Kip similarly was a fan of transparency and total illumination. No matter what question Penny asked, no matter how strange, Kip would do his best to answer it.

Nothing was off limits.

It was through Kip that Penny first learned that she was a medium. It did take a while, however, since Kip didn't exactly volunteer information and instead had to be asked about a subject before he could educate her on it.

Because of this, it took several years for Penny to suspect that she had a special relationship with the dead. All of them.

But especially Kip.

After the Whisper Street Affair, and especially after Gretchen dropped Kip's name, Penny knew she had to talk to him. She didn't know exactly what questions she was going to ask. But she was tired of being in the dark.

Karen felt Penny's absence viscerally. It woke her from sleep, the sudden flooding of emotions slapping her in the chest like a screen door hits a house when someone leaves it in a hurry.

It was mostly dark in their bedroom, although a bit of street lamplight filtered in through a set of blinds that wasn't completely shut. Karen felt the bed beside her. Penny normally slept in the middle spot, partly because she had always been the strongest link between Karen and Viv and partly because Penny had an iron bladder and rarely had to get up to use the bathroom in the night, a more difficult task when you're flanked by sleepers on both sides.

Karen felt only sheets and blankets beneath her hand. No Penny. She was gone. And not just gone from the bed, but likely gone from the house. Far enough away anyway that Karen's empathy wasn't dampened anymore.

From the atmospheric sense of anxiety she got, Karen knew at once that Viv was having some kind of bad dream.

Karen rolled over towards Viv, putting her arms around her, holding her. With the drastic differences in her heights, Karen and Viv looked less like a set of nesting spoons and more like Karen was strapped to Viv's back like a small jet pack.

Viv began to stir. "Karen?" she said. "What's going on?"

"Penny's gone," Karen said.

Viv sat up. "What do you mean she's gone?"

"She's not here. I can feel your emotions," Karen said.

"Well, don't be a jerk about it, okay?" Viv said.

"I won't," Karen said, although she wasn't quite sure what Viv meant by that and didn't like the sound of it.

"I didn't mean that," Viv said. "I mean, sometimes I end up feeling really dissected. Like it's unfair. That you can feel what I'm feeling, that I get no privacy, and I can't do it back to you."

"It's okay, Viv," Karen said.

"You know how you said it's like watching people play cards, reading their emotions?" Viv asked.

"Mmhmm," Karen said.

"It's hard sometimes, being on the other side of it, when you know," Viv said. "It's like I'm trying to play cards with you, and my hand is face up and yours is face down."

Karen felt Viv's vulnerability but decided not to say anything about it and instead to act on it. Karen held Viv tighter.

"Did Penny tell you she was going anywhere?" Karen asked her.

"No," Viv said. "I was hoping you'd have some idea."

"Nope," Karen said. "Sorry."

"Don't be," Viv said. She rolled over to face her. "I'm sure she's fine."

Karen nodded. "Penny always is."

"Maybe it's for the best," Viv said. "We're overdue to spend some time together alone, just you and me."

Karen smiled. She liked the sound of that.

The Public Gardens had long been a crown jewel of Skinner. Like many things in the Psychic City, it had changed considerably after the emergence of the Psychic Phenomenon. But unlike many other areas, everyone agreed that the changes to the Public Garden were squarely for the better.

It had always been a healthy gathering of plants, to be sure, but fairly standard among city botanical gardens, limited by what the regional climate could support.

The recruitment of psychic plant tenders had transformed it into lush sprawling oasis. The plants grew bigger and faster. Not only that, but now they could grow anything, whether or not it was native to the region or would normally thrive, or even survive, there.

This collection included a giant desert willow that shouldn't be growing in Skinner, especially not to its exceptional size, but absolutely was.

Penny had visited it many times in the past. She knew right where it was. She also knew that the western gate was usually unlocked, even after hours. Penny suspected that the staff didn't realize it was even there. Either that, or they forgot about it when it came time to close the park for the evening. In any event, the western gate was smaller than the others, and its tarnished metal blended it well with the bark of the trees that happened to surround it. It was difficult to see from any distance away from it and required a longer walk than any of the other entrances to use it, elements that when combined sufficiently deterred the public from sneaking in that way, arguably more than locking it would.

If you wanted to keep people away, making entry slightly more difficult usually did the trick, as most people stuck to pursuing the lowest-hanging fruit. A lock could provide that difficulty, for sure, but what most people didn't realize was that a slightly longer walk could just as easily.

The public was shockingly lazy. Most of the time anyway.

I'm not the public, Penny thought.

As she rounded the corner and slid behind the tree that mostly obscured the western gate, she noted the expected lack of a lock. She pushed on the gate, and it swung open easily.

From there, it was an easy walk to the desert willow. Kip was waiting for her as always, sitting beneath the tree. He was dressed in a pinstripe suit complete with a matching pocket square, as he always was, regardless of the weather. This time the suit was a deep charcoal gray and the pinstripes and square were violet. Penny hadn't seen Kip wear this particular suit in a long while, perhaps since childhood. The tree he sat beneath was in full bloom with the branches projecting blossoms that looked like fairies in the strange light of the garden, a haze of indirect streetlamps and moonlight.

He was reading a book, as he always was whenever she found him. He looked deeply engrossed.

"Hi Kip," Penny said.

"Ah there you are, little one," Kip replied. He shut his book.

It was curious. As captivated as he seemed by his reading, he never marked his place when she interrupted him. Penny didn't know if he had the kind of memory that made it so that simply remembered where he was or if he was reading the same book over and over again so it didn't matter.

She'd never asked. She considered asking tonight, as she had on many occasions that she'd seen him, but as usual, she had more pressing questions on her mind.

"I need to talk to you," Penny said.

Kip nodded. "You have more questions," he said.

"I do," Penny replied.

"If you didn't have questions, little one, I would worry. I wouldn't know if it were really you. I'd think I were dealing with a shapeshifter, an imposter." Kip smiled. He patted the ground next to him.

Penny walked over, sat down at the base of the tree. "It's funny you should say that," she said. She pulled out the card that the interloper to her kitchen had dropped when it beat its hasty retreat.

She handed Kip the card that advertised shapeshifting services.

"Change Patterson," Kip said. "Now that's a name I haven't heard in a very long time."

"But you've heard it before?" Penny asked.

Kip nodded. "He's older than I am. I knew him when I was alive."

Penny pondered asking Kip how old he was but like the other times she'd gotten close to asking just that thing, she decided she didn't really want to know the answer.

Instead, she looked up to see the light of the full moon shining through the branches. The tree blooms looked even hazier from this angle. In direct moonlight, their edges were rendered even fuzzier. The effect was otherworldly, as though the desert willow were growing at the connection between dimensions.

Maybe it is, Penny thought.

"What's on your mind, little one?" Kip asked her, and his face was so innocent and unguarded that she wanted to spill everything. She wanted to tell him about the entire sorry mess. The troubling signs, none of which were making any sense to her, but made her feel like there was some private joke being played on her. Something everyone else was in on – the ghost impersonator slash shapeshifter, the madam at the Warrens of Persephone.

She wanted to open up to Kip and spill it all. The whole thing. If she could have simply handed him her mind to review, she would have done so.

But that wasn't how she worked, or how Kip seemed to work. Instead, all she had were words. And wanting to tell him was making it really hard for her to do so.

It was a paradox that had dogged her for her entire life: It was easy to kid around. Make throwaway statements. It was easy for her to say things that didn't really matter, that she didn't care about. Particularly easy for her to say things that she didn't really believe or that she expected no one to take seriously. To make dumb jokes.

But when it came to things that really mattered to her, she wanted to get that right. And the pressure inevitably caused her to clam up.

Kip nodded as though he could hear and feel all of this with her. "That bad, huh?" To be fair, he'd known her for her entire life, and when you've known someone for a while, you pick up on things like that. You get to know when they're about to fall apart, even if they don't say a single word about what's actually going on.

Penny nodded. She began to cry.

Kip draped one arm around her. Like normal, Penny felt only a slight chill from his touch instead of body heat. Still, the effect was comforting because it was so familiar.

"Why don't we sit and enjoy the garden for a while?" Kip suggested.

Penny nodded again. She cried harder.

"So what's the deal with you and Roscoe anyway?" Viv asked Karen.

Karen winced. "Ryan Roscoe?" she asked. It was a pitiful attempt to stall for more time to figure out how to answer the question, but it was the best that she could do, especially in the middle of the night. It didn't help that the topic change caught her completely off guard. Nor that she'd been feeling so emotionally vulnerable prior to Viv bringing it up.

"Of course Ryan Roscoe," Viv said. "Who else?"

Karen sighed. "It goes back a long way. Back to the ranch."

"You with that ranch all the time," Viv said. "You're like one of those old cowboy shows. Meanwhile back at the ranch..."

Karen frowned. "Forget it. Let's talk about something else."

"Hey," Viv said. "I'm sorry."

Karen could feel that she meant that. That was one of the upsides to being an empath. You could tell when someone meant an apology and when someone was giving one defensively, as a way of saying, "Don't be mad at me. I didn't mean any harm. I'm a good person, honest!"

But that wasn't the feeling pattern Viv was exhibiting. Instead, there was a sincere remorse. And concern?

Yeah, concern, Karen decided. Concern was a vibe that could be very fuzzy, often resembled other internal states. Detecting concern always felt like a guess.

It was a genuine apology anyway.

"I know," Karen said.

Viv laughed. There was no cruelty in her laugh. And Karen felt no judgement coming from her, so Karen relaxed.

"Why don't you like to talk about the ranch anyway?" Viv asked. "It seems like any time I bring it up, you immediately shut down."

"It's complicated," Karen said weakly. Even as the words escaped her lips, she knew it was a pathetic answer. Far less than Viv deserved. And yet, she wasn't sure what else to say.

The answers to that question in fact were obscured behind a corner she didn't feel comfortable looking around.

But she tried again, this time addressing Viv's original question. "Roscoe looks a lot like another kid there. One who played a trick on me."

"Must have been a bad one," Viv said. "Kids were always playing tricks on one another at the ranch, weren't they? But this one was worse."

"It was," Karen said. "And they did. Lots of pranks. Dirty deeds. It was a madhouse in general, the ranch." She paused. "And I would know, having also been in my share of literal madhouses."

Viv laughed, surprised at the self-deprecating joke.

"None of the locked wards I was on ever compared to the ranch," Karen said. "There's something about being locked up with a bunch of teenagers that's unbearable. Especially ones who have been exiled from the rest of the world. And who are desperate to prove who they are."

"Is that how it happened?" Viv said.

"Hm?"

"Was the little shit trying to prove who he was?"

Karen nodded. "Of course." Then added, "We all were."

Viv nodded.

"I'm not sure I ever stopped," Karen said.

"You know," Viv said. "It was a really shitty thing for me to second guess you back there."

"When?" Karen asked.

"When we were interviewing Bronson Eck. When I called in Ryan Roscoe for the telepathic consult," Viv said.

"Ah," Karen said. What she didn't say aloud was that the reason she had to ask Viv "when" was because this was far from the first time Viv had second guessed her. If anything, it had gotten better in recent months. Viv had been especially bad about calling in consults to check Karen's work when she'd first joined PsyOps.

It had been bad enough that Martin had called Viv in to his office to make sure that he actually wanted Karen on their investigative team.

Karen was pretty sure she wasn't supposed to know that, but Penny had screwed up. Buoyed by several glasses of chardonnay, Penny had let the whole incident slip.

It had been humiliating for Karen. Not just to find out that Viv didn't trust her empathic powers, but also to learn that Martin had given Viv an out, an excuse to cut her loose.

Karen had trusted Martin, respected him. And she felt foolish in that moment to find that the trust hadn't run both ways. At least not in the way she'd expected.

The icing on the cake was finding out that no one had bothered to tell her about the incident, any of it. That she had to learn from her drunken girlfriend, when Penny drank most of a Wine of the Month package destined for someone else that had been misdelivered, unreturnable due to a missing address label. It was also humiliating that Penny presumed that Karen had been told already.

No, she had not been told.

And that was half the problem.

Karen ran over all of this in her mind as she lay with Viv in the dark. She considered doing as she always did, changing the subject, letting the matter slide, moving on with her life.

It was an attractive option.

There was a reason she'd done it over and over again, after all. It was the path of least resistance. Least short-term resistance anyway.

Drop it and walk away. Let the charge of the moment fade. Hope that it wouldn't be a live wire later when circumstance forced her to pick it up again.

But Karen was finding that instead of the charge dissipating and leaving the matter that the topic remained just as charged every time it came up.

And a deep resentment was starting to form within her. One whose potential power frightened her.

Karen felt the stirrings of it burn within her, even as she stared at Viv's face, at her ever-changing eyes, a sight that she considered one of the most beautiful in the world. If she could feel fury looking at the face of her lover, especially as she could empathically sense that her lover was actively projecting adoration and admiration her way, Karen reasoned, then things were out of control.

Karen swallowed.

"I'm sick of it, Viv," Karen said.

Viv didn't say anything. Karen felt something like shame mixed with anxiety emanating off Viv.

"I'm sick of being treated like I'm something lesser than you. Like my powers are no good. Like they're not important. You've known me for long enough that there's no excuse."

Viv swallowed. Karen felt the same mix washing over her. Shame and anxiety.

Good, Karen thought. *It's about time she felt it, too.*

Karen felt a little ugly thinking like that, but she continued anyway.

"Do you know what it's like coming into a situation like this?" Karen asked.

"Like what?" Viv said.

"Where two people have been together for years, and you're the new person in their lives."

Viv shook her head no. "Never," she said.

"Well, it shows," Karen said. "You don't know what it's like to come into a household where two people have already built up a life together. One full of memories, traditions, private jokes, routines. You don't know what it's like to try to find your footing in all of that. To try all the while not to upset secret taboos. It's like… moving into a minefield and being asked to join a group dance. One you don't know the steps to."

Viv nodded. "That had to be hard."

"Hard isn't even the Cliff Notes version," Karen said. "I wish I could go back sometimes, to when we first got together. And just tell you to knock it off. Demand that I be more included. Demand that you try to make me feel welcome, safe." She sighed. "But I didn't have a leg to stand on then. I showed up on the doorstep in the middle of the night like a box of abandoned kittens."

"You were just as cute," Viv offered.

Karen smiled at the compliment, in spite of herself. She willed herself not to, so she wouldn't get sidetracked.

"I was the third wheel," Karen said. "Do you know what it's like to be the third wheel?"

"You know," Viv said. "That I *do* understand."

Karen cocked her head.

"Love was always Mom's favorite," Viv offered.

Karen nodded. "There's a reason you moved out, isn't there? There's a reason that you don't live with her anymore, being offered off to eligible bachelors, trying to improve your mother's social standing like Love, right?"

Viv nodded. "Yeah. It kills me that I've made you feel that way."

"Made's a little strong. You don't have those kinds of powers. You can't make me feel anything," Karen said, and Viv laughed. "But yeah. You need to stop it. Stop second guessing me. You need to make more of an effort. "

Viv nodded. "Do you want to know where I was coming from?" she asked.

"Trust me, I do," Karen said. "I'm feeling what you're feeling right now." Remorse. Sadness.

"Well, you know my emotional process, but not my reasoning," Viv said.

"Emotions are more honest," Karen offered.

"Emotions are more automatic," Viv countered. "Aren't we more than our gut impulses?"

"Perhaps," Karen said. "But we don't ever really escape them completely, do we?"

Viv didn't answer that. Instead, she explained. "It isn't about my confidence in your abilities – or lack of it," Viv said.

"Then what *is* it then? What else could it possibly be?" Karen asked.

"...I'm worried about what other people will think," Viv said.

"You? Caring what other people think?" Karen said, laughing. But she could tell by Viv's emotional pattern that she meant it. That she was being sincere.

"I'm in love with you, Karen," Viv said. "Have been for a long time."

Karen smiled.

"*I* know what that means. Is love basically bias? Yes. Yes, it is. But does that bias leak over into my professional life? That's what I'm worried about. Or at least worried that other people will be worried about. And you know what bias does to psychic powers."

"It scrambles the signal," Karen said.

Viv nodded.

"Let me get this straight," Karen said, "You're worried that people will think you're biased and nepotistic because you hired your girlfriend to work with you."

"Something like that," Viv said.

"And you didn't worry about this with Penny?" Karen asked.

"Oh, I did," Viv said. "You weren't around for that. Ask Penny about it sometime, when she's not out being a cat burglar or whatever the heck she's up to."

"Raving at a graveyard?" Karen said.

"A rave yard, you mean," Viv joked.

Karen laughed. "That was such a Penny joke," she said.

"Spend enough time with someone..." Viv said, letting her voice trail off and smiling.

Karen smiled back.

"Anyway, I second guessed Penny just as hard. Hell, I wasn't even *sure* she really *saw* spirits until about a year after she took the comprehensive perceptive battery," Viv admitted.

"Really?"

Viv nodded. "I mean, I knew that's what *she* thought. But I also thought it was just as likely that she was having visual hallucinations and good at lying about it. Making up elaborate reasoning to explain it."

Karen boggled at this. "Wait, wait, you thought Penny was psychotic and a liar, and you still dated her?"

Viv nodded.

"Why?" Karen said.

"Because there's more to a person than their mental illness," Viv said. "And if she were going to lie about something, coming up with a narrative to explain her madness was about the most practical, least unethical lie I can think of."

"Huh," Karen said.

"After all," Viv said. "It's not like my mother hasn't done the same thing."

"True," Karen said. "But did you really want to marry a woman like your mother?"

"No," Viv said. "Of course not. Well, not in certain ways. A person can have something in common with someone you despise and still be quite lovable."

"Tell that to transference," Karen said.

Viv laughed. "Empaths have such a hard time of it, don't they? At least cancel culture is reacting to something. Throwing the baby out with the bathwater sometimes, sure. But empaths have to go even further. They have to precancel people not because they've done anything but simply because they remind them of people who have done things."

Karen shrugged. "I'd change it if I could."

"Nah," Viv said. "Don't change a damn thing. I like you the way you are. If you started 'fixing' things, who knows what would break in response? There's nothing wrong with you. And besides, it's a miracle you're even here... after all you've been through."

"The same could be said for you, Viv," Karen offered.

Viv's eyes reminded Karen of liquid mercury as they shifted silver. Viv smiled.

It was a beautiful smile, Karen noted, leaning forward and covering it with her own.

"It all started with the python thing," Penny said, when she finally had gathered herself enough to speak again.

"I take it that you and Viv still aren't talking about that," Kip replied.

Penny shook her head. "I don't blame her for not believing me. I probably wouldn't have believed me if I were in her shoes... Her thought was that I was reading too much Harry Potter, thinking I could speak Parseltongue, and I guess I was really into those books back then, but..."

"But the python really spoke to you, didn't it?" Kip said.

Penny nodded. "It sounds crazy, I know."

"Not to me," Kip said.

"Well you're dead," Penny replied.

"True," Kip said. "But that's not why. The truth is, little one, I've known you for years, and I've never known you to lie... about anything."

Penny hesitated at this, the way a person who is committed to telling the truth will when scanning their memory for times when they were arguably deceptive. Typically, there are no outright falsehoods in there. Maybe an omission or two out of tact. Or a time when they could have spoken up and corrected the record but either lost their opportunity to do so or chose not to (for whatever reason).

"Everyone lies," she said.

"Very good, little one," Kip replied. "But you lie the least of all the mortals I've encountered."

"Have you encountered many mortals then?" Penny asked.

Kip chuckled, the way he always did when she asked him a question he didn't want to answer. "Enough," he replied.

"That doesn't answer my question," Penny replied.

"I know," Kip said.

"I think the hardest part of it all," Penny continued, "is that I couldn't tell Viv the whole story."

"Because that would involve telling her about your other name," Kip said.

Penny nodded.

"That would involve telling her about your other life," Kip said.

"Well, I don't know about that," Penny said. "I don't really know all about my other life. Not really."

"You could though," Kip said. "All you have to do is ask."

Penny sighed. "If there's one thing I've learned from talking to you over the years, Kip, it's that I shouldn't ask questions I don't want the answers to."

"Fair," he said with a little laugh.

"Once you learn things, you can't un-learn them. Once you know things, you can't un-know them."

Kip nodded. "Once you hear things, you can't un-hear them."

"Exactly," Penny said.

"Okay, little one," Kip said. "I can keep a secret. Or twelve."

"Although..." Penny said.

Kip sat up straighter at this.

"I'm sick of feeling like I'm standing outside of everything," Penny said. "Like there's this grand secret that everyone else knows, and I'm the only one left in the dark. Like a private joke told at my expense."

"That's understandable," Kip said. "Although it's not everyone. Mostly it's just the dead who know."

"And that shapeshifter Change Patterson. If that's who he really was. What kind of shapeshifter is named Change?" said Penny.

"At the very least, it's truth in advertising," Kip replied. "Change is what you get with a shapeshifter, especially one who's been around as long as he has, who's seen the things he's seen, who knows as many people... and non-people... that he knows. I'm surprised to see he's freelancing though, enough to be making up business cards. Last I knew, he was an errand boy for the Macombers."

"*The* Macombers?" Penny asked.

Kip nodded. "They all have fixers, the Families," he offered. "People hired to hide secrets or make problems go away. I imagine that's how he knows who you are. People who do that kind of job learn a lot of things a person isn't supposed to know. Especially one who can transform himself to blend in anywhere."

"I guess that's fair," Penny said. "But it's not just him either, who knows my name. It was also that lady at the Warrens of Persephone today. She was alive. Viv and Karen could see her just fine," Penny said.

"All that means is that she has been talking to the dead, and they've let her in on who you are," Kip replied. "I assure you – your name is really only widely known among the dead."

They're the only ones who really know who you are. That you aren't who you tell other people you are."

"That's why they seek me out, isn't it?" Penny said.

Kip nodded. "It's related."

"But what about that python? Why a snake?" Penny said. She was simply wondering aloud, didn't really mean to ask him. But she'd said it before she was aware. And Kip was ready to answer.

"I'd blame your father for that one," Kip replied.

"My father?" Penny said.

"Do you really want to know, little one?" Kip asked.

"Would you want to know if our positions were reversed?" Penny countered.

"I'm not sure," he replied.

"Why not?" Penny said.

"You've built up a good little life here, little one. A cozy existence in the land of the living. The dead make some colorful cameos in all of it, sure. But for the most part, you're making your own way. Solving crimes. You've fallen in love not once but twice. With two very remarkable women," Kip said.

"And the secrets you know could change all of that?" Penny asked.

Kip nodded. "There would be no going back. No un-knowing. No un-hearing. No un-seeing."

"Oh Kip," Penny cried, "why does life have to be so damn hard?"

"Little one," Kip replied, "the afterlife is no picnic either."

Penny crept back into the house just before the sun started to come up. Karen by this time was out cold. Viv, however, heard Penny close the door behind her. The floorboards on the first floor creaked as Penny worked her way into the kitchen, even though she made sure to kick off her shoes and traverse the house in stocking feet.

Viv heard the coffeemaker springing to life. An ancient model, one that Penny had rescued from the front lawn of a neighbor who had moved without warning. One day the neighbors were in the house, the next they were gone, most of their belongings pitched unceremoniously in front of the vacant home.

By the time Penny had happened upon the welter of possessions, all the choice items had already been carried off.

But she was taken with the well-worn Mr. Coffee unit. It had a bulky square silhouette you didn't find much outside of the 80s. The years had sepia tinged the plastic base to a shade that matched her nostalgic recollections of commercials from the era.

It was precisely the kind of machine to drink coffee from when she was the age to be forbidden from doing so, told that it was far too adult for her.

That alone made the act magical.

Viv lay completely still in bed, imagining Penny rifling through someone else's trash. Viv didn't have to think too

hard about it, as she had a ready archive of still shots of
Penny doing just that, looking for a bargain somewhere
lowbrow and potentially un-hygienic.

You had to hand it to her, Viv thought, Penny was making
the most of a psychic detective's salary. Or the three that they
collectively lived on.

After what the State charged them for licensing, registration
fees, taxes, and provision for public safety (the result of
public referendums declaring that psychic powers were
potentially dangerous to the broader population and required
extra services to offset that risk), there was very little left. As
Green Stars, they had been provided public housing, and
with Martin's help and the sway of three stellar employment
records, they'd secured a much-coveted single-family home
and use of a company car.

Their grocery budget was laughable. They qualified for
rations provided biweekly, ones you couldn't exactly call food
but would keep them from keeling over dead on duty.

Coffee was a luxury. As was tea. As was anything palatable,
really.

They made it work though, between Penny's dumpster diving
and the active informal bartering system between intuitives.

Just barely though. Despite being at the upper echelon of the
psychic workforce, poverty was always just at their backs.

That was why they normally worked seven days a week. Any
less, and it was back to rations. Not having watertight shoes.
Playing games with the utility companies that resulted in the
electricity and water going out at random times.

But things were good today. It had been a good month. Penny
started to make pancakes.

Between the smell of the brewing coffee and the pancakes, Karen began to stir. With her eyes still half closed, she got up and walked downstairs.

Just like those old coffee commercials, Viv thought. *Raising the whole house from a dead sleep by brewing a pot.*

Viv thought about following her, but instead lay there a moment, listening carefully.

She could almost see them in her mind's eye – Penny and Karen exchanging hellos. Penny would look impeccable, despite being out who-knows-where until all hours of the night. She'd avoid the question of where if Karen asked – but Karen probably wouldn't ask. Because Karen knew better.

Karen would grab the giant chipped mug with the chibi-style panda on it. Because it was her favorite mug. She'd pour black coffee into it and take a sip from the mug, wincing.

Even though she didn't like black coffee, Karen always tried to drink it black because black was the cheapest way to drink it, and she didn't want to be a bother.

Before her second sip, however, Penny would emerge with a flourish, holding a pitcher of cream, half and half, or milk in her hand – whatever they could afford that week – and pour in a generous amount before Karen could protest.

Karen would fake resignation. "Well, if you insist."

They did this every time. Every single time. As though they hadn't done it hundreds of times before.

And as Karen took a few more sips, she'd spring to life, like the Tin Man after he'd been properly oiled. And together they'd build their cheeky wall of words, their frenetic joking back and forth that Viv had come to expect.

Viv made a big deal sometimes out of complaining about it, but secretly she found it *adorable*. They were both adorable as individuals and particularly adorable together.

The grouch act was mostly an act – although part of her sometimes worried that she was the odd one out. That Karen and Penny would take their bantering besties show on the road and leave her stranded behind.

Viv would be on her own, the dour serious one. The one who was no fun. Who needed someone like that? Who needed her?

Viv felt her chest ache in that familiar way. It was an old wound, the part of her that worried she wasn't good enough, that no one would ever want to be with her if given any other choice.

She heard their voices springing to life. The lilting banter. *The Tin Man rises*, she thought. *And he's all chatty Kathy with Dorothy.*

She listened to them for several minutes, unable to hear exactly what they were saying, but warmed by their tone and the familiarity of it, before joining them.

Good old-fashioned privacy is hard to find in the modern world. Pretty much everyone these days is in their share of databases. Their personal information is catalogued and out there for anyone to stumble upon if someone is so inclined.

The days of being completely off the grid are over.

Instead, a new kind of privacy has emerged to take its place: Data overload.

There's so much information available that as much as some worry about being exposed most people are lost in the clutter. There's just too much there for any one person to be a complete focus... of anything, really.

Detective work often posed a similar challenge for Detectives Dreadful, Lee, and Cross. In many cases, there was an abundance of leads – and that was half the problem.

They often found themselves looking at a complicated street map of leads, with many avenues that they could explore, but without a clear idea of which way they should head.

The list of clients Gretchen Mills had given them was helpful information, and they were glad for it.

But they would be even more glad if it weren't so damn long.

"Wow," Penny said, reviewing the list, "Is there anyone Heather hasn't given advice to?"

Some of the names were awfully familiar, too. For starters, there were a few Family members in the mix: A Macomber, an Eck, and even a Watson.

"No Skinners though," Viv noted. "I wonder if Heather discriminated."

"Not judging by the length of this list," Karen replied.

"Well, I'll be," Penny said. "Euphemia Tender Lee?"

"What?" Viv said, snatching the list from Penny's hands. Oh God. Yeah, her own mother was on this list. She handed the list back to Penny and held her head in her hands. "Does this mean we're going to have to go interview Mom?"

"Well, we can follow some other leads first," Karen said. "But possibly. Unless you want to call Martin and talk about moving the case to someone else."

"No," Viv said. "I'm not going to do that. I've never had to do that before. Not gonna start doing that now. Especially not because of her. If she wants to throw her money away on love readings, then that's her business." She paused. "Although it's awfully hypocritical, given her general stance on psychics."

"Is this the first time your mom has been hypocritical though?" Karen said. And then she quickly added, "Sorry, that was out of line."

"No," Viv replied. "That wasn't out of line. And no, it's not the first time she's been hypocritical. I'm sure you saw it, too, when you roomed with her."

Karen nodded but didn't say more. Nirvana Heights was still difficult for her to talk about. While it had made where she was today possible, it was the end of a chapter of her life she didn't really want to acknowledge.

"If it makes you feel any better, you're not the only one in PsyOps with a relative on the list," Penny said.

"Oh?" Viv said.

"Martin's sister. Darian Meek," Penny said.

"You're kidding me," Viv said.

"Nope," Penny replied. She pointed it out to both of them.

"That's the one with the record, isn't it?" Karen said.

Viv nodded. It had been a big stress on Martin, his older sister having so many run-ins with the law. Working for the State had given him a bit of wiggle room when he had to bail her out or advocate on her behalf, but it stressed him out to no end. He'd told them many times that if it weren't for pressure from his parents, he wouldn't bother. But Martin loved his elderly parents, even if they were unfamiliar with how the law actually operated and naïve about his sister's intentions, always giving her the benefit of doubts she didn't deserve.

He couldn't exactly blame them. After all, they were biased towards him, too. Love made it impossible for them to see things clearly, as it so often does.

"We've really got our work cut out for us," Viv said.

"Mm," Penny replied. "It seems like Heather was a one-woman Psychic Friends Network."

"Oh wow, that takes me back," Viv said. "I had forgotten all about that."

"Kind of funny how the first precogs showed up not long after that," Penny said.

"Almost like foreshadowing," Karen replied.

"Except foreshadowing doesn't happen in the real world," Viv said.

"Or does it?" Penny said. "Duh duh duh!"

"Sinister music isn't foreshadowing," Viv said.

"Or is it?" Penny said. "Duh duh duhhhh!"

"Duh duh duhhh!" Karen echoed.

They laughed as Viv rolled her eyes, but as she turned away from them, she smiled.

Poor as a Lizard-Eating Cat

Martin stood up from his desk, placed both palms on the surface, and let out an improbably long sigh.

He has more lung capacity than I'd expect from a short man who doesn't seem to be all that fit, Penny thought. There was a lot about Martin she didn't know, she realized. Especially since she'd known him for... four years? She did the math quickly in her head. They'd been a trio solving crimes for three years now, and she and Viv had been working as a duo for two years before Karen joined them with Martin having been on board for about half that time. Yup, four years.

How did you work for someone for four years and have so much you didn't know about them? Especially as they did, with the long hours and the danger involved in their jobs.

Maybe that was the whole point, and that's how you made it. You kept your most important secrets to yourself, away from the workplace and where they wouldn't be exploited as a vulnerability.

And Penny had to admit they'd been pretty secretive with PsyOps and even with Martin, especially at first. It's why it had taken six months for PsyOps to realize that she and Viv were even in a relationship. They'd hidden beneath the assumption that most people have when they see two women who are extremely emotionally close. The handy camouflage of "Oh, those two? They're just gals being pals."

Ah, gals being pals. Yeah, right.

It was an illusion that came in handy, even now. Outside of the people who knew them well, most assumed when meeting Karen, Penny, and Viv that they were just friends.

We are friends, Penny thought. Their system of relationships was made possible by a web of strong friendships woven between them. *We are spectacular friends. But not* just. *We are not just anything.*

Unless the detectives mounted one another in the middle of the grocery store, however, most people assumed their relationship began and ended in friendship. Which was just fine with Penny. It bothered Viv, who felt offended that it was so easy for outsiders to diminish or outright dismiss her romantic relationships just because they didn't look like the norm. But Penny appreciated her relationships being mostly invisible. She liked having the choice to either tell people or not.

It was hard enough dealing with the prejudice that came with being an intuitive. She didn't need to simultaneously battle over her sexual orientation or the way she structured her romantic life.

Besides, it wasn't like intuitives were legally allowed to marry anyway. Similarly, intuitives weren't allowed to bear children without express permission from the State. This involved a lengthy application process that was usually unsuccessful. The official justification for both of these restrictions was thin.

The cover story was something about the tax code and protecting the public good – same purported basis of restrictions on intuitives as the rest. So long as you were over the age of six, you knew the truth: It was based in prejudice. Envy. A fear that if citizens with psychic powers were allowed a level playing field that they would quickly conquer and enslave the rest of the population.

And the State wasn't about to allow that.

Instead, the State worked to keep intuitives in their place, installing systemic safeguards to quell public fears and also ensure they had a skilled workforce who would work for pennies, unless they wanted to surrender every last one of their civil liberties. If you could call them that, as watered down as the psychic version could be.

"Well," Martin said finally, snapping Penny out of her thoughts. "The right thing to say to you right now is that I'm glad you three came here. But I've known you long enough to be uncomfortable lying to you. And anyway, Karen would know."

Karen shrugged. "Well, not with Penny and Viv here. But I'm a pretty good judge of character even without my powers. And yeah, sooner or later I'd fully sense those complicated, conflicted feelings from you."

"And you'd make an inference," Martin replied.

Karen nodded.

"I'll be honest though," Martin said. "Might as well cut through the crap." A beat. "I'm not glad you came here. I wish you'd never come. You've put me in a difficult position, telling me this. By showing me this list of clients."

"Well, that's your job, isn't it?" Viv said. "To be put in the difficult positions."

"Maybe," Martin said. "Although if you surveyed all of the supervisors in this building anonymously, I'm sure you'd get a wide variety of answers, about what our job really is."

"I suppose you're right. I can think of quite a few that would answer differently," Viv replied, thinking specifically of the carousel of supervisors she and Penny had spun through in

the first year they'd been working at PsyOps, before they'd
been assigned Martin.

Martin was the first supervisor who had stuck around for
more than a few weeks. And the first who didn't express open
hostility to working with intuitives.

Before Martin was assigned their team, reporting to
management had been a dizzying, confusing experience.
They never worked with anyone long enough to be able to
anticipate how they'd react to news, let alone figure out the
best way to approach them.

It was a mercy, however, to have Martin on board and to have
worked with him for a year when Viv had asked about Karen
joining the team. She'd known exactly how to ask him, and
he'd known exactly how to challenge her on the wisdom of it.
How to voice responsible concern about possible conflict of
interests and bias without looking petty and pissing her off.

"But you're not those other supervisors," Viv said. "And that's
why we came to you."

"She's right, you know," Penny added. "You're the guy who's
good when things get complicated. You can make the tough
calls."

"Don't I know it," Martin said, standing up, leaning back,
and clutching his head. He stared at the painting on the wall.
His office was windowless, as all rooms in PsyOps were.
Not much to see when you were subterranean. Nothing that
wouldn't make you feel buried alive, anyway.

Martin had found the lack of a view depressing when he
first moved into the building, so he'd hung a painting that
simulated a window with a beautiful view of Skinner's
Business District in his office. The vantage point made it look

like he was looking out of a window in a high rise building on the 14th floor.

"It's why I was assigned you in the first place," Martin said. "The problem children."

"And look where we are now," Viv replied.

"What? With the highest rate of unsolved crimes in PsyOps?" Martin replied.

"Maybe," Viv countered. "But how many overturned convictions? How many exonerations after the fact?"

Martin sighed another interminable sigh. "Zero. Yeah. Okay, Viv. That's a good point."

"We do good work as a team, Martin," Viv said. "Even you have to admit that."

"You do," he replied. "I just wish that work were in a form that was easier to explain to *my* supervisors. Sometimes I feel like we're *all* Amarynth. Doing great work but not able to explain why or convince anyone of it."

Viv reflexively rolled her eyes at the mention of Amarynth. Martin saw it but knew better than to comment on it. Viv's ingratitude towards the Connection Agent's skills had always grated on him, but you had to pick your battles with Viv, and her strange feud with Amarynth was at best a second order concern. If that. Normally, third or fourth.

Martin had learned in his long career of managing teams that once you got a certain size there were always going to be a few interpersonal conflicts that were resistant to change. You couldn't eliminate every conflict. Trying to do so was often a waste of energy. If you couldn't learn to manage *through* conflict, you were screwed.

The best manager knew how to manage an imperfect team.

Martin never would have admitted it aloud – primarily because he feared other people would laugh at him, especially his wife, who continually complained that he didn't have a more prestigious job, one that impressed the neighbors – but Martin considered himself that kind of manager.

He kept his confidence in his own abilities to himself, clutched it close to his chest where he could enjoy it without anyone grabbing it out of his hands, throwing it on the ground, and stomping on it.

"The way I see it," Martin said, "We have a few realistic options here. The first is that you hand this case over to another team. This would avoid the perception of conflict of interest – and keep you from risking actual conflict of interest – but there would be downsides. You'd have to brief the other team extensively on not only the facts of the case but the web of inferences that you're working with. Ideally, Amarynth would also brief her counterpart, the Connections Agent consulting for this other investigative team. Theoretically, I suppose you could request that Amarynth work with this new team on the case, but..." He looked out his "window."

"No one wants to work with her," Penny said, completing the thought.

"You said it, not me," Martin replied.

"Don't hear you arguing though," Viv observed.

"Option one risks the case never being solved. You know as well as anyone that transferring a case inevitably risks a lot being lost in translation, especially with Amarynth trying to explain," Martin continued.

"You end up with a copy of a copy of the case at best," Viv agreed.

He nodded. "It's the safest option without a doubt, as far as not risking ethical impropriety. But you know as well as I do – and probably more immediately, based on what they've legally done to tueys in the last decade – that the State isn't exactly concerned with risking ethical impropriety."

"You can say that again," Viv said.

"They're concerned with what works, first and foremost," Martin said.

"That's a generous way of putting it," Viv cracked.

"Detective Lee," Martin said. "Do I need to remind you that you're not only in front of your supervisor, who works for the State, but also in a State-owned and operated facility? A building that could be wired. Where our conversation could be monitored."

Viv sighed, rolled her eyes. "You say that like I'm not a walking surveillance tool."

"Well, pulling a security tape is a lot easier than auditing an eideticist. You know that. Anyway, I'd be careful how you phrase things. You never know what tomorrow will bring," said Martin.

"We're not precogs, no," Viv said.

"Viv," Penny said. "This is pointless. Stop arguing with the man. I wanna hear what he has to say."

"Thank you, Detective Dreadful," Martin said. "Let's move to option two."

Viv felt irritated with Penny but held her tongue.

"Option two," Martin continued, "is continuing the investigation as a team but avoiding the encounters that could be conceived of as posing a conflict of interest. In our specific case, that would be the interviews of my sister and Viv's mother. With this approach, we'd have an additional choice to make – whether to skip the interviews altogether or to have another team conduct them in our stead and report those findings to us."

"This could be a good middle ground. Skipping them altogether is probably a bad idea, however. Not only would it look very biased and compromised – as though we are exempting relatives from the possibility of prosecution – we also risk missing valuable evidence."

"Now, I don't think my sister is going around murdering psychics, and your mother is the last person I'd suspect, Viv, but who knows what additional leads those interviews could generate? You know how it is. Witnesses will reveal small details that bust an investigation wide open."

Viv nodded. "My mother knows everyone. And she's a busybody."

Martin smirked. "You said it, not me," he said.

"We should get you a button to push that says that," Penny said. "You said it, not me. You said it, not me."

There are certain people in this world who have a knack of getting you to say the bold, outrageous thing yourself, talking up to the point where it becomes the obvious conclusion, and then gracefully backing away from actually stating it themselves.

Martin was particularly skilled in this area.

"The third and final option is that we proceed as normal, in spite of any perceived or actual conflict of interest. This has the obvious benefit of efficiency. We don't have to brief another team on the case en masse or coordinate with one for isolated interviews. It does run the risk of appearing improper, if anyone reviews this case looking for ethical breaches. I'll level with you. That's extraordinarily rare. If such a request comes through, it usually comes from way above me. Well, you all remember the Door-Winchester case."

How could they forget? The son of a high-ranking State official had been arrested and indicted as a result of a very well-conducted investigation. Instead of accepting that his son could have committed the crime, the official had declared the whole thing a witch hunt, started screaming about corruption in PsyOps.

The Door-Winchester case was audited with a level of scrutiny that was beyond anything PsyOps had ever seen. Even though their team had been far removed from the investigation (thank goodness), no one working in PsyOps had felt safe while the ethical inquiry was ongoing.

The official's lawyers worked so diligently at nitpicking minor procedural deviations that they were able to successfully throw out the case, only to have the same son reoffend within the following year. This time, investigators took every precaution and made sure to stave off a repeat fiasco. There was talk that the official successfully influenced the judge overseeing the case, however, as the official's son ultimately received one of the lightest murder sentences on record.

"Now, I haven't gotten any indication that this case will be a repeat of that. But you never really know what's going to be behind doors when you start opening them up," Martin said.

Viv nodded. "I know it isn't exactly scientific – and not within the scope of my powers – but something has felt different about this case from the very beginning. At least for me."

"Me, too," Penny added.

"Same," Karen chimed in. "It's not every day that you have a serial killer targeting psychics, er, intuitives."

"I'm going to suggest Option Three," Martin said. "I think we should keep this case in house as much as possible. I want to see it through."

The detectives all nodded in unison. Talking it over before coming to Martin's office, it was what they wanted to do; they just needed his blessing. Or, rather, the lack of his curse.

"As far as I'm concerned, I have no problem with my sister being questioned by you three. I trust you to follow the facts wherever they lead. And I trust you to know that even if they lead somewhere ugly for me personally, somewhere that would mess up my family life, that I won't take it out on you. Even if you needed to go around me in the reporting structure. Whatever you needed to do."

"I know, Martin," Viv said. "You're not the kind of guy who punishes people for the truth."

"Thank you," he said. "I think that's one of the nicest things anyone has ever said to me."

"Viv does the extremes well," Penny said. "Nice and mean. It's the middle ground that trips her up."

Viv laughed. "Fair."

"That basically just leaves one interview to talk about. Euphemia Tender Lee. I'm going to leave it up to you whether you feel like you can handle it. Whether you three want to tackle it. Or maybe Detective Lee stays out of that one. Or maybe that's the one interview you outsource."

"What do you think, Viv?" Penny said.

Viv sighed. "I... don't know."

"Well, you don't have to figure it out right now. It seems to me like you have plenty of investigative ground to cover before you have to worry about interviewing her, but give it some serious thought," Martin said.

"It isn't just impropriety that I'm worried about," said Marin. "I know bias can make it hard for psychic powers to work. Can generate interference."

Penny nodded. "That's generally true, although it's not much of a factor for eideticists or mediums."

"But it does affect empaths a bit," Karen confessed.

"A bit," Penny said. "But it's nothing like what happens to a precog or an invalidator."

"True," Karen said.

"Just something to keep in mind," Martin said. "I really should keep up better on my taxonomy if I'm going to keep herding tueys like this."

"I have a book I can lend you," Penny replied.

"*If* you're going to keep herding tueys?" Viv said suspiciously. "Something you're not telling us, Martin?"

"Oh, nothing new," he said. "You know my wife's always on my case about this job."

"You need to buy her a swimming pool or something. Maybe put an addition on the house. Give her an easy way to show off to the neighbors," Viv said.

"Maybe," Martin said. "Maybe that'd do it."

"Good meeting!" Viv said, raising her first in the air.

"Good meeting," Martin replied.

The three psychic detectives walked out of his office, wisecracking and telling private jokes in a rhythm that had become all too familiar to Martin over the years they had worked for him. They were as dear as the birdsongs that he heard waking up every morning as a young boy. As regular and known.

After the detectives left his office and closed the door, Martin sank down into his office chair.

"I hope they don't find anything on her," he said, thinking of how hard it'd be to explain indicting his older sister to his parents. Or his wife.

Talk about not impressing the neighbors.

He winced, feeling a sour feeling take over his stomach.

"Don't find anything on her," he said again, pressing his hands together.

"They won't find anything," he reassured himself, but he knew things had become grim. It was always a bad sign when his hands started praying without his conscious effort.

"Maybe I *do* have a bias here," he said. "But in the other direction."

Because something deep inside him gnawed at him. Warned him that this whole investigation was close to home.

"I might have a murderer in the family," he said aloud, hoping that admitting it would make him feel better. That accepting it would clear up the sour pit in his stomach.

It didn't.

It turned out that Martin's sister and Viv's mother weren't the only familiar faces on the list. The very first client they visited was an old college friend of Viv's.

"Martha Pointer!" Viv exclaimed when the door opened.

"Viv Lee!" Martha cried out, throwing her arms around Viv's neck.

Karen and Penny stared at them. This wasn't like Viv at all. Squealing. Girlish. Sororal.

It didn't last long.

"I must have the wrong house. I'm looking for a Martha Cooper," Viv said, after she'd collected herself.

"No, that's me. Married Doug Cooper," Martha replied.

"You don't mean..." Viv said.

"Yeah, whatever, *that* Doug Cooper."

"I always thought you'd marry another artist," Viv said.

"Did *you* marry another artist?' Martha asked.

"Well, no," Viv said.

"Oh, that's right," Martha said. "Tueys can't get married."

"Right," Viv replied.

"Glad to see you're still painting," Martha said, pointing to Viv's overalls, which were splotched with various paints.

"Oh," Viv said. "I'm not. These are old stains."

"Well, why not? Why aren't you painting?" Martha asked.

Viv frowned. It was an uncomfortable question. "Can we come in?"

"Sure," Martha said. She led them into a tastefully appointed living room, one where complementary shades offset one another beautifully in that effortless-seeming cascade that's often very expensive to achieve. Usually the work of a professional decorator. Every item of furniture and decorative ornament was well made, expensive-seeming, but impersonal. "I'd suggest you might like to take a look at my studio, but…"

Viv sighed.

"People change," Martha finished her thought.

"They do," Viv replied. "And they're allowed to. Even if it's jarring, when it doesn't square with how we remember them."

"Even if," Martha replied.

You've changed too, Viv thought but did not say. She flashed her badge instead. "I'm a detective now. Green Star. Level 3 Investigator, Department of Psychic Operations. These are my associates, Detective Dreadful and Cross."

"Dreadful, you say?" Martha said. "That's an unusual surname. What's the nationality? Are you British?"

Penny's nose twitched. "That's immaterial. And I think this interview will go better if you keep in mind that we're here to ask you questions. Not the other way around."

Martha blinked twice slowly. "So that's how it's gonna be," she said.

"You and I may go way back, but I'm afraid it's a serious matter," Viv replied. She pulled out a photograph of the deceased fortuneteller, not a crime scene photo but her senior portrait, the one that had run in her high school yearbook. "Do you know her?"

"Yes," Martha said. "Why?"

"When was the last time you spoke with her?" Viv asked, ignoring the question. Penny was correct. They were here to ask questions, not answer them.

"I don't know..." Martha said. "Maybe a month ago." She frowned. "Has something happened to her?"

Viv ignored the question again. "And what were the circumstances of that encounter?"

"It was a meaningless interaction. We had a conversation," Martha said.

"And what did you talk about?" Viv asked.

"It was a private conversation. About private issues. It was hardly a matter that concerns public safety. Nothing PsyOps would be interested in," Martha said.

"Martha," Viv said. "They found this woman dead a few days ago. She was killed by someone."

Martha gasped.

"I don't believe that you had anything to do with it. I really don't. But we need you to tell us everything you know. Even if it's embarrassing. You never know what's important. What will lead to something else. Something that will help us catch the person who did this. And stop them from doing it to others," Viv said.

"Others? What makes you think whoever did this would do it to others?" Martha asked.

This question Viv *did* answer. "Because this isn't the first murder like this. It looks like this is related to another attack that occurred several months ago. There's a killer on the loose."

"I see," Martha said. She took a deep breath, let it go. She turned her gaze to the wall, as though she preferred not to look the detectives in the eye as she spoke.

"I went to Heather for professional reasons. I'd hired her to tell my fortune," Martha said.

Viv nodded. "We suspected as much."

"I had started to suspect Doug was having an affair. Ugh," she stopped, rubbed her chest with the flat palm of her hand. "It's humiliating to even admit to you."

"Humiliating how?" Viv prompted.

"To be dealing with these sorts of suspicions at my age. I had always thought this was the kind of thing that I'd be wrestling with in middle age, not worrying about before my thirtieth birthday. But there were signs, you know... signs that troubled me. He'd changed. He was colder. And he stopped initiating sex. We were going weeks without being intimate, and I always had to initiate. Always. It's not an exaggeration. He'd put a lock on his phone. And was always popping off to meetings at strange hours. So yeah, semi-dead bedroom, locked phone, running off to who knows where... a woman starts to wonder. To worry," Martha said.

"So you hired Heather?" Viv said.

Martha nodded.

"How?" Viv asked.

"What do you mean how? I called up the Warrens of Persephone, made an appointment, came down to the facility, had a reading. I hired her the usual way. I'm not aware that there's another method," Martha snapped.

"No, no, I mean... did you ask for her specifically? Or did you just ask for any fortuneteller who could see you?" Viv said.

Martha hesitated. "I asked for Heather specifically," she responded.

"How did you know to ask for her? How had you heard of her? And why did you want to see her and not other fortunetellers?" Viv asked.

"People talk, you know," Martha replied. "The law's the law, so it's not exactly like you can go find a public directory of tuey fortunetellers posing as entertainers, but... people talk. People know. It's not that difficult to figure out if you talk to enough people."

"And if you make sure to reward the referral. With favors or a wad of cash," Viv said.

"That's a disgusting implication," Martha said.

"One that you're not directly denying," Viv observed.

"Nor one I'm directly agreeing to," Martha said.

"You don't have to," Viv replied.

It wasn't the first time in her line of work that Viv had run into this particular theme: If you had enough money you could pay your way out of following the law. Especially on smaller matters like the laws prohibiting the commercial use of psychic powers in sexual intercourse, regulations that didn't differentiate between sex and love. Although in Martha's case, Viv mused, it would seem that sex may very have been her primary concern. Both the fact that she wasn't having it anymore with her husband and the fact that he might very well be having it somewhere else.

This was a classic situation where flashing cash or pointing at the right social connections would make a crime essentially invisible. The kind of corruption that was not only excusable in the eyes of the most powerful (who made the rules) but expected.

After a few more minutes, Martha agreed to it, like Viv knew she would. She'd seen it many times in her line of work, that most people would eventually admit to ugliness but only after a song and dance, a bit of a struggle to show that they weren't exactly proud of the behavior.

Because it was one thing to admit freely to immoral behavior; it was another thing to do so begrudgingly.

To Viv, the difference didn't seem that vast, but to witnesses it often did. So she spun around with Martha, knowing the steps to this familiar dance a little too well. Bored but capable.

Karen dutifully recorded the highlights of the interview in the notebook.

As Martha led them to the door, she said to Viv in a soft voice, "I hope you paint again," before closing the door.

"That makes one of us," Viv said to the closed door.

There's a certain way that a person looks when they've been up all night. Their body starts to protest about it. Show less than subtle signs that it hasn't gotten to do its normal business.

There are, of course, the famous bags under one's eyes. The eyeballs themselves are known to act erratically after an all-nighter, darting one way and then another as though the person looking through them is incapable of sustaining attention on anything.

And at intervals, the eyes stop all activity, as the sleep-deprived person stares off into space. Almost like the brain is commandeering the body's machinery and trying to impose a sleepless sleep.

Darian Meek had all the signs of pulling an all-nighter but far more pronounced, as though she'd been pulling all-nighters for years.

Perhaps she has, Karen thought.

Darian's eyes themselves were jaundiced, the sclerae not white but closer to the shade of tea-soaked parchment. Her skin seemed at turns both tight and loose, as though she were wearing a face that did not belong to her.

Now there's a thought. Karen shuddered. Despite having visited many crime scenes, she hadn't ever witnessed a killing in progress. She'd never seen someone kill someone else, nor did she want to. Despite working as a homicide detective for years, she didn't imagine what murder must look like. She left that to Viv's starkly visual imagination and the work of crime scene technicians and the forensic unit. For the most part, she wasn't plagued by thoughts of the actual gruesome act of murder, let alone unsavory cousins like mutilation.

But sitting before Darian Meek, she began to.

Is this a sign? She wondered. *Have we found our killer?*

Perhaps there was something so lethal about this woman that one couldn't help but imagine dark acts.

"Martin's team, right?" Darian said after she answered the front door. Her voice was gravelly, but there was nothing hostile or defensive in it.

Viv nodded.

"Well come in," Darian replied. "I've heard a lot about you."

The detectives followed, tentatively. Darian's place was small, crowded, cramped, and dirty.

Piles of clothes dotted the single room. There appeared to be items under them but no way of knowing what. And none of the detectives really wanted to look, even if Darian had granted permission.

The dwelling smelled like a car does when you park it directly in the sun on a hot day, forget a package of steaks in it, and then return to it several days later.

Karen gagged. Penny discreetly covered her nose. Viv frowned at the scent and was glad she hadn't eaten in hours so there was nothing in her stomach to act up in response.

Darian darted to a small closet and pulled out four folding metal chairs. She set them up in succession, spacing them evenly apart with great care. Viv offered to help, but Darian waved if off. "No, I insist. Let me do this," Darian said, smiling wide. "You are my guests."

The chair backs were marked SPRIGLEY in permanent marker, the name of a local high school. *Either pinched or rescued from a dumpster*, Penny surmised, although noting they were in such a bad state, dented and discolored, that as much as she enjoyed the sport of dumpster diving, she would not have been tempted by them.

The detectives sat down on the chairs slowly, tentatively, not sure if the surfaces were clean and also worried that they might not be structurally sound. But the chairs held fast.

"I so rarely get visitors," Darian said. "That's what happens when you're the junkie sister." She laughed. "Oh shit, you're cops. Shit, shit. Forget I said that."

"We're not that kind of cops," Viv assured her. "We don't worry about little things like that."

Darian nodded. "That's what Martin has told me. But you never know. You relax, and people screw you. Once you fall down, it's hard to get up. No matter how much you try. You try to go straight, and people are always holding the worst thing you ever did over your head. You're defined by your biggest mistakes. They won't give you a fresh start. You're not allowed to be imperfect. So you start to ask yourself what's the point? What's the point of even trying if it's going to get you nowhere? Might as well fuck off and have fun if no one's ever going to forgive you."

Karen felt bad about coming. There was something pitiful about this woman... and in a way quite likeable. She didn't seem like a murderer.

Oh c'mon, Karen, snap out of it. People don't come conveniently labeled with a neon sign that reads "murderer." Even the most evil actor could be capable of charm in small bursts, Karen reminded herself. *Don't get sucked in.*

"I'd offer you some refreshments," Darian said, "but as you can see I'm not exactly swimming in money here. I'm as poor as a lizard-eating cat."

"Colorful," Viv said.

"Well, you have to have a sense of humor about yourself. Especially when you have little else," Darian said. "Anyway... I figure you're not here on a social call. So what's the deal? What are you looking into?"

Viv pulled out her investigative folder and pulled out a picture of Heather. "Do you know this woman?"

"Of course," Darian replied. "That's my love tuey. Paid her to help me figure out my love life. Good work. I heard the news. Real shame about what happened to her. She seemed like a nice girl, and her predictions were amazing."

"You hired her to give you relationship advice?" Viv asked.

Darian nodded.

"That's strange," Viv said.

"How so?"

"You're living here. You're as poor as a lizard-eating cat, as you just said. And yet... you somehow had the money to pay a Fortune-Telling Service," Viv replied.

"And why wouldn't I?" Darian said.

"What do you mean by that?" Viv asked.

"By your own logic, I shouldn't be buying drugs either. And well... just fill in the blank. I know you say you're not that kind of cop, but I'm not looking to confess to something that's not hurting anyone and is none of your business. Anyway, being poor and having no money whatsoever aren't the same thing at all," Darian explained.

"I see," Viv said.

"Not that tone again," Darian said.

Viv wasn't sure what she was talking about. What tone?

Darian rolled her eyes. "It's so easy to judge me. I know that. It's one thing when you can pay all of your bills comfortably and then afford things after that. But when there's no way to do it all, you make your choices. For me, it's a bit of escapism and looking for love. What's wrong with that? You'd probably do the same if you were in my shoes."

The detectives stared at her. Finally, Viv said. "Actually, I get it."

"What?" Darian said.

"You may have forgotten, or maybe you were never told, but intuitives are poor. And we're intuitives. So, no, I understand. We've set priorities, too, even if you wouldn't know by looking at us," Viv replied.

"I dumpster dive for furniture," Penny offered.

Darian brightened. "Oh." She visibly relaxed. Began to tell them of her time with Heather. "It could have been my imagination, but she seemed scared at our last session. I asked her what was wrong, but she told me she couldn't break any professional confidences."

"So the threats came from a client?" Viv asked.

"As far as I could tell. That's what I thought. She excused herself to take a call during the session. Probably rude of me to listen in, but I heard her saying something about damn rich assholes, too, to whoever was on the other line. That stuck out to me. Both because she was never negative about anyone, and I don't think I ever heard her swear before," Darian said. "I remember thinking 'damn right, damn rich assholes.'"

"Did you ask her about it?" Penny said. "About who called her, what it was about?"

Darian shook her head no. "I didn't dare. Didn't want her knowing I'd been nosy and listened in."

"It's a good lead," Viv replied. "Thank you. We'll have a look at her phone records. When was your last session?"

Darian told her. After a series of basic questions surrounding her alibi, any other things she may have noticed, the detectives concluded the interview.

"One more thing," Darian said, as they were leaving. "If you find the bastard who did this to her, you give them a kick in the balls for me. She was a good woman. I'll miss her. And I'll probably die alone without her."

"Thanks for your cooperation," Viv replied.

The team worked their way down the list, heading from interview to interview.

It was mind-numbingly dull. No one seemed to know anything.

Everyone seemed sad that Heather was dead. Many expressed that they were going to have a difficult time replacing her services.

Viv idly wondered the third time she'd heard that if they were only saying it because they were nervous about talking about hiring love psychics in front of police.

No, they weren't *that* kind of police. But people didn't always know that. And you couldn't blame people for being cautious or not trusting the Psychic State to tell them the truth about the real legal risks.

Besides, Viv thought, it could all change overnight. It had before. True, things were a lot more stable than in the early days of the Psychic Phenomenon and certainly a lot more stable as the Psychic State stayed independent and looked as though it wouldn't be reabsorbed into the union.

But you never knew.

Not even the precogs could see the future for sure.

And good luck waiting on forensics. It was true that when this murder cropped up with the same exact *modus operandi* as the Snow White case, the crime scene unit had collected more samples this time around. But it was also true that the lab was so backed up that it might very well be years before everything could be properly analyzed. Department budgets had started out tight at the time Viv had first joined PsyOps, and with each passing year, they seemed to be getting tighter.

Besides, forensics weren't nearly as much of a priority in the Psychic State as they were in their neighbor, the United States. DNA analysis would have to be shipped off internationally to an American lab, and tensions were tight. The Psychic State preferred to save such a favor for their highest-profile cases. And while these murders were certainly unsettling, Viv knew she'd be told they had bigger fish to try.

Everyone knew that things between the two nations had been tense following the War of Independence. The ceasefire was one thing; mutual respect was another. Peace itself was tenuous. Perhaps one day they'd be strong allies, but now was not the time. It was too soon.

So Viv was forced, as usual, to work with what she had.

She had worked her way through nearly the entire list of leads, growing increasingly more frustrated with each pointless, repetitive conversation with an apparently grieving client (who may or may not be faking said grief) when Martin handed her a note with her name on it:

Let's do lunch.

-Roscoe

Viv groaned and folded up the paper in her hand. It was the last thing she wanted to do, but they weren't exactly getting anywhere.

"Damn," she said.

She swallowed hard and rolled her eyes before whipping out her phone and drafting a quick email in response.

"I'm sorry, Karen," she said, as she hit send.

Viv had known it was a risky move, accepting Ryan Roscoe's invitation to lunch with him in the PsyOps cafeteria.

Even having lunch during a workday was a normal change of pace for Viv. She'd eaten there a lot when she was a rookie, but that was back in the time that PsyOps included a free meal with every shift.

Sure, they were pretty basic offerings – questionable meatloaf whose contributing animal (or animals) was never identified covered in a brownish-red sauce that tasted as though the last bits of several condiment bottles had been thrown into a pot and comingled. Overcooked green beans as tough as Pilates bands. Something Viv assumed was pizza but reminded her of sights she had witnessed at crime scenes.

Any sort of upgrade, the premium meals, had always cost additional money.

They weren't glamourous, but the basic meals were free, after all. Or had been. Now they, too, came with a small charge, just enough to scare Viv off.

Viv had considered complaining then, when free "food" was no longer available in the PsyOps cafeteria, but she didn't dare to. There had been simultaneous rumblings that PsyOps was considering taking away their work vehicles, gas, maintenance, and mileage.

If that went away, it would be a much bigger blow than some food that she couldn't swallow without grimacing. A much bigger financial hit.

It was better not to rock the boat, she decided.

Still, she wasn't about to pay for the work meals.

She'd rather take a chance on food that Penny rescued from dumpsters. After all, Penny could be quite clever and when seeking out meals targeted the hoity toity neighborhoods, supermarkets that specialized in imported goods.

Even though Penny never directly acknowledged it, Viv knew that Penny ate a lot of her haul long before she ever arrived home with food for Viv and Karen. Not that Viv minded. It was only fair, considering the effort Penny put in scavenging.

Besides, the extra calories had helped Penny stay curvy, even as starvation had whittled Viv and Karen down to bonier versions of their former selves. And that last thing Viv would ever complain about was Penny's curves poured into a pink jumpsuit. It was worth skipping a snack or two – even a meal – here and there.

And Penny did provide. After discarding a suspiciously rain(?)-soaked cardboard box, Penny had presented them with a full year's supply of protein bars. Good ones, too. Not even short coded this time but with valid dates well into the future.

It simply seemed as though the box had gotten damaged during the shipping process. "Probably left outside in a loading area and forgotten and rained on," Penny had said, presenting them.

After observing Penny to have eaten a few of these protein bars and noting that she suffered no ill health effects, Viv had begun to bring them every day for her lunch.

"It's such an honor to be the king's taste tester," Penny had joked about Viv's habit of letting her take the risks on salvaged food. But she had seemed pleased that Viv enjoyed the spoils of her hunt. "The *unspoiled* spoils," Penny had emphasized.

Today's protein bar was tucked into the pocket of Viv's paint-stained overalls the day that she sat down to lunch with Ryan Roscoe.

Because you never know, Viv reflected. *Always best to have a backup plan.*

It didn't take her long to second guess her decision.

"Really?" Roscoe said, reading her thoughts. "It's been *that* long since you've bought lunch here?"

Viv scowled. "You know, you'd think after an entire life of being able to read other people's thoughts, you would have learned by now that it's rude to answer them, as though they'd been spoken aloud."

Roscoe smirked. "I get that a lot," he replied.

"You get told that you're rude, and you keep on doing it?" Viv asked.

"Sure," Roscoe said.

"And why's that?" Viv asked. "If you know it's rude, and people ask you to stop, then why do you keep doing it?" Viv asked.

"Do you follow every order you're given?" Roscoe asked.

Viv didn't know what to say to that. No, she didn't. But she wasn't about to give him the satisfaction of admitting it.

"I didn't think so," Roscoe said.

Oh right, Viv said. *I don't have to admit it. Little bastard will extract it from me no matter what.*

"My parents were married when I was born, thank you very much," Roscoe said.

"Seriously, Roscoe," Viv fumed, "wouldn't it be a lot more efficient to engage with people in the way that they choose to present themselves rather than rifling around their subconscious and questioning them about garbage they'd rather throw out?"

He paused. "I've never really thought about it that way." Roscoe scratched his chin. "Every person I meet has a different distance between their thoughts and what they say aloud. I know it annoys you when I... rifle around in your trash, or however you put it –"

"However I *thought* it," Viv said. "I think the whole business of thoughts being translated directly into words is suspect anyway."

"I know," Roscoe replied. "You think it every time you're around me. At least once. Sometimes more."

Viv nodded.

"Anyway, as I was saying, when I rifle around your trash, I find that what you think is not that different than what you actually say," Roscoe said.

"Are you saying I'm a trash talker?" Viv asked.

"No, I'm saying you're honest. Blunt. A bit too much for most people, judging by what I hear them think about you," Roscoe said.

Viv winced at that idea, the reality that other people were thinking about her, whether she liked it or not, as well as the fact that not all of what they thought was positive.

"But it's refreshing to me. A break from the constant hypocrisy, the duplicity that most people have," Roscoe said.

"Some people call that tact," Viv said.

"People are good at justifying what they do," Roscoe said.

"Alright, whatever. I'll stay," Viv said. She poked at the Swedish meatballs on her tray tentatively.

"They're pretty good actually," Roscoe said. "I have no idea what's in the sauce, but the egg noodles are surprisingly decent."

Viv took a bite. He wasn't lying. Not bad. She took a larger second bite and felt her body react to how good it was.

"Well, as much as you hate having your thoughts read, there is one benefit," Roscoe offered.

Viv looked up at him, wondering what he was on about.

"You can eat as much as you want and still answer my questions without having to talk with your mouth full," Roscoe said.

Viv continued to eat.

"The reason I asked you to lunch is that I have a media contact who might be able to help you out on your psychic murders. Martin let it slip to my supervisor that you haven't been getting anywhere, really. Lots of data points but no way to draw a line through them. I think what you might need to do here is get some publicity. Let the public know what's going on. Someone's always seen something in cases like this. Anyway, you call up the station and see if they'll do a feature on the murders. True crime television brings people right out of the woodwork. People who'd like to be on the evening news as the hometown hero who solved the case," Roscoe explained.

Viv paused and thought, wondering who in the world Roscoe could know in television.

"Regina Withers," Roscoe said.

Viv sat up straight. *The Regina Withers?*

"Yes, *The* Regina Withers," Roscoe replied. He slid a business card across the table. "Just don't call her that when you talk to her. She hates that."

Viv slid the card into a pocket. *How in the world did Roscoe know Regina Withers, the queen of true crime?* Viv wondered.

"It's a family connection," Roscoe replied.

What does that mean? Viv thought.

"That's as much as I'm saying," Roscoe said.

I bet that bastard is glad this telepathy thing only runs one way.

"Yes, it comes in handy," Roscoe replied. "Although you're not listening well. My parents were married when I was born."

"Viv!" Penny called out, walking up to their table, with Karen following close behind.

"There you are," Penny said. She looked at Roscoe and then at Viv. "What are you doing... umm..."

"Having lunch with me?" Roscoe asked. "I'm helping out on the case."

"Not double checking your work again, Karen, don't worry," Roscoe reassured her.

"I didn't say anything," Karen said.

"You didn't have to," Roscoe said.

Karen sighed. It was a taste of her own medicine, being read in a way that she couldn't read. Usually she was on the other side of things, her empathy bringing to her one-sided insights.

"I envy you, you know, Karen," Roscoe said.

Karen frowned. "Really? Why's that?"

"I'd do anything to be able to turn off my telepathy, even for a little bit," Roscoe said. "Even if it meant I had to tag along everywhere to do it like the Poky Little Puppy."

"I don't know whether to thank you or hit you," Karen said.

"I know," Roscoe replied.

"I'm not sure you'd turn it off even if you could. Even with the constant din, I think you like knowing what other people are up to," Karen said.

Roscoe smiled. "Are you sure you're not telepathic?" he said.

Karen pulled two small plastic plates and plastic forks from her hoodie.

Roscoe boggled. "That thing's massive on you, but wow... Is it also a bag of holding?"

Karen frowned and ignored him.

Viv held her ceramic cafeteria plate forward and scraped two small portions on the plastic plates. Penny and Karen began to eat.

"You know, I should scout the back alley at Ballhaus again. They make an excellent Jagerschnitzel there. The gravy reminds me of this sauce. And they always make too much," Penny said.

Viv smiled. *Never change*, she thought affectionately.

"Oh don't worry, she won't," Roscoe replied.

"What?" Penny said.

"Never mind," Roscoe said.

He summarized the plan to the detectives as they continued to dig in, sharing his suggestion that they go to the media.

"Regina Withers!" Penny exclaimed. "I'm in."

Karen frowned. She found her mind drifting back to her years on the ranch, as it always did when she spent more than a few moments around Ryan. She thought of Matt-Mike. The way he always found a way to humiliate her. To insinuate that she was different than the rest of the kids.

He always seemed to know what she was thinking, just the way Ryan Roscoe did. And had a way of using it against her.

Roscoe met her gaze, seemed to register what she was thinking, and yet he said nothing aloud.

That's strange, Karen thought. *Why is this something he doesn't want to talk about?*

Roscoe glanced at her nervously.

"Best of luck, girls," he said. "And give Regina my love." He rose with his tray.

"Regina Withers," Penny said again, flushing. "If that isn't a lifelong dream." She smiled. "I used to watch her all the time, growing up. It was a way of taking of my mind off the shitty foster homes I was in. Murder's a Hell of a palate cleanser. Dramatic. Makes for a good distraction. And Regina... she's something else. She hasn't aged a day either. She still looks just like she did when I was a kid. I don't know how she does it."

Viv felt a bubble of jealousy in her chest. "Pancake makeup, lighting, and film editing, I'd imagine," she snapped.

"Maybe," Penny said, so excited still that she didn't register the venom in Viv's tone. "Guess we'll find out."

Straight Out of Central Casting

Afflicted with Christmas morning syndrome, Penny rose early on the day they were due to see Regina Withers.

Early even for early.

The sun had yet to come up. Astronomical dawn was a ways out still, let alone its followers nautical dawn and civil dawn.

Over the years, Penny had learned to distinguish well between all three dawn stages of morning twilight, along with their crepuscular nighttime counterparts – astronomical dusk, nautical dusk, and of course civil dusk.

Astronomical dawn is the state at which the sky is no longer completely dark. It is the very beginning of the lighting of the sky, becoming possible at the moment that the sun is still 18 degrees below the horizon.

Nautical dawn follows when the sun is 12 degrees below the horizon. Its name comes from it being the point at which sailors can see the horizon while at sea. During nautical dawn, the sky becomes just light enough to tell the sky from the land and sea.

When the sun reaches 6 degrees below the horizon, civil dawn follows. At this point, visibility increases to the point at which most objects are visible and that it's possible to begin to do some things outdoors. Not everything, but some things. A bit of activity commences.

Penny didn't want to look at a clock, but a simple glance out the window let her know that the sun was more than 18 degrees below the horizon.

She rose and crept down the stairs. She briefly considered making coffee, but worrying that the smell would wake the others, she instead began to boil water on the stove. The tea kettle was old, a gift from a former friend, a fellow dumpster diver and thrifter who had found it at a yard sale. When she'd been gifted the kettle, it had been painted caution orange with many bare patches where the paint had degraded over the years.

Penny had stripped the paint from its surface and repainted it a soft baby pink. More her taste for sure.

As usually happened whenever Penny couldn't sleep or got up early, finding herself faced with darkness, she felt strangely energized.

What is it about the darkness that attracts me? Penny wondered. It was inconvenient to say the very least, her natural tendency to want to be up at night and to sleep during the day.

It had all worked out a little more gently in the days when she was a college student. She would stay up for classes, taking multiple long naps in between, and then rise to pull an all-nighter.

But her work at PsyOps had placed her mostly on the day shift with the occasional investigative foray at an indecent hour of evening or morning. Ever-so-occasional.

Far less than she'd expected going into the profession. Different than what the television she'd been riveted to as a young girl had led her to believe. In those stories, a mix of fictional dramas and true crime documentaries, detectives were often portrayed as gritty nightwalkers who beat the darkest streets.

In her favorite programs, the detectives were there taping up the scene within moments of the murders, most of which took place in the wee hours of either morning or night.

Instead, her caseload unfolded much more haphazardly. It was actually quite rare that they were the first ones to a scene. And people seemed to kill others pretty much whenever they wanted to and the time it took for anyone to discover the body (or bodies) later varied widely, with an additional lag representing how long it took law enforcement in general to arrive, let alone her specific team in the event that they did get called in.

An awful lot of these summons seemed to happen during daylight hours. She'd willed herself to be on days as a matter of survival.

Workdays could be long. Naps were elusive. So much for the good old days of college all-nighters.

At least this awakening had been a sweet one. Penny had come to woven into a web of hands and arms, with Viv and Karen both wrapped around her.

True, it had been difficult to extract herself from this matrix, but it was a nice reminder that while her unconventional relationships sometimes carried headaches, it wasn't without its benefits. Ones that were hard to understand had you never been in such a situation.

Besides, the headaches were relatively minor. They mostly came from outside the relationships in the form of misinformed questioning from people who seemed to lack any sense of normal boundaries when they were presented with a novel model of interpersonal relating.

That a person could be non-monogamous, multi-committed, and happily, stably so was a foreign concept to a lot of people she met. And she could almost see a timer counting down from the moment that they first realized she was until the point that they felt comfortable asking her invasive questions.

The questioners sometimes posed these as real "gotcha, you're pulling my leg, it can't be as you say, tell me the truth," devastatingly incisive inquires, but they were actually pretty routine to her as the questioned.

They said the same things over and over again.

Some of them were working with a real learning curve. Their view of meaningful romantic and sexual love required a man and a woman and exactly one of each. Having more than one woman involved (no men, the horror!) was confusing enough for them without adding in stack overflow problems posed by three people being involved.

She wasn't sure how many times she'd been asked some variant of "How do you have sex without a man involved?" But she knew it had been a lot. And that this question had come from a diverse set of people, from a variety of different demographics.

If she had to come up with a singular unifying factor though, something shared by everyone who asked this question, it was that the person asking it either lacked a sexual imagination, underestimated the sensual potential of hands and mouths, or both.

As well as the emotional potential, Penny thought, as her water came up to boil. She switched off the stove before the kettle could whistle.

She thought again of how encased she'd felt as she woke, nestled between Karen and Viv. How safe and how loved.

Awfully good posture for a woman named Withers, Viv noted, as the TV host glided into the room for their afternoon meeting.

It's almost like she's on rollerskates, Viv observed. It was a peculiar thing to behold, how smooth her gait, a phenomenon rendered even more strange by the fact that Withers was wearing four-inch stiletto heels. Her long legs balanced improbably on minuscule points.

Roller-stilettos? Viv thought, stifling a laugh.

The laugh sounded disrespectful to Penny, who frowned and shot Viv a warning gaze. *Don't mess this up for me*, Penny thought, wishing for the umpteenth time that she were an expressive telepath and not hounded by checked out undead hordes. It would be ever-so-convenient to be able to silently tell Viv to knock it off.

Penny quickly turned her gaze back to Regina and proceeded to beam a smile at the host that made her look an awful lot like a sunflower who's just finding the sun.

"Sorry I'm late," Regina Withers said.

She was not late of course but precisely on time. But if there were one thing Withers had learned early in her life, it was that it was good to start out at a disadvantage the first time you were meeting someone new.

This was something she could never explain to other people, nor would she, preferring to keep the knowledge to herself as a secret upper hand. It was counterintuitive, the idea that you wanted to meet new people as humbled, less than them.

But she'd found doing so to be a powerful social accelerant. It caused others to let down their guard around her. And to open up to her in a way that they wouldn't otherwise.

This was truly important as her profile had risen over the years, being able to establish rapport quickly. Or to instantly effect something of a peer relationship.

Or at least an affected peer relationship.

Because while Withers had gotten great at delivering sincere apologies and humbling herself in front of others, she hadn't felt the corresponding emotions of chagrin, humility, or even self-doubt in years.

She was simply good at broadcasting those emotions. A broadcaster, not much of a feeler. Fitting for someone in television. Hadn't she been introduced at the last awards show she attended as "inveterate broadcaster?"

"We're on your schedule, Ms. Withers," Penny said. "No worries at all." She did her best to appear composed but was fangirling so hard internally that her stomach had risen up in her chest and she felt as though she might puke.

Penny's foster siblings had been a mixed bunch over the years, but there was one in particular that she'd been close to. A foster sister who'd also been orphaned and abandoned while still a baby, just as Penny had. There was a game that Penny used to play with her foster sister where they would fantasize about who they'd have as parents if they could choose anyone in the world.

Penny's choice for dream mother was Regina Withers. There was something soft, willowy, and incredibly feminine about the TV host, and yet Withers didn't have a hint of submissive surrender. No sign of weakness anywhere about her. Withers had a readily apparent steely reserve. Withers was beautiful, warm, and intelligent – and simultaneously took no shit.

Her hair flounced and shone without a single strand ever going out of place. Withers always looked perfectly put together and yet showed no outward signs that she cared at all about her appearance, a combination that Penny had tried hard to emulate over the years.

In her fantasies, Penny imagined Withers not as a stay-at-home mom who drove her to activities and baked cookies but as a professional mom working late or away on location, leaving Penny either by herself (ideally) or in the care of a stream of competent nannies. Mommy Withers wouldn't always be around, but when she were she would be present and attentive and take a great interest in everything going on in Penny's life.

And when she was away, Penny would be able to watch her on TV.

Her foster sister had pointed out how strange it was that even in her fantasies Penny had dreamed up a mom who was part time.

Penny responded to this observation by calling her foster sister a name, starting an argument. Unable to fully grasp, let alone explain, that she would feel suffocated with a helicopter parent or even a more, normal full-time situation. That she was the kind of latchkey kid who found doors she couldn't unlock to feel like readymade prisons.

Regina Withers represented her perfect mom: Busy enough to keep from smothering her but caring enough to continually check in.

Standing before the celebrity in the flesh was surreal, particularly because the TV host had barely aged in the many years since Penny had first seen her on television.

The phone on Regina Withers' desk beeped.

"Excuse me, ma'am," the timid voice of her secretary ventured.

"Yes, Allison?" Withers replied.

"I have a Mr. Orson Eck on the line for you, ma'am."

"Tell Mr. Eck I'll call him back," Withers said. "I'm in a very important meeting."

"Yes, ma'am." The phone beeped again.

Penny beamed at those words. Regina Withers – *The* Regina Withers – thought it was important to meet with her? (And yeah, okay, with Viv and Karen, too. Whatever.)

Wow!

Viv, however, wasn't flattered. "What are you doing talking to the Ecks?" she asked.

"I didn't know that was against the law, detective," Withers countered, smirking.

"Yeah, Viv. You don't have to be rude," Penny said.

"No, no, it's fine," Withers replied. "He's one of the talent, you see."

"Talent?" Viv said.

"He's a cast member. On *To Heck with the Ecks*," Regina said.

"I've heard of it," Penny said. She almost added on (truthfully), "But Viv won't let me watch it because she says it's trash." But she caught herself just in time, feeling that Viv was in bad enough of a mood already. No need to make it worse.

"What does that have to do with you?" Viv asked pointedly.

Regina Withers sighed. "I take it you're not a fan."

"I don't watch it, no," Viv said. "I don't watch reality TV at all if I can help it." To Viv's thinking, *To Heck with the Ecks* was just another permutation of an idiotic trend, a camera crew following around the rich and famous and then desperately splicing together scenes in a vain attempt to make some kind of vaguely watchable programming.

Viv wasn't about to admit it to Penny – lest she be called a hypocrite – but Viv had seen exactly one episode of *To Heck with the Ecks* while out visiting her mother, who was a raging fan of the show, and all reality TV for that matter. The Ecks were incorrigible playboys. Filthy pigs about it, really. The episode she'd seen had them trying to lure unsuspecting drunk women back to their mansion and get them to strip down in the hot tub before asking them to leave in the meanest way possible.

No sex required. Just debasement and humiliation. Although they did have their way with some of them before insulting them and kicking them out.

The Eck boys were engaged in a competition. Both scored the women on a number of different factors that made them worth more points: Appearance, fame, wealth, intelligence. She forgot what else.

The whole thing had made her sick. A couple of adolescent-acting boys treating women like hunting trophies.

Viv's mother, however, had laughed heartily at the women's humiliation. "Stupid tarts," she'd said, chilling Viv's blood.

Like you're any better than them, Viv had thought but knew better to say.

"Ah, not a viewer? Well, that's okay. Can't have everyone watching, can we?" Withers said. "I'm the executive producer."

Viv's face fell. She didn't have to say *how could you?* aloud. Her expression did all the work for her.

"Look," Withers said, reading the message loud and clear. "I know it isn't high art or anything. But it pays the bills. And it keeps me in the loop." She paused. "It's not fair, but there seems to be a hidden expiration date to be on television as a woman. One must have backup plans."

"You don't look a day over…" Penny began. Then she stopped, not wanting to venture what number to say, not knowing what age it would please her idol to be mistaken for. Especially since she'd ventured such guesses in the past with others and had been excoriated for saying one too high, or in some cases so absurdly low that they recognized the bald flattery and lashed out for *that*.

Withers cocked her head as people always did when you started a sentence this way, waiting for the number.

Penny felt like an untrained carnival barker taking a stab at a mark. It was an awful feeling, so she changed course.

"I mean, you look the same as when I first saw you on television," Penny replied.

Withers brightened. "And when was that, dear?"

"When I was a girl," Penny said. "In the 90s."

Withers's face fell. "Oh dear, you are young. Do you even remember when the first precogs were announced?"

Penny shook her head vigorously. "And I remember your coverage, your interviews. You were phenomenal."

The host beamed. "Thank you. That seems like a lifetime ago. In some ways, it was."

"What do you mean by that?" Viv asked.

"When you get to be my age, you'll understand," Withers replied. "When you start to feel like you're going off. Overripe. Like a fruit left for too many days on the counter and getting all sunken in and spotty."

"Oh stop that," Penny said. "You look fantastic."

"That's the thing," Withers replied. "It's all find-and-replace. You substitute new parts of you for the bits that are falling apart. After a while, you stop and take stock and wonder if there's any of the old you left, or if all rotted off somewhere along the way."

"I know what you mean actually," Viv replied. "My mother's gone through the same thing. She's heavily refurbished."

"Thank you," Withers said. "It's rare that young people understand. But it would seem that you're very observant. I bet you make a lot of people nervous."

Viv nodded. "I think that's half of why I have my job. The photographic memory is nice, sure, but that's nothing a good video camera couldn't do."

"Well, video cameras make people nervous, too," Withers replied. "You should see how people act when you turn up with a camera crew. They're ready to change their entire lives, completely remodel themselves, for a second on the air."

"Or completely remodel themselves for an entire career on the air," Viv countered pointedly.

"Viv," Penny said. "That was uncalled for."

Withers chuckled in a stunned, wounded way. "No, it's alright," she said. "Anyone afraid of the truth has no business being in journalism."

Viv smiled. Maybe she'd misjudged this woman. Lumped her in unfairly with all the vain fame-obsessed talking heads that seemed to clog up the celebrity world. Maybe there was some substance after all under the layers of shiny veneer. Withers was doing a good job at least of offering up real talk to her. Whether or not that was an act, Viv reflected, remained to be seen.

But she could talk a different talk than Viv had expected going in. And that alone was something.

"Anyway," Withers continued. "I'm tired of the find-and-replace game. Everyone constantly scrutinizing my face, my weight, my clothes. It'd be great to eat what I want and wear what I want. I'd like to age gracefully, fade into off-screen obscurity but still be involved somehow. That's where producing comes in. True, I have to break in with reality TV tripe, but everyone has to start somewhere, right? And the ratings on this program are great. It'll be easy to leverage into another show after a few seasons."

"Even if it's garbage?" Viv asked.

"People like what they like," Withers replied. "Who am I to tell them what they should like? Who died and made me the keeper of taste?"

"Well, I'm glad you're still on the air," Penny said, desperate to change the topic, to steer the conversation away from potential conflict, "After all, we're here to ask for your help publicizing a case of ours."

"Yes," Withers said. "Mr. Ryan told me about your situation. I'd be happy to help."

"How do you know Roscoe anyway?" Viv asked.

"Does it matter?" Withers asked.

Viv didn't have a good answer for that. It mattered to her, sure, but not for professional reasons. Not for reasons she was eager to admit. "Honestly, I'm just curious," Viv admitted, feeling a bit small.

"I'd be careful with that curiosity of yours," Withers answered. "You're smart women. How do you think Roscoe affords those suits of his on a psychic detective's salary? He has powerful friends. We have some of the same. That's about all I'm willing to say about that."

"Is that a threat?" Viv asked.

Regina Withers ignored the question and pulled out a notebook. "Okay, so I think we could add your case to the episode we're filming three days from now as an Unsolved segment. There's a yawner of a child abduction case that's been played to death that would be fine to bump. I'll check with the director, but he owes me several favors, so I think we'll be fine."

Withers snapped the notebook shut with unnecessary force. She smiled sweetly as if to punctuate the act.

"Now then," Withers said, swiveling her body towards Penny and removing Viv from her line of sight. "Why don't you tell me all about the case?"

Penny sprung to life, narrating what they had learned so far. Withers made copious notes. Viv tried to interject a few times to add in details, but it was though neither of them heard her.

Karen sat mutely and watched, only speaking up a few times to echo the corrections Viv introduced. When Karen spoke, Regina recorded it dutifully.

Great, Viv thought, *are we in middle school?*

"Perfect," Withers said. "I think we have it."

"When will the episode air?" Karen asked.

"Next Thursday," Withers replied. "Unless it gets tied up in editing and we have to air a rerun. But the editor owes me several favors."

"Who doesn't owe you a favor?" Viv asked.

"Thank you for coming," Regina Withers said. "And now if you'll excuse me, I have to return a phone call."

"What a loon," Viv said, after they were safely in the car.

"I've always really liked loons," Penny said.

"They had them out at the lakes in Maine where I grew up. You could hear them at night all the time when I was a kid," Karen replied.

"That had to be a trip," Penny said. "Like the dead having a yodeling concert."

"I don't think it'd bother you much," Karen replied. "Aren't you used to that by now? Don't the dead sing?"

"You'd be surprised," Penny replied.

"Anyway, when you grow up hearing loons, you aren't bothered by them. There's something reassuring about them then. They sound less haunted and more sad. I understood that sadness. Made me feel less alone to have it reflected back at me," Karen said.

Viv frowned. They had erected one of their conversational walls again. One that she didn't really feel like she could be part of. Her temples began to pulse. She closed her eyes and leaned her head against the car window. It was a long drive home from the studio and too sunny today. Better to try to nap than risk a migraine, especially with it having rained the day before.

Sunlight and rain had a way of conspiring, blinding her first, and then chucking needles into her brain. No thank you.

Penny drove while she and Karen talked, with Karen leaning forward over the center console so Penny could hear her better from the backseat.

Karen sometimes wondered why Viv didn't just sit in the back on long car rides, especially when she didn't feel well, but the one time Karen had dared to ask Viv had given her a glare that could fry ants so she had let the matter drop.

Karen knew that Viv worried more about being surpassed or replaced by her – or by anyone – than she let on. Like a lot of people who beamed out easy confidence, at the core Viv was rather insecure and unconvinced of her own value.

Karen had sensed this in the times when she and Viv were alone together but still hadn't come up with a meaningful way to put that knowledge into practice.

When others found out that she was in a relationship with not one but two other intuitives, they'd often say things like, "Boy, I wish my boyfriend and I were both psychic. That'd fix a lot of problems in our relationship."

Karen would nod politely, knowing they meant well, and preferring this harmless comment to other common ones she liked a lot less. But she knew the truth of it: Knowing how your partner felt was only the start of knowing how to approach them. Or what to do for them.

There were many times when someone you cared about felt something they weren't ready to admit to themselves. And while she could theoretically pull the empath card, it never went well when she did. People didn't like to be told they were feeling a way that they didn't want to feel and didn't want to admit to anyone else.

She'd heard a million times that honesty was always the best policy and that nothing couldn't be fixed by open honest communication. Solid advice in some scenarios, but in others it just wasn't helpful. Sometimes things were imbalanced, precarious, fragile. Sometimes you needed a little strategy to navigate it all.

And while having a good view of what was actually going on was helpful, it was far from everything she needed to set things right.

Sometimes she wondered if her empathic powers hadn't been a hindrance, a barrier to naturally developing those skills. Maybe if she didn't have such a clear view of what everyone was feeling, she would have been forced to learn more complicated interpersonal strategies. Methods that would be a Hell of a lot more effective than sitting paralyzed by the complexity of the feelings of everyone around her.

Besides, there was another large downside to dating another intuitive that would never occur to normals. The shame.

Karen had spent a lot of time wondering if she was a broken doll. Sometimes she wondered if all three of them were broken dolls. Or bits and pieces of broken dolls, more like. Each of them were strong in the ways others were not, but all of these strengths came with weaknesses.

Were they snapped all together, those bits and pieces, to make a powerful whole?

And if so, how strong *were* those connections?

The hardest part of being with another intuitive, another psychic, was sharing your lover with their own self-loathing. It didn't matter if you accepted it within yourself; if they hadn't gone there in their own mind, then all bets were off.

It was a lot like dating a person who hated themselves because they were overweight. All was fine and good so long as they hadn't internalized those societal messages about unworthiness. But if they had, good luck. You'd spend years being pushed to the edge of their psyche. They'd spend lots of energy fighting what they were and feeling like they didn't deserve to fully enjoy their life until they became something else entirely.

Always postponing their life until they could get a better handle on it.

Viv kept on postponing vacations until she could better control her powers, like someone else might say they wouldn't go to Hawaii until they fit into their old bikini. She'd say something about wanting to save up a little more money, just in case the roof on the house needed repairs. Or the furnace broke.

But Karen knew what was really going on, could sense it when it was just the two of them. Viv worried about getting swallowed up in her visions and never emerging.

Until the day that fear went away, Viv wouldn't relax. Couldn't enjoy herself.

Sometimes Karen felt like someday was never going to come.

It had been a great relief to Viv when they first got together that Penny was an orphan. Not that Viv was exactly eager to admit that aloud.

It sounded callous. After all, who would wish upon their lover a life without parents?

And yet... Viv had found dating quite difficult before she met Penny. It wasn't anything she'd been warned about, but people who were close to their parents often had a hard time accepting other people who weren't. Viv had thought it was a fluke the first time a promising romantic prospect had abruptly cut things off when Viv had admitted she wasn't terribly close to her mother.

"Family's important to me," her lover had said.

"I can respect that," Viv said, "even if my life's a little different."

"Well I can't respect that," her lover had replied.

It was weird enough when it happened that first time.

And then it happened again.

Viv had begun to wonder if she should start lying about it. She could start by lying by omission and then if push ever came to shove, maybe she could hire an actress to play her mother.

Hell, she could hire someone to play her father, too. That would be something, wouldn't it? Viv wasn't even sure who her father *was*, but she could pick someone else to play him in front of prospective suitors.

But then she'd met Penny and fallen in love with an orphan. While Viv couldn't begin to understand what that was like – let alone what it must have been like to grow up in foster care – Penny didn't need her to. Penny looked to Viv primarily for what Viv looked for in her: Basic acceptance of the fact that neither of them fit into the Hallmark trope of smiling mother-daughter pair. That neither of them could earnestly exclaim, "My mother is my best friend in the world!"

And when Karen had shown up with a mother who'd abandoned their family and a tense relationship with her own father (or "the cult leader," as Karen usually called him), she'd fit right into their Judgement-Free Zone.

All three of them understood how easy it was for people to mistake the rejection found in dysfunctional parental dynamics with the normal ebb and flow of adolescent disembedding, the fount of most teen rebellion, a developmental stage in which adolescents create emotional distance from their parents in order to better understand their emerging self.

It was easy for some to confuse a teen's "ew, Mom, I'm not anything like my mom," with Viv's need to create distance from someone who had repeatedly harmed her and others around her.

As a result, people often mistook her state of semi-estrangement as a sign that Viv was immature. That she'd never developed beyond a teenage level of understanding her mother. Because of this, they were quick to suggest that she repair that connection. That she throw herself into a full-fledged mother-daughter bonding.

They didn't realize how strenuous and difficult the little contact Viv had with her mother was.

It was a sore spot, even now.

That's why when Penny and Karen came to Viv asking about interviewing her mother that Viv nearly tore their heads off.

"Jesus, what's wrong with you?!" Viv said.

Penny blinked. She'd asked as gently as she could. Had taken great pains to frame the question as delicately as she could, because they had to make a decision on how they were going to conduct the interview, and yet Viv had still exploded at her.

Viv caught herself. "Oh geez, I'm sorry."

"It's okay, Viv," Karen said. "We all have something we're a little crazy about."

Penny nodded. "I know I do. More than one thing, actually, if I'm being completely honest."

"At least yours makes sense," Karen said.

It was meant as a comfort, but Viv found herself mentally asking, *Does it though?*

"It does," Penny said.

Viv noted mentally that Penny would probably be pleased to know she'd answered her unspoken doubt. Penny was always saying she wished she were a telepath, after all.

"Are you sure you're not a telepath?" Viv said aloud.

Penny blushed.

Viv sighed. "So the options again are that we can do it as a team. Or I can let you two do it without me. Or we can outsource it to another team, right?"

Penny nodded. "Right."

"Or anything else you can think of," Karen added.

Viv frowned. She brought up the image mentally of her mother's face, largely unchanged since childhood. Her mother's voice. She visualized the bodies of the victims they'd found. A series of other faces flashed before her eyes, witnesses they'd interviewed.

It was only a few moments, but to Viv, caught in the barrage of mental images, it felt like an eternity.

"You two do it," Viv said.

"Okay," Penny said. "You can count on us."

"Are you sure?" Karen asked.

"Completely sure," Viv said. "Now shut up before I change my mind."

Viv gathered her things. "I'm going for a long drive," she told them. "Make sure it's done before I get back."

Karen could feel the nerves raying off Penny with an intensity she was not at all used to feeling.

Not in her own emotional life and certainly not from Penny.

"I can make the call you know," Karen offered. "If you need me to."

A jolt of irritation from Penny. Aloud, Penny said, "It's fine. I'm fine." She frowned. "Oh why bother. You see right through me."

"It's not exactly seeing, but yes," Karen replied.

"Not exactly seeing? Didn't you say once that reading people's emotions was like watching a card game? One where you were positioned to see the entire table," Penny said.

Karen nodded. "A bit. And yes, I did say it." She paused and thought. "That's more how I explain it to other people. It really depends on the emotions and feelings. And how close I am to people. Sometimes, feeling is less like watching cards being played and more like I'm *in* the cards as they're being dealt."

"Really?" Penny asked.

Karen frowned. "Well, sort of. Not really."

Penny frowned back.

"I really wish I could explain it better," Karen said.

"Me too," Penny replied.

Karen thought for a second. "Have you ever been so choked up you couldn't speak?" Karen asked.

Penny nodded. "Of course. Happened all the time when I was young." She smiled, remembering. "I was a little crybaby until middle school."

"You?" Karen asked.

"Yeah, believe it or not. I had to learn the brave face later. When I was a little girl, I was an absolute mess. Messy, believe it or not. A total klutz, too. I was always skinning my knees," Penny said.

"Wow. Little Penny Dreadful with both knees skinned and tears streaming down her face. Must have been a sight," Karen said.

Penny shrugged.

"Well, take that choked up feeling, where you're so overwhelmed with emotions, and make it last for *years*," Karen said.

Penny furrowed her brow. "I'm not sure I can imagine that actually. Well, I can... but just imagining it makes me want it to end. And that's just as a thought experiment."

"There's something about psychic empathy that steals your words," Karen explained. "The act requires you to be passive, open, receptive. It comes from a part of me where there aren't words. A part of me that actively blocks out words. A part of me that words would interfere with. And when I go back into those experiences and try to explain them in hindsight, I find the words resisting me again. Even the vague memories of the emotions are so intense, I get overwhelmed. Choked up."

"It's like you're explaining a dream you only half remember?" Penny offered.

"Exactly like that," Karen replied.

"Maybe you're not as bad at explaining things as you think you are," Penny said.

Karen smiled.

"Probably for the best anyway, that you're not terrible at explaining, after all. Wouldn't want to encroach on Amarynth's territory. Poor thing needs something to be the queen of," Penny joked.

Penny's nerves fell away in that moment, with an empathic crash like a beaded curtain hitting the floor of Karen's mind. Percussively resolute.

Penny picked up the receiver and dialed the number to the Lee Residence.

Penny had been prepared to tangle with Tender, but the servant who answered the call put Viv's sister Love on the line instead. "What do you want?" Love said curtly.

"Hi Love, it's Penny. I'd like to speak with Tender, if I could," Penny said.

"And why exactly would you want to do that?" Love asked.

"Do I need a reason?" Penny challenged her.

"This is the first time you've ever called our house. I'd say you need a reason," Love countered.

"I need to ask Tender some questions about her schedule," Penny replied.

"Well, you can ask me if that's the case," Love replied. "Her day planner's right here on the desk. No need to bother Mom."

"I'd rather talk to her though," Penny said.

"You can't," Love said.

"Why's that?" said Penny.

"She's out," Love replied.

"Where?" Penny asked.

"With a friend," Love replied.

"A gentleman?" Penny asked.

"What does it matter?" Love asked. "Mom's popular. She's not here... so if you'll excuse me.."

"Know when she'll be back?" Penny asked.

"Tomorrow morning, I believe. She prepped like she wasn't going to sleep here. Packed a bag," Love replied. She intoned this information sounding half-bored. It was clear to Penny that she'd had a lifetime of practice watching her mother disappear to spend the evening with a "friend." Explaining it to others who wondered about her mother's sudden exits.

It squared well with stories Viv had told Penny, especially on nights Viv had a little too much wine and her usual armor surrounding her mom fell off with a clang.

"Alright, well could you do me a favor?" Penny asked.

"Another? I've done at least... three for you already on this call," Love said.

Penny wasn't confident in Love's math but let it slide. "If you could grab that planner and let me know what your mom was doing two Thursdays ago in the afternoon, that would be great."

"Fine," Love conceded.

Penny heard her place the receiver down on a hard surface. Or at least that's what she hoped were happening. She wasn't sure at first whether Love had hung up on her. But then, she heard Love pick the receiver back up and sigh copiously, communicating just how put-out she was being asked to do something so arduous.

Love asked a few confirming questions about which Thursday precisely Penny was asking about. And a few more about what constituted "afternoon" in Penny's estimation.

Finally, when she had clarity, Love exclaimed, "Oh, that's an easy one. Mom was at the hairdresser then. She spent three hours there. Getting her hair dyed and styled."

"What was the name of the salon?" Penny asked.

"Atria," Love replied. "She sees Evelyn there. A total wizard with color." A beat. "Oh no," Love said.

"What?" Penny said.

"Forget that I told you she dyes her hair. Mother would hate that," Love replied.

"Well, of course she does. At her age, it would be unnatural to not have any grey or white hairs," Penny said.

"At her age?" Love said. She snorted. "I'm glad I spoke with you and not her. What a disaster you are. So callous. Uncouth."

"Well, Love, I know how old Viv is, and I can do basic math," Penny replied.

"Oh, shut up," Love replied. "You're so nasty. Viv deserves you."

A slamming noise and then a dial tone.

Love had clearly had enough of Penny's call.

"Well, it would seem Tender has an alibi," Penny replied. "She was getting her hairs did," she said, mimicking Tender and Love's syrupy accent.

Karen giggled.

If it hadn't been for Penny, the team might have never thought to check back in on Regina Withers and the true crime broadcast of their case to date.

But Penny had marked the show time in giant fluorescent letters on their calendar. So giant that Karen almost missed her PsyOps physical that morning, obscured as it was by "REGINA WITHERS SHOW." Thankfully, Martin had made a note, too, and so her Green Star status was safe on medical grounds. For another year anyway.

Penny served a suspiciously nice dinner that evening. "Do I want to know how many dumpsters this one took?" Viv asked.

"Enough of that. It's nothing you need to worry about," Penny said. "Just eat. It's a special occasion."

And eat they did. They feasted as Viv could not remember feasting… ever? For years anyway.

At five to seven, Penny quickly cleared the table and swept all the plates into the sink. She ushered both of her partners to their couch and turned on their old television, already tuned to the appropriate channel.

Viv marveled at this. "Wait a second," she said. "We don't get cable."

"Shush," Penny said. "There are ways. Especially if you only need it for one night. I bartered well for this."

The program fired up.

"Doesn't she look incredible?" Penny exclaimed, as Regina Withers came onscreen.

"Ssssh," Karen said. "If you wanted to talk, you should have put on close captioning."

Viv thought idly that she knew how to do that but decided quickly that it was probably better if she left things the way they were. Penny's fangirling was enough to deal with in short bursts during commercial breaks. It might be unbearable if left unabated, aided by close captioning.

So the three women sat mostly in silence during the program, although Penny's silence still managed to be quite excited and enthusiastic. Karen had to avoid looking at Penny directly or risk laughing. Viv also had to avoid eye contact so that she wouldn't audibly scoff.

The cases Withers commented on at the beginning of the program were older cold cases, ones that they were all quite familiar with. At this point, they were practically historical.

Still, Withers managed to breathe new life into them as she interviewed witnesses that had not before been on the record.

"And you're sure that it was a navy blue Ford pickup," Withers pressed an older gentleman who looked disconcertingly pale, to a degree that stretched credulity. He looked as though all the color had been adjusted out of him by moving tinting knobs at least a few clicks too far. If Withers hadn't also been on the screen, Viv would have thought there was something wrong with the television.

"No, ma'am, I'm not sure of anything," the old man replied.

"Then why did you tell the detectives that?" asked Withers.

"You ever had a team of detectives backing you into a corner? Screaming into your face? I would have told them I was the Queen of England."

"A mistake that no one would make," Withers commented.

The old man on the screen winced. Viv stifled a laugh.

Damn, she thought, irritated that she was enjoying the program. *She's so good I can't help myself.*

Withers shuffled through a number of other cases. They seemed to get progressively more obscure and more recent as the program went on.

"I bet she'll do ours next," Penny said.

But the last featured case wasn't theirs. It was instead an unsolved child abduction case.

As the credits rolled, Penny frowned.

"They didn't get to us," Karen said, stating the obvious.

Penny's eyes began to well with tears.

"Penny, I bet she just forgot," Viv said, hating to see Penny upset.

"You don't believe that," Penny said. "You never liked her."

Viv didn't have a good answer for that.

"I bet Viv's right," Karen offered.

"Thanks, Karen. Tell you what, Penny... tomorrow we'll call Regina Withers, we'll find out what happened. It was probably just a stupid mistake," Viv said.

Penny brightened. "Really?" she said.

"Really," Viv and Karen said in unison.

"Jinx," Karen said.

"Oh stop, nobody does that anymore," Viv replied.

"I do. You're jinxed. You're not supposed to talk!" Karen protested.

Penny smiled. "I don't know what I'd do without you."

"I see," Viv said the next morning, as she listened to the explanation offered by Regina Withers's secretary. "I figured it was something like that."

Penny studied Viv's face carefully. The words coming out of Viv's mouth sounded okay and should have been comforting, but Viv's facial expression didn't quite match.

"Coming from where?" Viv said.

A pause.

"Well, surely you can tell me generalities at least. Does it involve a sponsor? A business partner? A relative?"

Another much longer pause.

"Sure," Viv replied. "I understand. Thank you for your honesty."

"Well?" Karen said, as soon as Viv had hung up the phone.

"So I spoke with her secretary. She told me that they couldn't run the story," Viv said. "Had to pull it last minute."

Penny frowned. "Did she give you any reason why?"

"Yes," Viv said. "She said there was a conflict of interest with her and the case. That she realized once she did a followup background check that she couldn't ethically run it."

"Did she say what the conflict was?" Karen asked.

Viv shook her head no. "Not even in general terms."

"Damn it," Penny said.

"Maybe it's for the best," Viv said.

Penny frowned. "How do you figure that?"

"It's risky opening a case up to the public. Sure, you get a lot of leads, but most of them turn out to be garbage. Is it possible we would have gotten some valuable intel? Sure. But would we have been able to sort through all the garbage to find it? Who knows," Viv said.

Penny agreed with Viv about this but couldn't bring herself to agree aloud. She was bent in knots, feeling quite disappointed in her hero but didn't want to say that aloud either.

It sounded so unprofessional. Weak, even. That she could be so swayed by a virtual stranger. So disappointed in her actions.

But it was the truth.

"And besides," Viv continued. "This conflict of interest gives us information. It tells us that Regina Withers is close to this. The question is: How? And why?"

Penny scowled. "The Queen of True Crime is not prancing around town murdering psychics."

"Well, no," Viv said. "But someone she's connected to is involved somehow."

"I guess," Karen said. "But we don't have a lot to go on. We don't even know where the conflict is."

That would be remedied the following morning when Viv brought in the mail.

In with the normal smattering of advertising and coupon circulars was a very official-looking envelope.

From the law offices of Shane & Wiley.

Viv opened it quickly and laughed.

"What?" Penny asked.

"It's a cease and desist letter from the Eck Family," Viv said. "Specifically cites the unaired television segment."

"Woah," Karen said.

"If they don't have anything to do with these murders, then why the heck do they care?" Penny asked.

"Exactly," Viv said.

Move-In Ready

It doesn't rain often in Skinner, but the storms have a violent temper. When it comes to storms, the Psychic City is very much like anywhere else in the Psychic State. It doesn't rain without torrential downpour and flash flooding. Baseball-sized hail is common.

As is the occasional tornado.

And yet people still live here, Penny thought, staring at a rain-soaked window in what seemed to be a rather low-budget realty office, given the franchise's purported stellar sales record.

Outside the office, thunder boomed and crashed unpredictably, requiring parts of the conversation to be repeated.

I'm glad Viv found some covered parking, Penny thought, as she heard pellet-sized hail beginning to hit the ground and anything else between the sky and the ground outside.

The first time she'd heard hail, when she'd first moved to the area for college, Penny thought it sounded like a giant dropping a bag of marbles. And then another. And then another.

Viv had laughed at her when Penny told her about this later, during the first hailstorm after they'd met. "No one has that many marbles," she'd replied. "Not even a giant emporium."

It was well known that the first precogs were exclusively situated up and down Tornado Alley with the highest concentration, the epicenter of psychic activity, clearly centered around one of the most tornado-prone areas in the world.

Including the area that would eventually become the Psychic State.

Some had wondered aloud if the energy from the storms was somehow involved. Perhaps they had charged people up with psychic powers, so to speak.

This explanation was dismissed and people who entertained it aloud were labeled conspiracy theorists and laughed at. But during particularly violent storms, Penny found herself wondering if there weren't some truth to it. Perhaps turbulent weather churned out turbulent people. People who were just as unpredictable.

People like her.

"Wonder if we'll have another tornado on our hands this time around," the realtor said.

This storm brought the second tornado watch in a fortnight. The first advisory had been the day of the murder. The citizens of Skinner were used to tornado watches, with most of them developing into nothing more than a few violent gusts of wind in a nasty downpour. Like the Boy who Cried Wolf, the weather reports were normally overly dramatic.

But not this past storm. In this case, the wolf showed up. A tornado emerged just in time for the next murder to take place. The building where the body had been found was right in its path and had been torn to shreds. It was now structurally unsound, a haphazard pile of building materials that bore little resemblance to the large home that had stood just moments before the tornado smashed into it. No one was going to live there. Not much to look at even anymore. The structure caved upon itself miserably, splinters of beams sticking out at unnatural angles.

It looked like a bomb had gone off.

"EF3, I hear. Big fella with 140 mph winds," the realtor said. "Thankfully, there were no other casualties, at least not that the news is reporting."

"Well, and Ms. Harris wasn't even a casualty," Viv corrected him.

"Hard to tell that, isn't it?"

Viv shook her head no. "Going by stomach contents, it's clear that time of death was well before the storm. And her pattern of injuries isn't at all consistent with being killed in the storm."

"Ah," the realtor said.

"I imagine you get close to the agents who work with you," Viv said.

The realtor nodded. "We're a work family. Some of it's tied to business. We give each other referrals, match buyers with sellers. Recommend contractors. That kind of thing. But it's more than that. I went to Ms. Harris's son's wedding just last month. You spend enough time with people, they really do become like family. It's not an expression after a while. I'm sure you three must understand that, working so closely together."

Penny stifled a giggle. He clearly didn't know they were an actual family, not a work one. A common misconception, one she attributed to a combination of the professional distance they affected with one another while working as well as certain people's tendencies not to see romantic love between women unless it were thrust in their faces in the most explicit terms. That good old "gals being pals" illusion again.

This often came in handy. It at least prevented their unconventional relationship structure from being a distraction to witnesses.

"Can you think of anyone who would have wanted to kill her?"

"I know it's insensitive to go this route," the realtor continued, "but certainly not me."

"We weren't saying—" Karen began.

Penny shushed her. *Let the man speak*, Penny thought and tried to communicate with a sharp glare at Karen. They could see what came out of his mouth and then mop up any lack of allegation later if it proved necessary.

Penny wished again that she were an expressive telepath. It would come in so handy. Karen didn't look like she understood the gaze and instead simply looked rather sad.

"Her death has created quite a headache for me at the office, you see," the realtor explained.

"A headache?" Viv said. "How?"

"That house she was found in? The one the tornado crashed into? The sale on it closed *three days* before the storm. The new owners were about to move in. The sale was finalized, everything was set. Now they're calling me day and night insisting that they want to nullify the transfer. That's not how real estate works. This isn't something the buyer could have foreseen and failed to disclose," the realtor said.

"It isn't?" Viv asked.

"How could she?" the realtor said.

"Well, wasn't Ms. Harris a precog?" Viv said.

"So?" the realtor said.

"Isn't it possible that she could have seen the tornado coming?" Viv asked.

The realtor frowned. "I'm disappointed in you. You work for PsyOps, so you're tueys yourselves, aren't you?"

Viv nodded.

"Then you must know that precognition isn't exact. Even if Ms. Harris *had* gotten a premonition, she wouldn't have known if she could trust it or not. Particularly if it affected her directly, which this sale most certainly did, as the psychic home inspector."

"Do you know the other victim?" Viv asked.

"Other victim?" the realtor asked.

Oh dear, Viv thought, not sure if she should proceed.

"Are you telling me another one of my agents got caught up in this? I haven't had time to check in with everyone. Perhaps I should," the realtor said.

"When I say victim, I'm not talking about another murder," Viv said. "But another one of your agents was found wandering the streets. He'd forgotten who he was. Temporary amnesia. They were able to identify him by the contents of his wallet."

Viv tactfully left out the rest of the story. That this roving agent seemed quite mad. Had even argued with the police officers who picked him up when confronted about his identity. Had insisted he was everyone and nobody. And that the name they kept saying wasn't his.

He was currently undergoing psychiatric evaluation.

"Ah," the agent said. "It's probably odd to you that I didn't know that."

Viv shrugged. "You see enough in our line of work to find very few things odd," she offered.

"My agents work rather independently. If business is slow or if it's running smoothly and they don't need any assistance, it can be weeks sometimes before I have to check in with someone," the agent explained.

That's odd, Penny thought. N*ot exactly the picture of a happy little work family you painted a few minutes ago. Sounds more like ships passing in the night.*

"So you say this house just sold?" Viv asked.

The agent nodded.

"Who were the sellers?" she asked.

"Just a moment," he said. He looked up the information on his computer.

The lights above them flickered as he worked.

"Don't worry," he said. "I have good surge protection. And the building has a backup generator."

"Handy," Viv said.

"Ah yes, here it is," the agent said. The printer began to work. It spat out a few sheets of paper. He walked over, picked them up, and handed them to Viv.

"There are a lot of names on here," Viv said. "And percentages."

"The home was crowdfunded," the realtor said.

"Crowdfunded?" Viv asked.

The relator nodded. "A bunch of individuals all invest a small amount through a company that manages the property until it's sold. Everyone on this list got a share of the sale. Actually, give that back to me," he said.

Viv returned the paper to him.

He carefully wrote on the back of one of the sheets of paper. "This is the investment firm who oversaw the crowdfunding. I doubt you'll need it but just to be clear."

"Thank you," Viv said. "We'll be in touch if we have any more questions."

In theory, a licensed realtor with psychic powers should have been illegal.

It was illegal, for example, for an intuitive to practice law or work as an investment banker. The government had decided that there was too much risk involved, that the involvement of psychic powers threatened to destabilize the legal system and economy.

But the real estate industry, while being heavily involved in both money matters and the law, had lobbied hard for the right to employ psychics.

They argued that the inclusion of precogs would actually be a profoundly *stabilizing* force for the housing market. That their ability to look beyond the current moment and make projections could protect both buyer and seller from fluctuations that would normally elude normal realtors.

With the help of deep pockets and political leverage, the real estate industry had won that fight.

And it was now virtually unheard of to be running an agency without a few intuitives working as negotiators. They were as common as notaries during the closing process.

True, it set back closing dates an average of an additional two days, but nobody wanted to take the risk anymore of not consulting a precog.

Most precogs found steady work in real estate by performing an additional psychic inspection that typically followed the normal home inspection of the house's basic structure. One that focused not on the state of the property as is but the state of the property that could be in days, weeks, or years.

"You know," Penny said as she turned the key in the ignition, "If the perp's goal was to get lost in the clutter, I'd say they did a damn good job."

"You can say that again," Viv said.

"You know, if the perp's goal –" Karen began.

Viv shot a warning glance her way.

"Okay, okay," Karen said.

"That sort of joke hasn't been funny since Peewee Herman," Viv said, "and you know it."

"It wasn't funny then," Penny added.

"Well, I wouldn't go that far," Viv said.

"Anyway," Penny continued, "I have a feeling we're going to hit the same roadblock as we did chasing down Heather's client list. Dozens of interviews. Lots of leads, many promising, but nothing that really seems *more* promising than the others."

"Unfortunately," Viv agreed.

"Well, maybe we need a different approach then," Karen said.

"And that would be?" said Penny.

"Stop looking at little things and focus on something big," Karen said.

"Easy to say," Viv said. "But that would suppose there's something big that we're looking past."

"Which is always a possibility," Penny said.

"True," Viv replied. "But if we're looking past it at the beginning, what's to say that we don't *keep* looking past it. Considering it too obvious, too atmospheric to investigate."

"Or maybe," Karen said, "It's bias we're looking past."

"What do you mean by that?" Viv asked.

"Maybe we're shying away from certain solutions because they seem too easy. We keep looking for some minor detail, some small person hidden in the mix. What if... the killer is exactly who a lay person would think they are?" Karen said.

"What if the butler actually did do it?" Penny asked.

"Exactly!" Karen said.

"Or what if the husband really did kill his wife?" Viv asked.

"Yes," Karen said.

"Or what if a powerful family really was going around murdering people in order to hide some kind of terrible secret?" Penny asked.

"That's what I've been thinking, too," Karen said. "There are too many dots to connect that involve the Ecks. They seem threatened whenever we get close. It can't be a coincidence."

"I don't know. Rich people are easily threatened, period. I've found them to be rather paranoid. Especially when it comes to anything that can affect their reputation," Viv said. "I'd say a murder investigation certainly qualifies."

"Okay," Karen said. "Paranoid enough to be scared by a normal investigation. That's fair. But does that mean that they're also paranoid enough to kill?"

"Possibly," Viv said. "But if that's the case, then why haven't they come after any of us?"

Penny thought suddenly of the odd visit from Change Patterson. "There was that one... thing that showed up in the kitchen, don't you remember? Pretending to be a spirit, dropped a business card that said he was a shapeshifter. I don't know if it qualifies as an actual threat, but I felt threatened at the time."

"I love you, honey, but that's not saying much," Viv said.

Penny glared at her.

"He could have been sent by the Ecks though," Karen offered. "Like an errand boy."

Penny thought about that for a moment. True, Kip had said he was hired help, linked to the Families. But he was linked with the Macombers, not the Ecks. The two families were sworn enemies, so why would the Ecks send a Macomber stooge to scare them off?

No, it didn't make sense.

She considered bringing this up as an objection but stopped herself, since the intel came from Kip, and Kip was a part of her life she found hard to explain to *anyone*, even Karen and Viv. A lot of Penny's life stayed private, known to her alone, not out of a desire to deceive others but due to an unwillingness to explain things that others hadn't seen and a worry that they wouldn't believe her in the event that she tried.

She could have shared all of this aloud right away, but she didn't.

"Any other ideas?" Viv said.

"Well, there's the letter from the lawyer," Karen said.

"Sure," Penny said. "And it's also possible that they've been on our tail in other ways, ways we may have missed."

"Now there's an interesting thought," Karen said.

"I guess it's not just rich people who are paranoid," Viv joked.

Penny glared at her. Now she *really* didn't want to talk about Change's background and how it contradicted their focus on the Ecks.

"Anyway," Karen said. "I mean it. Forget the donor list. Let's go bigger. It has to be bigger."

Viv had a headache and Penny was tired of talking, so they rode the rest of the way home in silence.

When they got home, Viv did a little digging.

"Oh jeez," Viv said. "Karen, you're a genius."

"I am?" Karen asked. "Why?"

"The crowdfunding platform. Guess who founded it?" Viv said.

"Who?"

"Bronson Eck," Viv said.

"You're kidding me," Penny said.

"Nope," Viv said. She showed Penny.

"That can't be right," Penny said.

"Look, Penny, sometimes it's really that straightforward. Sometimes it's just that obvious," Karen said.

"That isn't it…" Penny said. "There's just so much that doesn't line up."

"Like what?" Karen asked.

"Was there an Eck on that client list?" Penny said.

"Yes," Karen replied. "And if Heather did get a threatening call from some rich person, then Eck would fit that perfectly."

"But Karen, you didn't get a sense off Eck that he'd done it, did you?" Penny persisted.

"Well, no," Karen replied. "But maybe I was wrong. It can happen."

"Roscoe came to the same conclusion though. What are the odds that you'd both be wrong?" Penny said.

"I don't know," Karen admitted. "But I'd imagine it's possible."

"And why would the founder of an app care about a tornado hitting a house after it closes? He'd get his money either way," Penny said.

"Ah, that one's actually not so farfetched," Viv chimed in.

Penny looked at her expectantly.

"It's a viral story waiting to happen. Bunch of investors thwarted by a tornado that an unsavory agent probably foresaw. Horrible publicity," Viv said.

"And a murder with your app's name attached to it isn't horrible publicity?" Penny said.

"Well, you've met Bronson Eck. He probably didn't think so far through things," Viv said.

"Not to mention he's been in prison the entire time," Penny said.

"So he sent hitmen," Viv said. "Honestly, Penny, it's not hard to imagine."

Penny sighed. Actually, yes, it was very hard for her to imagine. Even setting the shapeshifter aside, none of the pieces really fit, not without an awful lot of force being applied to jam them in.

And that was something as an investigator she tried to never do.

"Okay," Penny said, switching strategies, "Let's say that Eck ordered all of these murders. That he hired professionals."

Viv nodded.

"We still don't have a trail," Penny replied. "And we're not taking down someone that powerful without an airtight case."

"True," Viv said begrudgingly.

"Besides," Penny continued, "I don't care how much of a rich asshole he is, I'm not putting anyone behind bars unless I'm absolutely sure. And I'm just not sold that Eck's our guy."

"Eck and company," Viv corrected.

"Right," Penny said. "The whole Eck angle just isn't coming together for me."

"Well," Viv said thoughtfully. "In that case, Penny, I'll see what I can do."

There was another important break in the case that soon followed. After the third set of murders, the higherups at PsyOps decided the balance had shifted. They were now ready to ship the blood sample – blood which most likely was the killer's – to the United States for DNA analysis.

"No promises on how long it takes," Martin said.

Viv threw herself into retracing the case as it was. She started with the idea that Eck had ordered the murders and went over the available evidence over and over again, trying to construct a case.

She'd learned from experience that this sometimes worked, starting with a solution and then moving backwards to find the path towards it.

She knew Eck was the killer. She could feel it. Now she just had to find a way to prove it.

The DNA test came back within the week, shocking everyone with the speed.

"I've never seen anything like this," Martin said. "That's the fastest turnaround I've ever seen." He paused. "Maybe peace has a chance, after all. Maybe the US will leave us alone. No more war."

"I wouldn't count on it," Viv replied.

"Oh?" Martin asked.

"You hurt someone that bad, they don't forget. Maybe they pretend they do, but that doesn't mean they won't find a way to get back at you when they see the opportunity," Viv said.

"I don't know how you date this woman. She's scary sometimes," Martin said to Karen and Penny.

They laughed.

"Anyway," Martin continued, "I'm sorry to say we didn't have an exact match."

"Of course not," Viv said. "That would be too easy."

"It's awfully hard to develop a comprehensive DNA database for a population when you have to depend on your ex-sovereign for testing," Martin said.

"I don't know why we just don't develop the technology ourselves," Viv snapped.

"Yes, you do," Martin said. "Tech is expensive. And people are cheap in the Psychic State. Detectives. Manpower."

"You mean, *psychics* are cheap in the Psychic State," Viv corrected him.

"Yeah," Martin said. "Psychics are people though, right?'

"You wouldn't know it sometimes," Viv replied.

Martin frowned. "Do you want to hear the results or not?"

"Viv," Penny said. "Let's just hear what he has to say."

Viv sighed. She nodded.

"Thanks, Penny," Martin said. "Anyway, we didn't find an exact match on anybody – since we don't have a lot of info to compare. But we do know one thing: Our killer is female."

"Really?" Viv said.

Martin nodded.

"Well, unless there's something important Bronson Eck isn't telling us, it's not him," Viv said.

It was a really terrible joke, kind of offensive and not even funny, but Viv seemed so depressed that Penny or Karen didn't point that out.

All That Withers Isn't Old

"So it isn't Eck," Penny said after they'd left Martin's office. "Fine. I know you're disappointed about this, Viv, but it's important information."

Viv sighed. "Sure." She sighed again. "How many times have I heard that? Important information... a detective's least favorite euphemism."

"It's like AFOG," Penny said.

"AFOG?" Viv asked.

"Another Fucking Opportunity for Growth," Penny replied.

Viv laughed. "Yes. It's exactly like that. Important information is the detective's AFOG."

"A woman," Karen said. "That takes us completely off our radar."

"Wasn't suspecting that at all," Viv agreed.

"Where does it bring us?" Penny said.

Viv brought out her notes on the case and spread them before Penny and Karen.

"Geez, Viv," Penny said. "This is busier than Amarynth's board. Guess you learned more than painting from your old art teacher... what was his name again?"

"Mr. Herman," Viv said. "And I suppose so." She smiled thinking about the old guy. He was old when he'd taught her over a decade ago and in those days never well for more than a few days at a time. She suspected he'd passed by now, but she could remember all too well his love of conspiracy – and his flair for visually representing it.

An entire wall of his home studio had been plastered in a wide variety of maps – over which he'd pasted news articles about strange happenings, tracing a spidery network of ley lines between them. Conduits of power, he'd called them.

It was all a little spooky Viv'd had to admit, but of all the people who seemed troubled by the emergence of the Psychic Phenomenon, Mr. Herman had found a more constructive outlet than most. Or at least, a pretty darn harmless one.

Mr. Herman had also let her know that he met with other likeminded folks, people who were attempting to pool their knowledge and find a way to explain the psychic emergence. The Web Spinners, they called themselves. To Viv it seemed more like a supernatural fantasy football league. They got awfully invested in their analyses, but at the end of the day, that knowledge wasn't ever applied. They adjourned, split up, and went to their respective everyday lives – which remained largely unchanged by their extracurricular activities.

And the world at large barely knew they existed.

When she'd dropped out of art school to join PsyOps, Viv had quickly forgotten all about Mr. Herman and the Web Spinners. But Penny was right. It appeared that something about that experience had stuck, and she'd internalized a way of organizing complex, contradictory information that made sense to her but to a third party looked pretty darn cracked.

Viv riffled a stack of papers through her fingers as she thought.

"Okay," she announced in as resolute a voice as she could muster, hoping that feigned confidence would convince herself as well as her audience, "if we're looking at women, that narrows the field considerably. We have just a few suspects that haven't been ruled out."

"Martin's sister, Darian Meek," Penny said.

Viv nodded.

"It isn't her," Karen said.

"And just how do you *know* that?" Viv asked.

Karen frowned. "Viv, it's all wrong. All of my intuition is telling me it's not her."

"Karen," Viv said in a small voice, "I don't mean any offense by this but..."

Karen steeled herself for Viv to say something rude, as pretty much every time someone started out by saying "no offense," offense was sure to follow.

"...intuition isn't enough to rule out a suspect. Especially since you haven't done a proper feel on her. This isn't even your empathy talking. This is just your gut, isn't it?" Viv finished.

Karen sighed. She nodded. "But you know, Viv, you know better than anybody else how strong a gut feeling can be."

"I do," Viv replied. "But strong isn't the same thing as reliable. And anyway, subjective strength certainly doesn't make for a convincing case for conviction."

"Tell that to some other PsyOps teams," Penny muttered. She was right of course. Their role as PsyOps agents did allow them more leeway to accuse, arrest, and even charge than the normal police force. All you had to do was claim a gut feeling came from your psychic intuition and wave your fingers mysteriously, and the non-intuitive mucky mucks in the Psychic State government would look the other way – provided of course, the arrest didn't run afoul of their own personal interests.

Corruption ate both ways. Given the proper set of circumstances, it was possible for the innocent to end up condemned and the guilty to be set free. Everyone knew it.

But that didn't mean anything to Viv.

"Look, the State might be okay with putting away innocent people in order to look more efficient or to help the president win another election, but I'm not," Viv said. "And I never will be."

"I know," Penny replied. "And I know you're right." She got a faraway look on her face. "I just don't know how long it's going to be okay to think like that."

Viv frowned. "Don't go there," she said. "I know it's been bad the past few years, with all the changes. The cutbacks, the extra regulations. But the war is over now. There are other changes happening, too."

Penny didn't say anything.

"There are," Viv replied. "Has it been getting worse? Sure. But at any moment it could get better. There are still good things in the world, even if you have trouble seeing them sometimes. Even if they're crowded out by darkness, pettiness, fear. People are creating and inventing and living happy lives. There *are* good things still in the world, things that are moving forward. And those good things aren't just going to stop developing and going exciting places because the wrong people are in charge."

Penny and Karen didn't say anything.

"And while that happens, I'm going to keep acting like corruption's days are numbered. Not just because I can't stomach becoming one of the monsters – although I suppose that's true – but because I really do believe that there's hope.

I feel like we're on the edge of something big, and nobody – not you, not me, and not even the people in charge – knows what we're going to tumble over into next. All I know is that the future is uncertain, so uncertain that an entire army of precogs couldn't predict what's ahead of us," Viv replied.

Penny nodded.

"Regina Withers," Karen said.

"Hm?" Viv said.

"That's the other suspect that makes sense," Karen said. She pointed to a small web that Viv had traced between various facts. "Think of it. Proximity to Bronson Eck. She's the producer on his family's reality TV show. She has a vested financial interest in his being freed from prison, right?"

Viv nodded. "Yes, I suppose she does." She didn't say it aloud, but she was a little irritated she hadn't thought of that first.

"She's also potentially a 'damn rich asshole.' She could have been the one on the other end of that suspicious phone call that Heather took," Penny said. Phone records had been less than helpful. There was a call at the time that Martin's sister had reported, but the number traced back to a burner phone. Nothing they could tie to a suspect.

"Although," Viv said. "We only have Darian Meek's word for *that*. And she could have lied about that to direct suspicion away from herself."

"True," Karen admitted. "But let's just take a second and stay with Withers for another minute."

"Okay," Viv said. "She wasn't on the list of crowdsourced investors, for one."

"No," Karen said. "But Bronson Eck was."

Viv frowned. "Why would she kill to cover his interests again? That doesn't make sense."

"Well, not as we're thinking about it now, no," Karen said. "But let's make it make sense."

Viv groaned. "I hate this game."

"I know," Karen replied. "But it's worked well in the past."

"Fine," Viv said, because Karen was right.

"Okay, what would make Regina Withers willing to kill *multiple times* for Bronson Eck?" Penny said.

"Bias," Viv replied.

"Hm?" Penny said.

"The big kind of bias," Viv said.

"Maybe they're lovers," Karen said.

"Oh please," Penny said. "She's classy. Powerful. Accomplished. He's a sleazy trust fund baby who can't keep it in his pants."

"I've seen stranger matches," Viv replied.

"Viv!" Penny protested.

"What?" Viv said. "I know she's your hero, but when it comes to their love lives, people sometimes have really questionable taste."

Penny frowned. "I could say something really mean right now, but I'm not going to."

"I know," Viv replied. "I'm evidence of your questionable taste. It's fine."

Penny sighed. "It's no fun when you say it for me."

Karen giggled. "Anyway, I think that's where we should look next. We need to check on the alibis of Darian Meek and Regina Withers."

And so they did.

Checking Darian's alibi turned out to be a rather quick affair. Department of Corrections could account for her whereabouts at the time of the third set of murders. Darian had unfortunately indulged *once again* in illegal substances, and at the time the crime was committed, she was being held awaiting trial, behind bars, a guest of the State.

Martin told the team that he'd briefly considered springing his sister out via bail but was perturbed enough this time to let her sit in there and think for a while.

"Besides," he added, "when she's in jail, at least I know where she is."

He'd felt cruel making the decision, he told them. The way he was raised, you weren't supposed to let your family suffer in such a way. "But I guess I ended up doing her a bigger favor," he said. "Since she's been cleared of suspicion."

"Funny how these things work out sometimes," Viv had replied. It was a frustrating development. As much as she liked Martin and didn't want anything awful to happen to anyone in his family, it would have been a much simpler matter seriously investigating someone like Darian Meek than a high-profile person like Regina Withers.

With his sister cleared of suspicion, however, Martin was happy to call in some extra favors, even if it meant exposing the department – and his team in particular – to more scrutiny.

Still, confirming Withers' alibi took days. Even with Martin
on board pulling very important strings, there was a
tremendous runaround as their calls were directed through
a vast network of industry representatives, in charge of
coordinating filming schedules and travel arrangements for
network talent.

However, at the end of the paper chase, a firm alibi hadn't
emerged. There remained ample time for Withers to have
committed all three murders. It would be tight – but possible.

This was enough for Martin to push a court order through
to obtain a sample of Regina Withers's blood. They braced
themselves for Withers to hire high-powered lawyers and
begin a prolonged court fight.

However, this didn't happen. Withers showed up at the
appointed time and voluntarily gave a sample.

"We've got her!" Viv exclaimed.

"But if it's her," Penny said. "Why isn't she putting up more of
a fight?"

"I don't know," Viv replied. "Maybe she's cocky enough to
think she can beat us post-arrest. It wouldn't be the first time
that's happened."

Penny frowned. It was true that she'd pedestalled Withers for
decades at this point, and that did skew her impression of her
in a way that was undeniable, but her fandom also meant she
was quite familiar with Withers. What she would know. How
she operated. This was no legal amateur. This was the Queen
of True Crime they were talking about.

Withers knew all about how suspects were investigated,
how the State built its cases. In certain segments of her TV
programs, Withers even gave advice to viewers about how

they should act when suspected of a crime, and such advice was tailored based on guilt or innocence.

If you were guilty, Withers advised, you surrendered nothing to the police. You made the entire process as onerous as possible.

Hell, Penny remembered, if you were innocent but felt ill equipped to prove it, Withers advised similar. Make headaches for the police at every possible opportunity. Force them to pay more attention to other targets that were less of a hassle (and if you were innocent, these would also be targets that were more likely to have actually committed the crime).

If Withers were guilty, she wasn't following her own advice. She was acting as though she were innocent, and that time would easily prove it.

That's why Penny wasn't surprised when the blood test results came back later that afternoon: Wrong blood type. Not a match. Martin wasn't going to bother to send it to the United States for DNA testing. No need to squander *another* favor when it wasn't going to lead anywhere.

Viv was crushed. Their last promising suspect was cleared.

How were they ever going to solve this case?

Taking a Flyer

The very next day, still feeling the sting of reaching yet another dead end, Karen wandered through a maze of shops, ones she'd never seen before and wasn't sure she'd ever see again. Skinner could be like that sometimes. Certain neighborhoods were a risky place to open a business. It wasn't as though the locals could afford to buy most of what they were selling, confined to a paltry psychic allowance, a pittance after they were taxed for existing.

Really, the businesspeople were at the mercy of business travelers and tourists. People who were in Skinner for the day, a weekend, or perhaps a week conducting business or gawking at the native tueys, like a busful of visitors to Amish country would gape at the locals.

Karen suspected tourism was the true golden goose that businesspeople were chasing, just based on the establishments that seemed to do the best. Keep the busiest. And stay around the longest.

The more tourism-centered a business venture was, the more successful it was. The crown jewel of Skinner's Chamber of Commerce was arguably the Museum of Psychic Innovation. Priced just beyond the budget of most intuitives, even the comparably monied Green Star variety, the museum chronicled the emergence of the first precogs, the still developing frontier of psychic taxonomy, and as the brochures boasted, the way that the government had "cleverly harnessed psychic power to build a better society."

Yes, it actually said that.

More like exploited us, Karen had thought the first time she had stumbled onto one of the brochures. One that had flown away from someone's hand and stuck unceremoniously to a trash can, demonstrating why such pamphlets are often called flyers.

Lost in her own thoughts and taking random turns down streets without thinking, she almost missed a familiar face sitting out on the patio at Cambria, a bougie café just outside Skinner's psychic inner ring, a place that boasted of serving genuine Italian espresso but whose baristas also couldn't be bothered to seem excited about doing it.

Karen almost missed the familiar face but not quite.

It was Viv's mother, Tender Lee. Sitting across from a man in a business suit. Tender was predictably engaged in a kind of obvious pantomime of adoration. This was her default behavior around men, especially ones that appeared wealthy. Her breasts swung under a dress that managed to simultaneously showcase impressive décolletage and also to be loose enough that the rest of her spectacular figure was obscured enough to instill intrigue. She laughed at regular intervals, a throaty passionate laugh, but one whose authenticity you would begin to doubt if you looked into her eyes and saw her smaller expressions and lack of reaction, not all of which could be attributed to Botox.

Still, Viv's mother looked spectacular. A good 30 years younger than the age that was likely on her birth certificate. Not that she let anyone see it.

That woman really knows how to dress, Karen thought, lifting her hood and pulling up the strings on her hoodie tighter. Tightly enough so that they'd obscure her face should Viv's mother look in her direction.

The last thing I need is a run in with Viv's mom. Their interactions were always tense, awkward. And besides, Tender was *clearly* busy entertaining a man of great interest.

Even as she hid beneath her hood, however, Karen found it hard to look away from Tender, as she always did. Tender was nothing if not eye-catching. There was something wildly improbable about her appearance. Karen noted Tender's makeup was flawless, her blonde hair impeccably coiffed – except…

Karen stopped dead in her tracks. Gray roots peeked up from Tender's scalp. Enough gray showing that Karen could see them from where she stood across the street from the café.

Enough undyed growth to make it evident that it had been months since she'd had her hair colored.

But that was her alibi, Karen thought. *That's why we ruled her out.*

Tender's hair looked nice enough other than that, but it was clear that she hadn't seen a colorist in quite some time.

As she walked closer to Tender and her gentleman friend, Karen felt their emotions simultaneously. With concentration, however, she was able to quickly sort out which emotions belonged to which person. The man felt pride and a hint of sexual arousal. Tender felt bored.

At that very moment, Tender turned and spotted her. And her boredom flicked over to rage.

Karen took off running. Her feet carried her all the way home. She didn't stop or look back. Although emotions assailed her every second of the jog, coming from random people on the street, in cars, even people relaxing in their homes just out of her visual sight, Karen didn't digest or process them. She flew, operating on blind instinct.

Besides, the din seemed relatively muted compared to the screaming in her own chest. The anxiety. The dread of everything that could follow if her instincts were correct.

It can't be, she thought, her own breathing becoming heavy as she ran, the blood rushing into her ears. *It can't be. But it is.*

When she reached their house, the wall of other emotions fell and she was left with her own. Viv and Penny looked up at her, their faces dropping into unison demonstrations of relief.

A pantomime of *Oh there you are. We were so worried about you. We're glad you're safe.*

Knowing that Viv and Penny had been worried about her made what Karen had to say next even harder to say.

Suffice to say Viv didn't take the news well. She screamed at Karen, telling her that she was full of it, ran up the stairs, and shut herself in the upstairs bathroom.

Penny stood there numbly, frozen like a statue.

"Say something please," Karen said after a while.

Penny shook her head.

"Well, then don't go anywhere," Karen said.

Penny screwed up her face. "Where would I go?" she said.

"You have a way of wandering off like a cat," Karen replied. "Don't play dumb about it."

Penny scowled so deeply that Karen noted she looked almost ugly. *A real feat for her*, Karen thought idly. Penny was normally so radiant she seemed to emit a slight glow.

"We have to confirm this," Penny said. "We have to confirm she wasn't at the salon. We can't jump to conclusions based on something you saw while you were out wandering around who knows where."

"I know what I saw," Karen insisted.

"For all we know, she got something else done. Maybe she didn't have her roots done. Maybe she had a spa treatment. Got a trim. Maybe..."

Karen stared at Penny. "Since when does someone as vain as Tender go to a salon and leave her grey roots visible?"

"I mean, it's unlikely," Penny said. "But we can't just go arresting people based on unlikely. We need more proof."

"Then I'll go to the salon," Karen replied.

"Like Hell you will," Penny replied. "I think you've done enough."

"We need to follow up on this lead," Karen said.

"*We* aren't going to do anything," Penny replied. "You're going to stay here, and I'm going to check on this alibi."

"But Viv..." Karen said.

"You're a big girl," Penny said. "You can figure it out. I mean, you're an empath, after all. You'd think you would be halfway decent at calming a person down."

"Or letting them be upset if they need to be," Karen said.

"Yes. Or whatever," Penny said.

"Or whatever," Karen agreed.

As Penny walked out the door and got into the car, Karen was nearly bowled over by the emotional equivalent of a primal scream. Suicidal urges. Existential angst. Rage.

Karen knew it was coming from upstairs.

"Hello, do you have an appointment?" the receptionist asked Penny as she walked through the door.

"No, I'm actually here on some PsyOps business," Penny replied. She flashed her identification at the same time she flashed what she hoped was a winning smile. The last thing she needed when following up a lead was for any apprehension she felt to get in the way of finding the truth, no matter what that truth was.

"Detective Penelope Dreadful. I'd like to ask you a few questions about your appointment book."

"Aww, that's too bad," a stylist working nearby called at her. "You have beautiful hair, honey. I'd love to get my hands on it."

"Well, I've seen your rates," Penny said. "Not exactly scaled to a PsyOps salary."

"Maybe we could work something out," the stylist countered. "You never know."

"Sure thing, detective," the receptionist responded. "Now what would you like to know?"

"I wanted to check in on a client of yours. I believe she's a regular. Euphemia Tender Lee," Penny said.

"Ah! Miss Tender! What a character," the stylist interjected.

"She comes here a lot. What were you looking into?"

Penny asked her about the date and time in question.

The receptionist flipped open the book to the appropriate page. She stared at it for a moment. "Ah yes. Tender Lee was scheduled for that time."

Penny felt a wave of relief. *Of course. Of course she was.*

"But it says here she never showed up. There's a note here that I called her about it, and she said she'd pay double the next time she came in. I remember that happening now. And come to think of it, she *still* hasn't rescheduled. I'm gonna have to call her again here and ask about that. So it's a good thing you came in."

Penny's heart sank. *A good thing? Well, maybe a good thing for you.*

"Thanks for your help," Penny said. "I'd start tracking things in another appointment book if I were you."

"Oh?"

"I have a feeling that one's going to be subpoenaed and entered into evidence," Penny said.

"For what it's worth, officer, I always thought Tender was a nasty bitch!" the stylist interjected.

Penny reflected on how easy it was to find fair weather friends, as she trudged off to her next location.

Fear Visits

Karen had always hated how emotionally reactive her face was. No matter what she was feeling, it would soon be broadcast in her facial features, plainly visible for all the world to see. If she were lucky, she could catch the expression quickly and force her muscles into another configuration in an attempt to mask her true feelings.

But there was always going to be a microexpression that leaked through. One that flickered across and could be easily viewed by people who knew her well and those trained in detecting such facial fluctuations.

When it came to people who fell into both categories, Karen was frankly screwed. It had been that way ever since she was a little girl.

Because of this, there had been a number of personal relationships throughout her life in which she simply had no emotional privacy to speak of. Furthermore, tact was a rather strenuous undertaking, requiring extensive rehearsal before a difficult interaction and usually an anchoring thought to get her through it, something she could focus on while she spoke to the other person that would be sufficient to distract her from really absorbing what was said to her in real time, thereby lessening her microexpressions.

Developing empathic powers should have been a boon, but in this reality, Karen couldn't escape a painful sense of irony at the fact that her own emotions were so easy for even normals to read. Empathic detection should have been an advantage like looking at people through one-way glass.

Instead, the glass was practically two-way. Perhaps there was a slight tint on her side, but most of what she felt still could be seen. She felt nearly as exposed as those she viewed with empathy. More exposed actually, whenever her powers were dampened by the presence of Viv and Penny.

True, that's what had enabled her to fall in love with them in the first place, that vulnerability, that sense of calm that made every emotional act involving them feel like a blind leap of faith. At the same time, however, it had been unsettling and terrifying.

She'd managed to adapt over time, even developed auxiliary compensatory strategies for times when her empathic powers were dormant. She got quite good at reading microexpressions herself. That, at least, was a relief.

Some emotions were easier to detect than others. Karen found Fear the easiest. Not everyone found Fear so easy to read. The face of Fear was often confused by others with Surprise. Understandable, really, as both expressions included raised eyebrows.

But that was where the similarity ended. After all, anyone could see that Surprise's raised eyebrows took on a different shape. Surprise's eyebrows were curvier and raised higher, as though they were jumping into the air suddenly.

Fear's eyebrows were flatter and lower, almost as though they were a creature crawling along on its stomach to get away or making itself as small as possible to shelter in place.

The eyes also opened wider in Fear than in Surprise. More of the sclera was visible. When someone was afraid, you saw more of the whites of their eyes.

Plus, there was a difference in the mouth. A fearful face had tension in the lips. A surprised mouth opened and hung slack.

No, the faces looked nothing alike.

That's why Karen knew precisely who had entered her home when she looked up from her own misery, suffering in the intensity of Viv's emotions, and saw the visitor.

"I hope I haven't scared you," Fear said. She attempted a smile, but what happened instead was an unsettling rictus.

"No," Karen said. It was true. There had been no jump scare. No feeling of being startled. Even though the visitor had seemingly materialized from nowhere. "But I guess that's to be expected. You tend to show up when I'm *not* feeling you but should be. Not the other way around."

Fear nodded. "You are teachable, after all," she said. "Anger wasn't so sure."

"Well, Anger's inpatient," Karen said.

Fear squeezed her face into that unsettling grimace again. It looked like a smile would if it were left out in the sun in a car on a hot day and allowed to partially melt. "That she is," Fear said. "Always so certain of herself. Righteous about it. Doesn't understand that's not normal, or that anyone else could feel a different way."

"You don't have to try to be human," Karen said.

"I know," Fear replied. "But you don't know that."

Karen laughed. "Oh, trust me, I know I'm human."

"Do you?" Fear challenged her.

Karen gestured in Viv's general direction, where she was holed up in the upstairs bathroom. "I'd love to be able to do something about that... *situation*."

"Who's to say that you can't?" Fear said.

"Oh please," Karen replied. "I've stepped in it enough today. I'll only make it worse if I go up there."

"Defeatist," Fear noted. "If you don't stop stealing my lines, I'm going to have to charge you."

Karen scoffed. "I'm not afraid of Viv," she protested.

"No one said you were afraid of Viv," Fear said.

"Well... you said I was stealing your lines, and you're here, so clearly you think I *should* be afraid of something," Karen said.

"Aren't you?" Fear asked.

Karen stared at her. She didn't respond.

"That's fine," Fear replied. "I'm used to being everyone's dirty little secret."

Karen chewed on her lip and tried to conjure up an anchoring thought. She focused on trying to remember the last twelve books she had read, the exact order, the spelling of every author's name. Some of them had rather long, difficult surnames. She hoped it would be enough of a masking task.

"I used to think it had something to do with me, you know, the fact that people didn't ever want to acknowledge me. I thought it meant that I was a weaker emotion than the others, lesser. Everyone was acting like they were ashamed to be associated with me, so there was clearly something wrong with me, right? I was weak. Forgettable," Fear said.

Karen avoided Fear's gaze. She switched to doing math in her head. Counting down from 600 by nines.

"But then I realized it was the opposite," Fear continued. "People didn't want to admit that they had fears because then the next thing everyone would be asking was *what* they were afraid of. And when people know your fears, that knowledge becomes a kind of leverage."

Karen lost count. She started again, from the top.

"But that's only if you let them be leverage. It's difficult to shame a person who isn't ashamed. It's easy to manipulate someone with fear if they're unwilling to acknowledge that they have any fears. That's when I realized how powerful I am."

In spite of her attempts at distraction, the words cut through the mess in Karen's head. "Sounds like it was a good day for you," she said glibly.

"Yes," Fear said. "But an even better day for anyone who would join me."

Karen sighed.

"I've been here all along, darling," Fear said. "You've just been ignoring me. It's starting to hurt my feelings, you know."

"I don't want to make it worse," Karen said.

"I know," Fear replied. "That's what you're afraid of."

"Can you promise me I won't make it worse?" Karen asked.

"No," Fear said. "I can't promise you anything."

"Fantastic," Karen said.

"I'm not in the business of making promises," Fear said. "And even if I *were*, it's not wise to count on promises made out of fear."

Karen thought about that and begrudgingly realized Fear was right. Every time she or someone else had made a promise due to fear, it had dissipated the moment that the fear did.

Fear wasn't known for its loyalty – or, more fortunately, its staying power, provided you didn't cater to fear or feed it too vigorously.

"I think," Karen said hesitantly, "that the world would be a better place if everyone could see you folks. If everyone entertained regularly visitors like you and your friends."

"Maybe," Fear said. "But I like it this way. Besides, I'm busy enough as it is."

Karen laughed.

"Stop resisting me," Fear said. "You can be afraid *and* do what you need to do. They're not mutually exclusive."

"I just wish I felt naturally brave," Karen replied.

"No such thing," Fear replied.

"You don't have to say that," Karen said.

"No," Fear insisted. "There really isn't. Bravery isn't something you feel. Bravery's what you do. Have you ever been visited by Bravery?"

Karen thought about that. "No, I haven't."

"Neither have I," said Fear. "Haven't even heard of such a being. Probably for the best, too."

"Why's that?" Karen asked.

"I'm fairly certain that whoever it is would be my competitor. Or worse, my sworn enemy."

Karen laughed.

Fear sighed. "I am what I am, I suppose… and so are you." Fear snapped her fingers.

Karen felt terrified, overwhelmed, like she wanted to hide. The emotion was so intense that it matched Viv's projections and in a few moments swallowed them whole, overtaking them.

Karen leaned against the wall with one hand, feeling as though she might vomit. As she steadied herself, she took several long deep breaths, deliberately slowing her breathing.

"Okay," she said to herself. "It's time."

She climbed up the stairs.

"Hey Martin," Penny said.

"Penny," he replied. "I thought you were off today."

"I was. But breaks happen when they happen. You won't believe what's happening in this case."

She told him.

As he listened, the blood drained from Martin's face.

"Penny," he said finally. "We're way beyond conflict of interest here. You're all in over your heads. You have to hand off the case."

Penny nodded. "I don't see any other way... but I need one thing from you."

"Name it," Martin said.

"Let me be there when she's arrested," Penny said.

"No, the team can't be there when that happens. Especially not Viv."

"No, Martin," Penny said. "Not Viv, not Karen. Me. I want to be there."

Martin sighed. "That we could probably do. But can I ask why?"

"You can," Penny replied. She didn't say anything else.

"And can I get an answer to the question?" Martin persisted.

"Because Viv needs to know how it happened. And she needs to hear it from someone she trusts. At this point, I think the list is just down to me," Penny replied.

"Oh geez. Viv and Karen having a tiff?"

Penny nodded. "Viv's basically shooting the messenger. I'm not an empath, but I'd be willing to bet she's really angry at her mom and herself, for not figuring it out sooner, for not suspecting. But all of that is too painful, so it's easier to just be mad at Karen instead. To displace that anger and frustration on a safer target."

"Alright, Penny," Martin said. "I'll see what I can do." He lifted the receiver of his VoIP phone and began to navigate the bureaucratic maze that Penny had seen him deftly maneuver so many times.

She did a quick salute to him as she stepped towards the door to leave. Martin waved at her with the same motion that he might swat away a fly.

Once Penny had closed the door behind her and was standing in the empty unmarked hall outside of Martin's office, she began to cry. She squeezed her eyes shut, hoping to arrest the tears, but it only made it worse.

She stood in darkness for about a minute before wiping her tears away.

"Hey," a woman said. Penny recognized it as Amarynth's voice.

When she opened her eyes, she was in Connections.

Penny didn't remember walking to Connections, but she must have. Her feet must have taken her there. It was curious to her sometimes how much of what happened inside of her body wasn't under conscious control. She'd had to learn a lot about the human brain as an intuitive living in a normal world and as a detective. The more she learned, the more amazed she'd been that so much of what we do, what we are, happens automatically and actively defies logic.

Meanwhile, the conscious mind fumbles to make sense of it all, becoming a defense lawyer for indefensible, inexplicable behaviors.

We want to make sense so desperately, Penny thought. But we don't.

"Penny, you look like someone tried to make a copy of you but failed," Amarynth said.

"What?" Penny said.

"You look like Hell," Amarynth said.

"Geez, Amarynth," Penny said. "Tell me what you really think."

"I always do," Amarynth replied. "Someone has to. And sometimes someone has to look like Hell. Today it's you."

Penny sighed.

"Want a donut?" Amarynth asked, gesturing to a box next to her.

Penny noted that every single donut in the box had a bite taken from it. Even the filled ones, which oozed custard from their puncture wounds.

Penny frowned. "Have any intact ones?"

"These are from the shop downstairs," Amarynth says. "I tried each one out of fairness, but they were so gross, Penny."

"Then why are you offering them to me?" Penny asked.

"It's all I have," Amarynth admitted. "And you look like a person who needs something."

"Amarynth, you know... sometimes you are awfully sweet," Penny said.

Amarynth ignored that. Instead, she said, "I'm sorry by the way, about how this whole thing shook out."

"You of course knew the whole time," Penny said, feeling irritated.

"Like always, yes," Amarynth said. "As much as I ever really know anything. I knew it had to do with Viv. I've always known."

"Which probably put you in a bad situation, seeing as you're not Viv's favorite person or anything," Penny said.

"No, Viv's favorite person would be you. Or Karen. Depending on the day and what kind of mood she's in," Amarynth said. "I'm near the bottom of the list. And it's a very long list."

"Detective Dreadful?" said a voice from behind Penny. She turned around. It was one of the interns, a normal majoring in Intuitive Behavior. A shorter man with dirty blond hair

and ears that looked far too large for him, he was pushing a
mail cart.

"Yes," Penny replied. "That's me."

The intern handed her a beautifully wrapped package. "For
you." Noting the surprised look on her face, he added, "Don't
worry. It's been properly screened. I wouldn't put you at risk."
He blushed, before pushing the cart away at an increased
clip.

"I think he likes you," Amarynth said.

"Thanks, Captain Obvious," Penny replied.

"More like Captain Can't State the Obvious," Amarynth said.

"Hey," Penny said. "It's not so bad."

"Aren't you going to open it?" Amarynth asked. "Or do you
not want an audience?"

Penny laughed. "Oh, I don't care." She untied the ribbon
and slid the top of the box off. A whiff of perfume hit her
nostrils. The scent reminded her powerfully of the Warrens
of Persephone.

In the box was a pomegranate and a slip of paper that just
read "COME HOME."

Penny froze in place, holding the paper. Half of her knew that
it was important. The other half was afraid to acknowledge
that it was. Both halves warred, leaving Penny in a state of
mind that defied logic.

"I'm not going to ask," Amarynth reassured her, soothing a
fear she hadn't even voiced aloud.

But that was Amarynth for you, for better or worse.

The Devil Was Beating His Wife

It was raining a few hours later when a PsyOps force visited Tender Lee's house. It wasn't a normal rain storm, however, but a sunshower. The team of arresting PsyOps officers assembled in the kind of watery sunlight that Penny noted usually set off Viv's migraines. *Another reason I'm glad she's not here,* Penny thought.

"Oh, look, the devil's beating his wife," one of the other agents remarked. Penny stifled a groan. She hated that expression. But now wasn't the time to make trouble. There was serious work to do.

Penny realized as she waited that this was one of the few arrests that she'd ever made during the daylight hours. Usually, they took suspects in at night when they were sleeping, but when she'd told Martin, he'd wanted to act more quickly. No waiting until nightfall once they had the go-ahead.

Besides, Tenny often napped in the afternoons. Penny remembered Viv saying that one time, that her mother was a creature of the night. Maybe they'd get lucky, and she'd be sound asleep when it all went down.

Penny didn't know the other officers, but she was glad Martin had made room for her at all. Besides, it was arguably easier to make the arrest surrounded by relative strangers and not people who were in her inner professional circle.

People who would otherwise be tempted to gossip.

Before setting out, she'd been properly introduced to each of the other five members tasked with bringing in Tender Lee. She'd been told their name, their rank, their intuitive specialty.

But as they came upon Tender's house, all of that information rushed out of her mind. And all she could think of was the gravity of what they were about to do. And how it would upset everything in her home life.

She also noted that she hadn't encountered a single spirit since Karen had broken the bad news.

Penny couldn't remember a day that she hadn't run into at least two or three, even old familiar undead faces. Ones that she had run into dozens of times.

It seemed like the spirit world was giving her a berth, for whatever reason.

Is it an omen? Penny wondered. *Am I on the wrong track?*

Or, she thought suddenly, *is my bias finally getting the best of me?*

Everyone knew that bias was a threat to psychic vitality. And this case couldn't hit any closer to home if it tried to.

Had her job finally broken her?

Was there any coming back from this?

Penny was so lost in her thoughts that she missed her name being called. "*Detective Dreadful,*" one of the team members said. By the tone, Penny knew that it wasn't the first time.

"Yes. Yes. Sorry," Penny said.

"Glad to have you back on Earth," the agent replied.

Penny flushed with embarrassment.

"Any reservations?" the agent asked.

"No, none at all," Penny replied. "As my superior, Martin Meek, indicated in the filing papers, I'm part of the original investigative team but not here in any operational capacity. I'm simply here to observe. This is your show. However you want to tackle this, it's fine by me."

"Understood."

Penny lagged behind the group as they approached the residence. Knocked on the door. Asked for Tender.

As Tender was informed she was under arrest for the murder of three people and the assault of three others. As she was read her rights and handcuffed.

As Love screamed like a person possessed and struck one of the officers. As Love was taken in for assaulting an officer, with more cursory rights spat at her like curses.

Penny stood back on the lawn and watched it all unfold.

"Bunch of inbred weirdos in that family," one of the agents said to her as they climbed into the squad car after the deed was done. "Except for Detective Lee, of course," he added.

It was too little, too late, Penny decided. The kind of thing you say because you realize how offensive your actual beliefs are and want to do a half-ass cover-up.

This case was going to affect their reputations. In the short term, yes, and perhaps for the foreseeable futures. It could very well make an already difficult job even harder. There was nothing for it. No taking any of it back.

Penny glared out the window as they drove through the watery sunlight back to the station, wondering how in the world she'd explain any of this to Viv when she got home.

Emotional Vampires

Tenny had noticed that time changed first. It moved so much more quickly than she was accustomed to. She found herself bored less as well.

And then her energy waned. She had to stop more often, at points that would have been unthinkable before.

Then her libido. Her passion.

Her drive.

She woke up one morning realizing she had become a senile old dog, like the one that was always on her grandfather's porch. Smiling. Mouth open wide. But with the emptiest expression. Staring out into the fields. Never unsettled or barking.

It must have been easy for the men who robbed her grandfather's homestead to sneak past a dog like that. Which was why it was so curious when the dog was found dead later.

Some days Tenny worried she would end up just like that dog.

"It's a fine thing for all these legends to talk about drinking the blood of virgins," Tenny told the inspector assigned to oversee the case in Viv's stead. "But they're all wrong, you know? What you really need isn't blood. It's a fresh brain. That's what keeps you young."

"Their brains?" the inspector said. "What do you mean by that?"

"You really don't know, do you?" Tenny said. "Well, I suppose there's no blaming you for that. We've existed for decades, you know."

"When you say 'we', you mean...?"

"The psychics," Tenny said frowning impatiently. "The *first* precogs, my ass." She laughed in the low part of her throat. "Oh, excuse me. That's hardly a way for a lady to act. Where are my manners? Tell me, inspector, are you married?"

"No," he replied. "Not anymore. So when you say –"

"I've been married a lot of times. I forget how many," Tenny said. "That's the problem. I keep forgetting important things. Things I should remember."

"So you say you're a tuey," the inspector said. "But that doesn't explain the bit about brains."

"Ah," she said. "Well, there are many kinds of us, I'm sure you've noticed."

He nodded. "I have."

"I forget the word for what we are. The original one that was used anyway. I keep forgetting things, you see. That's part of my condition. That's part of who I am," Tenny said.

"What condition is that?" the inspector said.

"I believe they're calling us derangers now," Tenny replied.

A *deranger*? The inspector's blood ran cold. "I thought that was something mothers made up to frighten their kids into behaving."

"Oh you poor dear," Tenny said, "don't you know that the real world is scary enough that mothers don't have to make up anything to scare their kids into behaving? You'd think with your job you'd get that."

Complications of Taxonomy

While much that has been unearthed since the emergence of the Psychic Phenomenon has largely benefitted society as a whole – and the Psychic State in particular – like any new discovery, it has come with attendant dangers.

Society of course has been well aware of these potential dangers; they are the root of anti-intuitive prejudice. Like most prejudices, these sentiments are tragically overgeneralized and misapplied. However, also like most prejudices, they originate from a basis of truth, however limited and specific.

Taxonomists are now grappling with the task of identifying and classifying psychic powers that so gravely violate social norms and mores, that their practitioners would be classified as monsters, abominations who wouldn't be out of place in a horror film.

A few complicating factors makes this task very difficult and daunting.

First of all, these monstrous intuitives are understandably secretive about their powers. With general anti-intuitive sentiment and psychophobia as widespread as they are, intuitives of all stripes have been known to hide their powers due to stigma. However, those who possess more dangerous or destructive powers are especially prone to hiding them, as the stigma involved with having those abilities – whether or not they are actually ever employed or used – would typically immediately result in Black Square status and permanent imprisonment.

The very existence of destructive intuitives is treated by the government as a crime against nature, regardless of what they do (or don't do) with those talents.

Secondly, a number of false reports have been made about destructive intuitive powers. They are particularly popular in Internet forums known for propagating urban legends and in some instances even creating them whole cloth for "entertainment purposes." Readers may remember the Slender Man incident, in which an urban legend inspired adolescent normals to attempt the murder of their close friend.

Unfortunately, as these urban legends are shared well beyond their original source, the citation and critical thinking ability of lay people becomes quite unreliable, and the relevant scientific agencies frequently receive anecdotal reports of certain psychic powers which in fact do not exist. Unfortunately, these are often mixed in with credible reports of destructive intuitive events, leaving the agencies evaluating them unable to meaningfully distinguish between urban legend and truthful accounts.

Or, in other words, we have trouble knowing from civilian reports whether we're hearing about a fiction like Slender Man or the true monsters in our midst.

Thirdly, these destructive intuitives are potentially quite dangerous, making proactive discovery and classification a much more daredevil task than it is at default. Few taxonomers want to risk exposure to various psychic assaults simply to add to the collective knowledge of intuition. The qualification few is key here, however, as there do exist brave taxonomers working on this field of endeavor, who make it their business to proactively investigate reported phenomena, no matter what the risks. But they are the exception and not the norm.

As a result, many of psychic taxonomy's reports about the dark side of intuition have filtered into the scientific community by way of the Department of Psychic Operations, a government agency devoted to employing intuitives in the investigation of crime, as well as other law enforcement agencies who make incidental reports when they encounter irregularities in the line of duty.

Their assistance helps us to solidify our working theories about reported destructive intuitive powers and meaningfully sort through what we suspect to be true and what we suspect to be the product of urban legend.

However, there are a number of intuitive types that are beyond rumored to exist by the frequency and credibility of the reports and at the date of this writing are simply waiting to be confirmed by empirical study before they are added to official taxonomic classification.

The author of this book would caution the reader at this point to understand that the following example, while likely, is offered as an uncertain one. The reader is cautioned that while taxonomists believe that this type is likely to exist, they still lack outside confirmation meeting the standards of the scientific community. Time may very well contradict the existence of this example and show the reader that either the intuitive type in question does not exist or does exist in a different form, one that has been misinterpreted due to insufficient or misleading information.

As mentioned in previous chapters, while many intuitives manipulate mental forces in general, there do exist a number of intuitive specialists who are attuned to certain psychic energies to the exclusion of others. Ostensibly this could be very limiting; however, it does seem that a counterbalance does exist. The most narrowly specialized intuitives do indeed seem to achieve a greater intensity with their admittedly quite specific powers. Even though intuitive specialists are limited in the scope, they are often quite powerful in what they *can* do.

One notable example of this is a theoretical/rumored intuitive type known as a deranger. Believed to be limited to the manipulation of sanity, one could possibly expect that a deranger's impact would be far more limited than an empath, precog, or telepath.

Instead, even a single deranger could be quite devastating. While to date there have been isolated reports, a picture is now beginning to emerge of what this intuitive type – or prototype – could entail.

Derangers are reported to possess the ability to essentially siphon off the sanity of their targets, draining wellbeing and coherence from them and absorbing it into themselves. This process would leave a mess of empty emotional and mental husks in their wake but leave the deranger quite high functioning and thriving, despite a mass of victims.

If a deranger were mentally healthy themselves, these victims would be only slightly harmed, mostly miffed, perturbed. Perhaps some of the less resilient victims would develop dysthymia or limited bouts of depression and need talk therapy or pharmaceutical intervention. However, a deranger who is generally mentally healthy would likely pass unnoticed, blending in easily with the kind of difficult personalities frequently found among the normal population.

However, if a deranger were they themselves quite mentally ill at baseline, it would theoretically become necessary for them to draw upon larger quantities of sanity in their targets, as a result leaving their victims psychotic or perhaps even dead.

It is rumored that certain deaths that have been formerly declared suicides may very well be the work of errant derangers.

Empirical confirmation is needed.

Our agency continues to work in concert with law enforcement and the media in order to obtain this.

from Insecta Psychica: Towards an Intuitive Taxonomy by Cloche Macomber

"You don't have to watch this, you know," Penny said to Viv.

"Just shut up and start the tape," Viv replied.

"Viv," Karen said.

Viv swiveled around to glare at her. Karen didn't say anything else. They'd managed to make up but only just. Karen didn't want to do anything to upset the fragile alliance.

"Viv, I don't think this is a good idea," Penny said. "I don't think you should watch her confession. Nothing good can come from it. It's only going to damage you."

"And why's that?" Viv challenged her.

"You're not like other people, Viv," Penny said gently.

"No, I'm not," Viv agreed. "I'm stronger."

"That's not what I meant," Penny said.

"You're very strong, Viv," Karen said.

"What I meant," Penny continued, "is that if you watch this tape, it's going to be with you forever. Stored in your visual memory. For a normal person, it fades. You're different. If you watch this tape, you'll never be rid of it. You've told me it yourself so many times. You can't un-see what you've seen. Forgetting's a luxury you don't have."

"You think I don't know that?" Viv said.

Neither Penny nor Karen answered that.

"That's why I want to watch the tape," Viv explained. "There's a video in my mind starring every person I've ever known. For some people, say, a person I met in passing on the street who face-planted, they're just quirky shorts. For other people, they're more like sprawling epics. Like my memories of both of you."

Karen and Penny both involuntarily smiled at this idea.

"There's a video in my head of Mom, too, of course. A drama. And right now, it's lacking an ending. I don't care what's on this tape. I have to see it. Because if I don't, all there will be is an empty space, a place where the film just cuts out. And if there's one thing I've learned from life is that I'd rather know

what's behind a closed door rather than be left wondering
what *could* be there. My imagination is much scarier, much
more potentially damaging than reality, than memory, ever
could be," Viv said.

"So what you're saying is if you don't watch the tape, anxiety
will fill in the blank that's left," Karen summarized.

"Exactly," Viv replied. "There's always going to be something
unpleasant there, occupying that empty space. Given the
choice, I'd prefer it's what actually happened."

"Okay," Penny said.

She started the tape.

The confession room camera produced astonishingly grainy
tape, but Viv's mother was discernible, as was the investigator
in charge of eliciting the confession.

The audio quality was considerably better than the video,
and every word rang loud and clear.

"What about the blood?" the investigator asked Tender.

Tender smiled. "What about it?"

"There were inkblots on the chest of a victim at every crime
scene... and yet, when the coroner examined the victims,
he couldn't find a link between that blood and the cause of
death. Autopsy revealed aneurysms to be the cause of death.
Aneurysms that wouldn't have led to any external expression
of blood."

"Your autopsy results are correct," Tender replied. "They
were bloodless deaths."

"Fine," the investigator said. "That's consistent with the evidence... but if the blood didn't come from their murders, then why is it there? Where *did* it come from?"

"It was mine," Tender replied.

"Well, that's what testing says so far," the investigator replied. "Your blood type matches the sample, and we've sent it out for DNA analysis in the States, for a more exact match. But that doesn't explain *why*. Were you wounded? Were they fighting back?" the investigator asked.

"Those are two questions. With two very different answers."

"And those answers?"

"It's not easy to absorb all of that psychic energy at once, you know," Tender said. "It's unnatural. It's not the normal way someone like me would feed... if I hadn't gotten so much hungrier all of a sudden. And if I weren't forced to take such things underground. If I had my way, I wouldn't gorge myself all in one go. Instead, I'd take little sips. Ladylike ones."

Tender paused, considering this, before continuing, "Actually, what's the difference now? I'm going away for life. It doesn't take a precog to see that. I'll be honest. That's how I used to do it. I used to take small pieces of people as I went along. Enough to keep me going. Enough to hurt them. But not nearly enough to kill them. And not so much that they'd know exactly what I did."

"And who were these people?" the investigator asked.

"I can't remember now, all of them, exactly who they were, but generally? Pretty much every man I ever dated – and trust you, there were a lot of them. Random women I didn't like. You know, the ones who judged me. Who said mean things about me when they *thought* my back was turned."

"What about your children?" the investigator asked. "Did you ever feed on them?"

Viv inhaled sharply, dreading her mother's answer to the question.

Tender frowned. "I don't want to talk about that."

"Of course she doesn't," Viv muttered.

Penny laid her hand on Viv's arm, but Viv pulled away from her, rejecting the comfort.

On the tape, the interview continued. "Okay, so it was your blood. You got nosebleeds because you were... feeding on too much energy at once... is that about right?"

Tender nodded. "That's how it works. My body couldn't get handle it."

"But why the inkblots? At every scene, the blood resembled a psychological projection test."

Tender smiled. "To be perfectly honest, I'm not exactly sure why. It was like a high, you know? Draining people's energy... especially that much at a time. I'd get too high and I had blackouts. And then later I'd come to, and there they were. Dead, bloodied. For all I know, I was fingerpainting. Maybe that's just the way the blood fell. I'll never know."

The investigator stared at her incredulously, as though he didn't quite believe her. But it was a minor issue. He trudged on to more important matters.

"So we've established that there was a need. That you needed to find a source of sanity. Why did you leave the second victim alive in each case?" the investigator said on the tape to Viv's mother.

"Isn't it obvious?" Tender replied.

"No," the investigator said.

Tender pursed her lips together impatiently. "Take a look at me. Take a look at this figure."

"Ma'am," the investigator said, "I don't see what your physique has to do with the case."

Tender let out a frustrated sigh. "I don't have enough of an appetite to finish off two intuitives all by myself," she said.

"Is that a joke?" the investigator asked.

"No," she replied. "The truth is that I can only absorb so much energy at a time before I burst. Some of us can fully deplete the minds of two, three, or even four people at a time. I have a more petite reserve. One and a half is about my limit. Any more and I risk bursting. Really, one at a time is ideal, but I didn't have that sort of luck, and I couldn't risk leaving a sane witness to rat me out. You understand."

"I'm beginning to," the investigator said. "And why these victims?"

"It was a mother's duty," Tender explained.

"How so?"

Tender scoffed at the question. "I wouldn't expect you to understand," Viv's mother said.

"Why's that?" the investigator said.

"You've never had a special child, have you?" Tender said.

"Well, I think all children are special," the investigator said.

"You know that's not what I meant. I'm talking about... a kid who's different than others. Who needs extra help. Who isn't suited to deal with the world like a regular kid," Tender said.

"You have two children, don't you?" the investigator asked.

"Yes, Viv and Love. Love's a joy, really. I named her well. Always there for me. Always in my corner. Love's brought me nothing but joy."

"And Viv?"

"Something's missing from Viv," Tender said. "Always has been."

"What do you mean by that? What do you mean when you say there's something missing from Detective Lee?" the investigator asked.

"She's like me. She's a tuey. It's funny. There are some people who say that tueys are different but that they're better. Buncha kooks, if you ask me," Tender said.

"Why do you say that?"

"They see that we can do things that they can't. That we have extra abilities. Powers, some people call them. That's the most misleading name I can think of for them. What has happened to us isn't extra at all. We don't have something you don't. Instead, we're damaged. Like a wall with a big crack in it. Sure, the sunlight's shining in, and it's easy to be blinded by that. But there's nothing powerful about us at all. We're just conduits. And the only reason we can conduct these so-called powers is because we're damaged enough for it to leak through us. We don't have the normal filters someone like you does," Tender said. "It's easy for other things to leak in, too. Nasty stuff."

"Interesting theory," the investigator responded. "I still don't see what this has to do with the murders."

"The first one was a fluke, really. I was hungry, hungrier than I'd been in decades. I remembered those guards from my time at Nirvana Heights. I was an inpatient there for a bit, several years ago, back when this problem started but before it got really bad. Those guards were real bitches. Always laughing at me when they thought I couldn't see them. Doing impressions. Mean girls," Tender said.

"So you attacked them?" the investigator said.

Tender nodded. "I was hungry. I had to destroy someone. Couldn't think of better candidates."

"How did you find them?" the investigator asked. "They weren't even working at the hospital anymore."

"Oh that?" Tender said, flipping her hair. "That's easy. I know a lot of powerful men, dear. I'm popular."

"So you just asked around?" the investigator said.

Tender nodded. "Wasn't hard. You'd be surprised how easy it is to track someone down if you know the right people and the right questions to ask."

"Not really," the investigator said. "You forget who you're talking to."

"Ah, law enforcement, you're better than hunting people down than anybody," Tender replied flirtatiously.

"In the best of worlds, that would be true," the investigator replied, "but as you've noted, there are criminal ways at the same information."

"Criminal?" Tender said. "That's a little harsh."

"Have you forgotten where you are, Ms. Lee?" the investigator asked.

Tender frowned. "What a cruel thing to say to a woman with a condition. And no, I'm perfectly aware of my circumstances. But not all people who are jailed are criminals, sir."

"What about the other victims? Why them?" the investigator said, steering the conversation back on course.

"Like I said before, those were a mother's duty," Tender said.

"You still haven't explained exactly what you mean by that," the investigator said.

"When I attacked those bitches, I didn't realize they were within Viv's PsyOps district. That she'd be the one put on the case," Tender said.

"Normally she wouldn't be," the investigator said. "The crime scene was located outside of PsyOps jurisdiction. But according to her report, Detective Lee had a premonition that the bodies would be there while she was out visiting you. And once she called in the case, PsyOps took it over."

"That girl and her stupid visions," Tender grumbled.

"Do you have any reason to doubt that Detective Lee is telling the truth? You didn't tip her off to the scene of the crime, did you?" the investigator asked.

"I didn't tell Viv what I had done, no. She's telling the truth. Like I said, there's a crack in her that lets the light in. That's how she saw it. That's how she knew what was there, after I left." Tender chewed on her lip.

"...but...?" the investigator prompted Tender.

"She came to see me later. And she told me about the case, just talking about her job in general. She talked about other cases, too. I could tell she didn't know I had anything to do with that scene. But as she talked, an idea came into my head. I knew that I'd be hungry again and soon. The emptiness was building. I guess in a way you could say that the crack in me was splitting open wider, and soon I'd spill out everything I had inside of me."

"I don't need metaphors, Ms. Lee. I need answers," the investigator said.

"I got to thinking... what if I fed in Viv's territory? What if I gave her a little something to do? What if I drummed up business for her? Gave her a chance to shine, you know."

The investigator frowned. "Skinner-Watson is a dangerous place. PsyOps has enough on its hands to keep them busy for quite some time. Detective Lee didn't need your help."

"Of course she did," Tender replied. "I'm her *mother*."

The investigator paused, taking this in. "Okay, so let's go over this again. Exactly how did you approach your victims? How did you attack them?"

Penny glanced over at Viv. Viv's face was puffy and red, as though she'd been crying. And for the first time since Penny had known her, Viv's irises had gone completely black.

Upsetting the Balance

They had taken a lot for granted, Karen realized. How well their powers meshed. How well they all got along.

The days following Tender Lee's arrest seemed to belong to a different reality, one in which everything wasn't so well balanced.

Viv's medication stopped working the day of the arraignment. Karen was glad about this timing but felt guilty about it. After all, Viv was confined to a PsyOps medical ward for the day, postictal and fuzzy after an early morning seizure.

Karen knew Viv was in good hands with the team of specialists running tests on Viv. She wasn't happy that Viv's condition had taken such a sharp turn for the worse, but it did mean that Viv didn't have to permanently commit yet another unpleasant day into her indelible eidetic memory.

It gave Karen comfort to know that there would instead be a mélange of strange visions and what Viv had once described as "smeary slowness" afterwards in that place.

Viv would never have to hear her mother's arrogant plea of "less guilty than the rest of this kangaroo court, that's for damn sure." Nor would she see her once-refined mother spit on the ground after saying so.

Viv would never have to see her mother unnervingly disheveled at the initial court appearance, a real shocker if Karen had ever seen one. Karen had expected Tender to turn out impeccably dressed as always, coiffed to the point where she looked like she should be arguing someone else's case, not appearing to be charged.

"I can't work out what's going on with Tender showing up to court looking like that," Penny commented after the hearing.

"Me neither," Karen admitted. "She's got a good lawyer. It would be easy for her to find a way to clean up for court. And you'd think she'd want to, after all. I never saw that woman without makeup on before today."

"Has she given up? Is she angling for an insanity plea? Or has she legitimately lost her mind? I can't see any other way a woman like that, with her values system, lets herself go... It just doesn't add up," Penny said.

Karen nodded. "Maybe she's starving to death in there."

The State had heavily drugged Tender post arrest and continued to do so while she was in jail awaiting trial. Every day she received a mix of chemicals designed to depress intuitive powers, doled out in what seemed to Karen like incredibly irresponsible dosages.

Another thing she could not tell Viv, Karen told herself. The list was growing rather long.

In fact, they didn't talk much. Even after Viv was given a clean bill of health ("for now," Viv stipulated glumly) and discharged home, Karen found herself talking to Viv less than she ever had.

They stuck to mandatory communication:

"Here's your medicine, don't forget to take your dose."

"You're in my way."

"Can I use that after you?"

There was far less mandatory communication than normal, too. They didn't have work to talk about. And wouldn't for a while.

In light of recent events, Martin had approved a leave for the team. "A short leave," he'd said, which had set Karen up with modest expectations.

"Short" turned out to be four weeks, however.

Four weeks off.

Karen couldn't remember the last time she'd had four weeks off, not since her time in mental institutions, which in some ways was its own kind of work, staying alive and afloat there. It was hard, after all, to survive when you didn't want to.

Visions of elaborate vacation floated through her head.

They'd talked about it for years, the three of them, fantasized aloud about all the places they'd go if they could just have enough time off. When Martin had broken the news, he'd said that he'd be willing to kick in some of his own personal funds if they had a place they wanted to go.

Karen's heart had soared. Penny beamed.

But Viv had only grunted. And that should have probably told her something.

And now Viv had started to break down, to get sick. She slept later and went to bed earlier every day. Some of that was likely due to the new meds. Karen could remember how drowsy some of her own psych meds had made her. But was that all of it?

Karen wasn't so sure.

The first week disappeared with Viv primarily living through dreams. Or at least that's what Karen assumed, since Viv wasn't talking to either of them.

Karen also noted with increasing alarm that the presence of Viv and Penny wasn't blocking her empathy the way that it had always done before. It did seem like they were turning down the intensity and the volume of what she felt psychically, but bits of emotions were making their way through.

It was like a curtain had been nudged slightly out of alignment, and shafts of light were flowing into a previously dark room. A room that had once been calming, relaxing, tranquil.

A place where she could rest.

The same time that Viv was plunging into darkness, Karen found herself assaulted by unbidden glaring light.

Or maybe it was how Tenny had put it in her confession: Maybe the wall itself had cracked and was letting the light through.

"I wonder if we'll all ever be in the same emotional place ever again," Karen found herself wondering aloud, to no one. It sounded dramatic to her as she said it, but she couldn't shake the feeling that something had fundamentally changed, maybe forever.

Whatever the case, her family life didn't feel the same.

And home didn't feel like home anymore.

Come Home

On the ninth day of their leave, Viv's phone rang during the thin sliver of time that she was actually awake. Penny and Karen traded worried looks as Viv answered the call.

"Oh, it's you, Withers," Viv said. "I should have expected you'd call. You're like an ambulance chaser. Of course you can't wait like a decent person would. All the money in the world can't buy class, can it?" she snapped.

A long pause.

"Not a chance in Hell," Viv said. "You missed your opportunity." She hung up the call.

Viv turned to Penny and Karen. "Of course that bitch wants to air a segment about our case now that an arrest has been made. Now that it's not threatening her financial interests. I'm not having any part of it."

It was the first words Viv had spoken to either of them in days. With that, she climbed up to their bedroom to go to sleep.

It was 2 pm. Viv had woken up just three hours earlier, at 11 am.

"You know," Penny said brightly to Karen after Viv had left, "Maybe there's something to be said for a staycation. What do you say?"

Karen thought for a moment. "I think, Penny... that you could be happy anywhere. And that I could be happy anywhere, so long as I were with you."

Penny beamed her brightest smile, but as Karen went off to take a shower, she let the smile fall away.

Penny's cheeks ached from pretending everything was okay. That she was happy. That things were fine.

They weren't.

She hadn't seen a spirit since that day.

There had been a point in her life when she'd felt pestered by the undead, positively hounded by them, like a celebrity overwhelmed by rabid fans who were demanding never-ending autographs and joint selfies while she just wanted to eat her meal in peace.

Now she felt like a *persona non grata*. A has-been. A former medium who had shrunken down to small, perhaps invisible.

And then Penny began to smell something foul. Something that neither Karen nor Viv could smell, when she asked them.

Penny searched the entire house multiple times before she finally zeroed in on the source: The package that she'd received at PsyOps the day of Tender's arrest.

It was in the front entryway under a pile of coats that had been stacked upon a bench meant to assist them when taking off or putting on shoes but which ended up being a good place to let things accumulate instead.

The ribbon on the package was gone, as was the note that told her to come home, both having wandered off to who knows where, but the fruit was still in the box.

Rotten and rank, she noted as she removed the lid. An overripe artificial sweetness that abruptly took a bitter turn assaulted her nostrils.

Penny held the rotten pomegranate in her hand. She walked over to the trash can. Standing over the bin, she squeezed the fruit in her fingers, softly at first and then with progressively more strength.

Finally, the fruit gave. A smell of decay permeated the room as the sticky innards dripped through her fingers.

She had expected the fruit to be brown and dead-looking inside, as rotten as it was, but it wasn't. Instead, the fruit was overripe and... seemed almost alive.

Outrageously red and warm.

At that moment Penny felt very much like a shaman engaging in human sacrifice. *Is this what it's like to destroy a human heart?*

She shook her head violently as the thought came to her, as if trying to shake the sentiment out of her mind.

She went to the sink. After summoning the hottest water the tap could manage, Penny rubbed her hands together vigorously under the stream until they turned red from rawness. The pillow of soap she'd lathered into existence did little to insulate her from the damage.

Her hands were red, so red.

Her skin burned, which should have bothered her. But instead it felt good.

Penny turned off the tap, finding herself short of breath... and excited? Well, that was weird. What was going on?

No more pomegranates, she promised herself, feeling faint, throwing the box it had come in into the trash as well.

And she meant it. No more pomegranates. She was putting this whole weird chapter behind her. Starting over fresh. Playing house with Viv and Karen. Nursing Viv back to health. Making the most of her staycation. And then going to work every day and doing a solid job.

No more pomegranates. She swore them off resolutely.

That was why she became so troubled when the fruits started showing up on their own. In beautifully woven fruit baskets dropped on the porch, enrobed in crinkly fussy cellophane. The kind whose rustlings would wake the dead from darkness.

When the first basket came, she thought at first a trick was being played on her. But who would the prankster be?

She had told no one of her self-promise to keep away from pomegranates. She'd made a point to not tell Viv or Karen. And while Karen was of course highly attuned to her emotions, it wasn't like she possessed the ability to pluck such a specific image from Penny's head.

No, she hadn't spoken about the experience aloud. She'd kept what she'd done and her powerful revulsion entirely to her herself.

But the basket came at just the right time, in one of the various twilight hours when she was the only one awake. It bore the card with her other name, the one no one was supposed to know.

Panicked, she started a fire in their backyard and sent the tiny slip ablaze, not wanting Karen or Viv to read it. This had of course awoken Karen, who joined her next to the blaze.

"If only we had some marshmallows," Karen said. "I'm not good at toasting them. Not patient enough. But I bet you anything that Viv is."

"Maybe I'll find some soon," Penny replied, willing her voice to sound as normal as possible, hoping anxiously that Karen wouldn't spot the one vestige in the fire that could give her true intentions away – a tiny slip of paper curled up and singed.

Karen didn't. Still, it was too close of a call for Penny.

When the next baskets came with identical cards, Penny ate the evidence each time, swallowing the paper. It wasn't exactly pleasant, but it was quicker, she concluded, drew less attention.

She dutifully filled the normally scantly filled produce drawers in the bottom of the fridge with pomegranates as they came. The left drawer first and then the right. When both drawers were full, she began to place the fruits on the bottom row of the fridge.

Penny wondered idly if you could pickle or can pomegranates. She couldn't bear eating them, and while Viv and Karen were eating a few stray fruits here and there, they weren't going through the batch nearly quickly enough.

"What's with all the pomegranates?" Viv asked.

"They're organic," Penny lied.

"Dumpster diving outside of the natural food store again?" Viv said.

Penny nodded.

She hated lying to Karen and Viv, but she was just starting to feel as though she could manage this strange unwelcome intrusion to her life when the situation escalated once again.

This time there was a messenger at her doorstep bearing the next fruit basket. An entirely unremarkable man that she almost mistook for a complete stranger, except for a few telltale signs around the eyes that let Penny know that it was him. It was Change, the "spirit" who had accosted her that one time in her kitchen with warnings about the investigation. The one whose poorly printed business cards boasted on "shapeshifting services," whatever that meant.

"Delivery for Rhea Stygius," the shapeshifter announced, thrusting the basket in her hands, before turning around to walk away.

Penny winced at the sound of her other name, grateful that no one nearby seemed to yet be awake.

"Thank you, Change Patterson," Penny called after him as she regained her composure.

Change spun in place. "Don't," he said. "Don't try to be cute. And don't keep ignoring this. You're going to have to deal with this. For once in your life, you're going to have to deal with something, Rhea. Instead of just changing your name and running away."

There was a familiarity in Change's tone that troubled Penny. It was as though he knew Penny well – or rather, that he knew Penny *as* Rhea well, which bothered Penny even more because she barely knew him. It was very much like hearing the words "Oh! I've heard so much about you," from a complete stranger and not knowing if it's a good thing or a bad thing.

"There's a point when everyone has to finally come home," Change said. "I'd say you're well past that point."

"Don't you know," she said to him, "That telling me not to do something is the easiest way to get me to do it."

"I sure do," Change said. "Why do you think I said it?"

Penny scowled at him and didn't reply. She didn't want to give him the satisfaction of a response.

After he left, Penny thought about this attempt at reverse psychology, at thrumming up reactance in her. Like all people who don't like to be told what to do, Penny was greatly angered by the overt attempt at reverse psychology. This set her on a course to reverse the reverse psychology.

How dare he try reverse psychology on her, Penny fumed.

She'd show him, Penny decided. She'd... Well, she'd *do what he said.*

In that moment, it never occurred to Penny that *this* could have been what Change intended all along. That he could have been like the villain who puts the poison in his own glass when you're drinking together, knowing that you won't trust him and insist the glasses be switched.

No, as happens with most people experiencing an emotional crisis, Penny's problem-solving field had shrunk down to a single point. No other alternatives existed.

Penny placed the last batch of fruit in the fridge gingerly, knowing what she must do.

She sprinted to the desert willow.

"Okay, Kip," she said to her old friend. "I'm ready to know. Who am I? Who am I, really?"

Later that morning, Karen and Viv woke up at the same time. The birds were singing outside their bedroom window. They sang the same songs as any other morning but perhaps a bit more quietly, as though they were further away than normal.

The light coming through their bedroom window also seemed dimmer than normal, not as bright or piercing.

"Penny's gone," Karen told Viv.

Viv frowned, not sure what to say. They descended the stairs together, holding hands.

On the kitchen table, there was a note in Penny's handwriting, scribbled on the back of a blank florist's card:

I've gone on a trip. Not sure when I'll be back. Give Martin my best.

The story continues in
Psychic Inferno

About the Author

Page Turner is the award-winning author of four books. With a professional background in psychological research and organizational behavioral consulting, Page is best described as a "total nerd." She's been cited as a relationship expert in a variety of media publications including *The Huffington Post*, *Glamour*, *Self*, and *Bustle*.

She clearly can't see the future because she didn't see any of that coming.

Due to her incurable wanderlust, she has lived many places, but these days she calls Dallas home.

Made in the USA
Middletown, DE
04 September 2020